SUSPENDED
VAGABOND CIRCUS ✦ BOOK ONE

SARAH NOFFKE

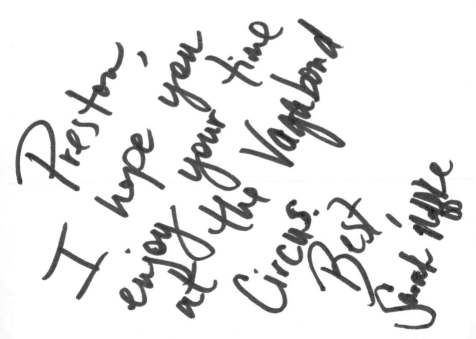

Preston,
I hope you
enjoy your time
at the Vagabond
Circus. Best,
Sarah Noffke

One-Twenty-Six Press.
Awoken
Sarah Noffke

Summary: When circus acts go above and beyond what skeptics
know to be the limits of human ability, the only remaining, logical
explanation is the least plausible of all—magic must be real.

Published in the United States by One-Twenty-Six Press
ISBN: 978-1523285440

Praise for Previous Works:

"There are so many layers, so many twists and turns, betrayals and reveals. Loves and losses. And they are orchestrated beautifully, coming when you least expected and yet in just the right place. Leaving you a little breathless and a lot anxious. There were quite a few moments throughout where I found myself thinking that was not what I was expecting at all. And loving that."
-Mike, Amazon

"The writing in this story was some of the best I've read in a long time because the story was so well-crafted, all the little pieces fitting together perfectly."
-The Tale Temptress

"There are no words. Like literally. NO WORDS.
This book killed me and then revived me and then killed me some more. But in the end I was born anew, better."
-Catalina, Goodreads

"Love this series! Perfect ending to an incredible series! The author has done this series right."
-Kelly at Nerd Girl

"What has really made these books stand out is how much emotion they evoke from me as a reader, and I love how it comes from a combination of both characters and plot together. Everything is so intricately woven that I have to commend Sarah Noffke on her skills as a writer."
-Anna at Enchanted by YA

For Kathy Cilley,
because people like you really spread
magic.

Table of Contents

SUSPENDED

VAGABOND CIRCUS ✦ BOOK ONE

SARAH NOFFKE

Prologue

There are those who come to judge the circus and then there are those who come to experience it. The latter go home satisfied. The former go home full of scrutinizing accusations. Those who experience the circus, taking it in and allowing themselves to be awed, have a richness built into their lives afterwards, almost like they've gained an extra day to their existence. Those who observe seem to have lost a day. They're the ones who tear down sandcastles. They're the ones who say clouds are just clouds when they are irrefutably in the shape of unicorns.

These skeptics are the people the Vagabond Circus caters to. The circus would shut their doors to the joyful and starry-eyed if their business didn't keep it running. The Vagabond Circus runs for two reasons and only two reasons: first and foremost to give the lost and lonely Dream Travelers a place to be great. And secondly, to show the nonbelievers that there's still magic in the world. If they believe then they care and if they care then they don't destroy. They stop the small abuse that day by day breaks down humanity's spirit. If the Vagabond Circus makes one person believe then they halt the cycle, just a little bit. They allow a little more love into this world. That's Dave Raydon's mission. And that's why he recruits. That's why he directs. That's why he puts on a show that makes people question their beliefs. He wants the world to believe in magic once again.

And yet, what his patrons witness is real. Real people, doing real things. Things that are inconceivable to most, but real nonetheless. That's because Dave recruits only Dream Travelers. People who can do what most can't. Unique people. They aren't magical. But to those who don't know the difference, they are an inspiration. They appear magical. However, what most believe to be real magic is only the extraordinary which defines the Vagabond Circus completely.

1

Chapter One

Rain pelted the big top, gliding down the tent and gathering in puddles on the muddy ground. The crew had worked throughout the night to reinforce the oversized tent from the winds and storms. The earth it was bolted to was threatening to melt away, sending the bright green and blue tent into a mound of chaos. The Vagabond Circus had been on the road for three weeks and this was its first night in Seattle.

Tomorrow the city's residents would have the opportunity to witness a show the people in Vancouver called "unbelievable," "unreal," and "more than a trick of smoke and mirrors." The critics were speechless, as they were every year when the Vagabond Circus came through town. There was little to criticize and more than enough of the show to overwhelm the senses. No one understood half of what they saw at Vagabond Circus, but still they never looked away.

And yet in this year's show there was something missing. The fifty people who came together to put on the show knew it. Its ringmaster, Dave Raydon, knew it. And the one person who could fill in the missing gap knew it after watching the show in Vancouver. But the audience had no clue there was anything lacking in the Vagabond Circus. They were ecstatic, leaving the big top with smiles that wouldn't fade for hours. They had seen what they thought were tricks, not realizing everything about *this* circus was real.

In the shadows a boy stood under an old oak tree, only partially protected from the heavy monsoon. He watched in the dark as performers sprinted to their trailers. They were intent on getting dry and rested before the sun came up, marking a day of three shows. The boy was wet, but didn't care. He was exhausted from hitchhiking and stealing rides on the train from Vancouver. But he was here. He'd followed Vagabond Circus. And soon he'd be ready for the next part of his plan.

Chapter Two

Steam rose off the flame-lit lantern when slanted rain trespassed into the open flap of the tent. Dave Raydon could have had his office in a trailer, like the ones he and most of the people in Vagabond Circus lived in. Instead he chose to erect a small, one-mast version of the big top for his professional space. It was large enough for a round table and a few chairs and decorated in the same neon green and teal blue as the big top which towered beside it. Dave could have also lit his office tent with the same electricity that powered the thousands of lights in the neighboring big top, but he enjoyed the charm of firelight. Dr. Raydon enjoyed the charm of many things that had died out due to technology. As the ringmaster of Vagabond Circus and also its founder, he was in essence "before his time."

"Open your eyes, Dave!" a slender man said, jabbing his finger at a piece of paper lying on the table. "Look at the numbers. They don't lie."

"Numbers may not lie, but they also only tell half the story," Dave said, leaning back in his chair and folding his hands over his rounded belly.

"Well, the only story I'm interested in is the one they're telling me," Titus said, tapping his finger repeatedly on the stack of figures detailing the hole the Vagabond Circus was quickly sliding into. "If you care so much about this damn circus then I encourage you to take this all more seriously."

"I don't just care about this circus, I have faith in it," Dave said, his voice even and a strange contrast to that of the gentleman standing over him red-faced. "We've been through slumps and we're going to weather this one." A smile crooked up the corners of his thin lips, a glint of hope in his eyes as he gazed out the open flap of the tent. "This storm will pass, just as the one outside will. Things will get better, just as the sun will rise and dry up the rain."

"Oh hell, would you stop with the metaphors! Now really isn't the time," Titus said, snapping his fingers in front of Dave's face. The seated man was almost lost in a daze as he watched the rain shift from a downpour to a steady sprinkle outside. "We need to charge more for tickets. We need to expand the show. Go bigger. Sell merchandise. Have more booths." Titus leaned down low, finally gaining Dave's attention, and when he spoke his mouth hardly parted for his words. "We need to evolve and stop operating like we did twenty years ago, don't you get it?"

Dave shook his head of short brown hair, unleashing the water clinging to its ends. Titus stepped back suddenly and shielded his face with a raised elbow from the spray of droplets. When the taller man lowered his arm the shorter man stood, a mischievous look in his small light-colored eyes. "Evolution isn't all that it's cracked up to be," Dave said. "It works for mammals and birds and fish, but in my opinion it isn't suited for all organizations or in this case, the Vagabond Circus."

"Your opinion is wrong!" Titus threw his hands into the air, his fingertips almost knocking into the low part of the ceiling overhead.

Dave took one large step, his short legs really reaching to close the space between him and the other man in only one stride. He threw his chin up and stared with bold eyes at the man who easily stood a foot over him. "I value your input, but at the end of the day my opinion, whether right or wrong, is the only one that counts. Is that clear?"

Titus didn't say a word, only stepped back and roughly shook his head, his lips pressed together in a hard line.

"I think we're done here tonight," Dave said, his voice cordial once more. He turned and made for the open flap of the tent. "Please close up, would you?"

Chapter Three

The outsider stood closer now, just under the eaves of Dave Raydon's office tent. The boy was disappointed that he couldn't hear the conversation going on inside the miniature big top. The rain prevented him from making out the two men's words, but he could discern that it was a heated conversation. When the shorter man strode out of the building the trespasser slid in closer to the tent, his shirt colliding with the wet material, drenching his backside completely. He stifled a curse and instead watched as the ringmaster trudged through the puddle-filled lane, head held high against the splattering rain. Dave's figure soon grew indistinct as he neared his personal trailer and the boy lost sight of him completely.

Dave, however, had excellent night vision and didn't even carry a flashlight at night like most in Vagabond Circus. He also knew his path so well he could find his way blindfolded. And this was impressive since the configuration of the big top and trailers and sleeper-row shifted slightly between each city. It always depended on the space allocated by that city and the relationships of the performers. Neighboring situations shifted, but only slightly. Dave had figured out long ago how to keep relations among his staff pleasant. This was because he'd learned the hard way that pleasant relations made for consistent performances and everything at Vagabond Circus relied on consistency. It's what kept the doors open and the believers and non-believers filing into the big top.

The rules were simple and no one ever forgot them and usually no one ever broke them, which was solely a result of the level of leadership Dave had over his employees. The rules, number one: everyone respects each other, no matter what. And two, no one dates each other, no matter what. Those were the rules and they weren't just easy to remember, but surprisingly easy to follow. People understood them. Followed them. Believed in Dave's reasoning. Mostly never questioned it.

Twenty years ago when Dr. Raydon started Vagabond Circus he was devastated by something that happened to his circus and the sole reason was he didn't have any rules. His primitive mission had been clear: to take in lost and wandering Dream Travelers. Encourage them to use the skills their race was born with to become someone great. Dream Travelers, starting at puberty, could utilize sleeping hours to take their consciousness anywhere and do anything. Too often the lonely Dream Traveler will waste away these skills. But Dave recruited and organized a band of young, rogue Dream Travelers. He instructed them to meet him every night in an empty field and practice various skills. To hone their unique abilities. It was in this field that Vagabond Circus was born.

Dave then bought the four-mast big top that the circus still used to this day. This was why he didn't want to take Titus's unrelenting advice. He still believed that what he created belonged inside that tent. That it didn't need to outgrow it.

Once inside his dark and empty trailer, the middle-aged man threw himself down in his plastic-sheathed recliner. Dave sighed to himself, his aggravation finally surfacing. He *did* firmly believe that the forty-eight-foot-diameter ring was still big enough. But proving this to the creative director was tough and growing more of a challenge day by day. Two big tops wouldn't make for a grander show, just more of a show, but that wasn't the key. And neither was merchandise. He hated stuff anyway. He hardly had more than the bare minimum in his tiny trailer.

Once, Dave had an estate and enough possessions to fill it, but it didn't bring him happiness. He wasn't going to take hard-working people's money in exchange for crap that would congest their closets one day. People didn't need souvenirs or mementos. They needed an unforgettable experience and that's all that Vagabond Circus offered.

Dave flipped open his recliner, not having to feel around for the handle but going straight to it. He smiled with relief when his damp head nestled into the pillow. *Yes*, possessions never brought happiness. Comfort *yes*, but that shouldn't be confused with happiness. He hadn't known true joy until he closed up his psychiatrist practice, sold his estate, donated his belongings, and started a new life.

His initial bit of happiness came when he located his first drifter, a Dream Traveler who had the ability to manipulate objects with his mind. The boy was underfed, disenfranchised by his years as a runaway and completely intrigued by the idea of being the first member of a circus. From there it was easy for Dave to grow Vagabond Circus. He simply put out a message amongst the homeless and transient population that he was recruiting those with extraordinary abilities. The ones who fit the bill knew who they were. These individuals lined up once they realized they'd be given food, room, pay, and, one day, a reputation of prestige.

Sometimes Middlings came for auditions—the other race, the one who couldn't dream travel and had no unique ability—but Dave quickly saw them for who they were. There was nothing wrong with Middlings, they were just a different caliber. Their circuses were great and based on talent but also flashy costumes and a bit of deception. Vagabond Circus was not flashy and didn't rely on bright lights and sparkly costumes. Its success, from the beginning, relied on the various Dream Travelers who all had unique abilities. And it also relied on a ringmaster who had them spend every waking moment and every dream traveling second honing these skills until they were super powers. That's what made Vagabond Circus the best in the world and Dave wasn't about to exploit it. He did, however, agree that his circus was currently lacking. Something was missing. Something that would keep the doors open without raising ticket prices or adding extra shows.

With a slow hand he slipped a bottle of pills from the drawer in the table beside his recliner. Fanny, the Vagabond Circus healer, had created the herb mixture a few years ago. It was for the nights when Dave chose not to spend his twilight hours dream traveling with his staff. Dr. Raydon could do almost anything, but for too many years he couldn't just close his eyes and sleep.

He popped the brown capsule into his mouth and swallowed it dry. The formula Fanny concocted wouldn't just put Dave to sleep but would also prevent him from having dreams, which was crucial.

The first troupe Dave started twenty years ago had phenomenal success but in less than a year it all crumbled. The troupe, through acts of betrayal and jealousy and greed, tore one another apart and Dave was left to pick up the pieces and start again. This was the reason for the rules and also the reason for the nightmares.

Dave's eyelids finally fell shut and within several seconds he was breathing with the rhythm of a person locked away in dreamless sleep.

Chapter Four

*T*he boy stepped out from his place hiding beside the tent. He wasn't actually quite a boy anymore, Finley would be eighteen soon. Maybe in a month, he guessed. He didn't know when his real birthday was, and he'd guessed at the year he was born. Perhaps he was about to turn seventeen or nineteen. The boy wasn't entirely sure.

Finley didn't follow Dave to his trailer. He had considered it. Considered confronting him then, but by the way the man moved, Finley knew he was tired and thus knew he wouldn't get the audience he desired. Tomorrow. Tomorrow he'd find the ringmaster when he was alone. That was the only way his plan would work.

He snuck out from behind the tent and stealthily moved through the RV trailers lining the back lot. The rain had calmed to a gentle mist now and the crew inside the tent sounded as though they were nearing the end of their work. It wouldn't do the trespasser any good to be seen. It might ruin everything. Finley wasn't concerned about being caught. That would be nearly impossible, but if he was seen then later he might be recognized. Tonight wasn't the night to take chances; it was the time for reconnaissance. There would be other nights for chances, once he knew more about these people.

Slipping between the gaps in the RVs, the boy slid up against a trailer echoing with noise. He pressed his ear up alongside the wet metal listening to the muffled voices inside. They were undoubtedly children's voices. Four or five distinct voices. And possibly a woman's. Hers was warm and low. Finley backed up and surveyed the RV trailer. It was larger than most, but by the sound of it there were more residents in this trailer than most. What he needed was to get a look inside, but after circling the compartment he learned there were no open window shades. They were all pulled down so tightly that the light within hardly found its way out. If the adult inside had just been as careless closing her window coverings as her neighbor then Finley would have what he needed for confirmation.

The neighboring trailer had all its window shades still open wide, the various lights within spilling out into the black night. Inside he spied movement, someone crossing the small living area within. Finding a spot beside a tree, Finley focused his eyes through the window. He was only fifteen feet away. This proximity provided him an unobstructed view of a girl. Maybe like him, almost not a kid anymore. He recognized her at once from the performance he'd seen in Vancouver. She was one of the acrobats. There was no doubt about it. Not many people had platinum blonde hair with a two-inch-wide bright pink streak running through it.

She was seated, perhaps at a table. The details around her Finley couldn't see without moving closer. His inhibitions wavered for only a second before he got control again and forced himself to stay hidden by the tree. Trespassing on the circus was one thing, but being spied peeping was another. He couldn't risk it.

The girl was chatting, her words flowing easily, as if the person she was speaking to she knew well. She reclined a bit and gathered her long hair in her hands and began twisting it. Again and again she twisted the blonde and pink hair into a tight rope and then absentmindedly she twirled it into a bun at the back of her head and stuck something slender through it. With her hair back, he noticed her long neck again. Finley remembered her lean muscles, no doubt a result of hundreds of hours of stretching, twirling, flipping, and gliding through the air.

When the girl erupted in sudden laughter, Finley realized he'd been staring at her without actually seeing her, his mind trailing back to her performance. Now he focused on her again. She didn't just laugh once, but instead seemed infected by it. He could hear the sound spilling through the flimsy door on the side of the trailer. It was a sound he was unaccustomed to. Laughter. People didn't laugh where he came from and never like this girl, with seemingly no end. Her face was now a shade lighter than the streak in her hair and her long slender hands glided under her eyes, pushing tears away. She was enchanting when she laughed. As unfathomable as it was to Finley, she seemed to grow even brighter. Her laughing smile soon lessened and after a few seconds of composure her passive expression reappeared. And still under her eyes she wore the joy connected to that fit of laughter, like it might burst forth again at any moment.

9

Finley wondered what would make a girl like this laugh so hard. More curious was *who*. She spoke to this person again, a now bashful look on her face. With a quick scan of the area Finley made an impromptu decision. He raced, as only he could do, crossing the space between him and the window. His pause was brief. It gave him just the information he craved and he was once again a blur of movement and back safely behind the tree. It was unlikely anyone saw him. His moment of indiscretion had been only a second or two. Besides, his speed was almost too fast for anyone to register in the dark.

And now he knew who had made the girl laugh. It had been one of the other acrobats. He was the one who Finley guessed had the ability of levitation. He wasn't sure what the girl's skill was. She had appeared almost like a normal acrobat in the act, like a Middling, but that couldn't be the case. There were no Middlings in Vagabond Circus. Everyone was a Dream Traveler and had one or more unique abilities they used in the show. Even the crew who tended to the big top were Dream Travelers. Maybe the girl's gift was that she was hypnotizing, because for some reason Finley couldn't look away from her. Didn't want to.

And then the girl leaned across the table and the spell was broken. If Finley didn't know who she was leaning toward, then he wouldn't have turned away. But he did know. And he felt cold shame for caring what two strangers were doing inside the privacy of a personal space.

Chapter Five

Zuma said a polite farewell to the other acrobat three minutes after Finley marched away. He was two rows away when she waved at Jack as he strolled to his own trailer. There was no long kiss goodnight, as Finley had imagined there would be.

With Jack gone the sudden need for privacy was overwhelming for Zuma. It always dropped down on her like a net. Being with her circus family nonstop, and having the public eye on her during every show, created a greedy need for decompression time. She pulled the shades of each of the windows as she passed to her bedroom at the back of the trailer. Her chest was still buzzing from the laughter. Jack always made her laugh. He had the beautiful knack of breaking through her tough exterior and making her appear almost human. Not happy, but almost human. Zuma didn't know what happiness felt like. She hardly knew what human felt like.

Zuma sulked quietly as she slid onto her bed, not even bothering to put herself between the covers. Just this once she wished she would have asked Jack to stay longer, to share more of his time with her. But they both knew, and had discussed, that this would only lead to one thing and that could never happen. They both loved their place within Vagabond Circus too much to take that risk. Even for each other.

The regret slid away as Zuma focused her thoughts. Tonight was a free night; she could dream travel to wherever she pleased. No dream travel rehearsal or meetings. Just her lonely consciousness and the world to explore. With her eyes closed she focused on a location. She'd learned about it from one of her clients in Vancouver. Their thoughts had been obsessed with this place and she now wanted to find out why. Most places had an energy that either pulled people in, locked them out, or did a little of both. Zuma was good at reading the energy of places, about like how she could read minds.

Her consciousness spiraled through the almost metallic tunnel. It pushed her like a comet through space and time, barreling her in the direction of her focused thoughts. Since she was twelve she'd been dream traveling, and the experience never lost its rush. How could the automatic transport through the latitudes of the globe ever grow boring?

This was her last thought before she arrived on a sandy beach and stood facing out at the waters of the Atlantic. Of course, her body was only there in ethereal form. The Middling tourists strolling through the sand couldn't see her. Only other Dream Travelers in the same form as her could. But she was finally alone after the long day. Middlings in the physical realm didn't really count as company.

Zuma let out a refreshing breath and then turned to the city. Her pink lips quirked up with a smile of delight. She instantly knew one of the reasons Cape Town had a draw. It didn't look like most cities. Most places she'd visited in physical or dream travel form weren't surrounded by tabletop-like mountains. How protected the residents of Cape Town must feel nestled in the bottom of a bowl, a beautiful archway of mountains on one side and a warm ocean on the other.

Chapter Six

A single spotlight glimmered down on Dave Raydon. He wore a teal blue three-piece suit with long tails in the back and a matching top hat nested on his plump head. His almost neon green bow tie matched the round carpet he stood on in the middle of the ring. Every eye in the big top was centered on him.

"Lentlemen and gadies! Goys and burls," he said, his voice booming through the speakers. Giggles tumbled out of everyone in the crowd. "It is my distinct privilege to welcome you all to Vagabond Zoo!" he said.

"No, no, no," the crowd echoed. Kids shook their heads furiously, covering chuckling mouths with tiny hands.

Dr. Raydon clapped his hand to his chest and furrowed his eyebrows. "What do you mean 'no'?" He looked around the tent, confused. "Doesn't this look like a zoo to you?"

"No!" a dozen kids yelled.

The Vagabond Circus was different from all the rest in many ways and the first was it had no clowns. Not a single red, round nose in the whole troupe. Maybe that was the reason Dave had decided he'd be the silliest ringmaster in all of history. His job was to lead and move the events of the show along but he was less a Master of Ceremony and more a buffer between the jaw-dropping acts.

"Not a zoo you say?" Dave said, running his fingers over his dimpled chin.

"No!" the audience sang again, punctuated by laughter.

Dave patted the air with his white glove and nodded like he had just realized his mistake. "Right." He coughed to clear his throat and held his arms out in a commanding fashion. "It is my pleasure to welcome you all, those short and tall, those fat and lean, those smart and dumb, and those undefinable, to the Vagabond Ranch!"

"Noooooo!" the crowd hollered, their glee and anticipation strong in the tent.

"Huh?" Dave said, pulling off his top hat and scratching his smashed down hair in confusion. The hat, which was as old as

Vagabond Circus, was covered in patches of varying shades of teal blue. "This isn't a ranch? Are you quite sure?" Dave asked the audience.

"Yes, it's a circus!" a few kids yelled from various places.

Dave shook his head, a mock look of offense on his face. "Oh, no, if this was a circus then I'd know about it."

"It's a circus!" they yelled again.

Dave strolled to a corner of the ring and fisted his hands on his hips, his top hat still clenched in one palm. "How dare you tell me how to do my job? This is a ranch. I know it to be true."

"It's a circus. Vagabond Circus," the boy he was staring at argued boldly, suppressing a grin.

"Circuses have magic though," the ringmaster said, throwing one finger high in the air above his head. "And I can guarantee you that what you'll see tonight isn't magic. It's real! So there you go, this isn't a circus."

"No! No! No!" the crowd now sang louder than before.

"It is a ranch, like I said."

"Nooooo!" they shouted in unison this time.

"If it isn't a ranch then let me ask you one question," Dave said, scanning the various faces.

The crowd fell silent at once, some leaning forward in their seats.

"If this isn't a ranch then why are there horses?" the ringmaster said, taking a step into the middle of the neon circle. And then a half dozen glistening Arabian horses sprinted into the ring. They had shot straight through the velvet blue curtain at the back. But to every crowd member's amazement the curtain stood still as though not jostled at all by the beasts that ripped through it. The horses galloped one behind the other around the perimeter of the ring, close enough to the front row that the audience could reach out and touch them. No one dared though; instead, everyone stayed still, eyes wide, mouth hanging open. Dave stood in the middle of the ring watching the animals as they made lap after lap, creating an unbreakable stream of galloping horses around him.

"Now how do you explain that?!" Dave said and his excitement and question broke the trance and the crowd erupted with applause and cheers. The horses then came to an abrupt halt and turned at once to face the crowd. Dave raised his hands in the air, top hat clutched in his right. "As I said before, ladies and gentlemen, there is no magic here!"

And there was no smoke. No change in the lights. No tricks to distract. In front of every patron's eyes the six full-sized Arabian horses vanished in unison. Cheers and applause shot out from the shocked audience.

"It is my immense pleasure to welcome you to Vagabond Circus!" Dave said, arms spreading out wide before he popped his top hat back on his head, a compelling glint in his eyes. And at once everyone's seat was emptied as the people at Vagabond Circus gave a standing ovation. If it was like most shows this wouldn't be the last one tonight.

And behind the teal blue curtain stood various performers at the ready. One of those would have to rest before his next performance. The Vagabond Circus used zero animals in their acts and therefore the horses, as the audience now suspected, hadn't been real. They had been Oliver's illusions. The pale boy stood in the wings, taking measured breaths. Creating illusions in the physical realm was draining, but he had at least half an hour before he'd have to go into the ring. Now was the acrobats' first act of the night.

Chapter Seven

*A*fter the last performance of every night the circus performers and crew all gathered for a BBQ by sleeper row. It was a tradition that Dave started eight years before and hadn't allowed anything but torrential downpours and snow to disturb. Other circuses had lines drawn between the crew and performers, but Dave never condoned such segregation. It took everyone in the circus to make the big top successful. How was anyone more important than another? In most circuses the tent crew could be replaced by anyone with a strong back and attentive personality, but not at Vagabond Circus. This circus should have needed a crew four times the size Dave employed. However, for crew he only recruited Dream Travelers from the streets who wanted a job but didn't have a star-worthy ability. These individuals worked by day and spent their night hours dream traveling to also work to put up the big top or take it down. To a person watching at night it would look as if invisible ghosts were doing the work, but it was only crew members in the other realm. This was also how Dave's performers became elite in less than a year. Middlings lose the nights to uncontrollable dreams, but Dream Travelers had a choice and his staff chose greatness. It was a part of the agreement they all signed when they started.

Although Dave had the intention to bring people together, the circus still was somewhat divided during the BBQ festivities. People inevitably want to be with those who do the same job as them. Costume and make-up employees chatted as they ate their baked beans and fresh rolls. Tent crew ribbed each other from the other side of the campfire. Performers took turns impressing the kids with stunts.

Fanny, the orphaned kids' nanny and homeschool teacher—as well as the circus healer—sat close by, watching with dazzling eyes. She'd watched the performances at Vagabond Circus a thousand times, but like a kid she never got tired of it. She said it was the kids who kept her young at heart, but her kids were more mature than most adults. Dave found them at orphanages and recognized them for their race immediately. He constantly visited the children's homes in every city they passed, looking for more kids who needed a place to belong. He spotted the special race of children usually by relying on Fanny's abilities. Her healing skill made it so she was attuned to people's energies. Dream Travelers, even before they came into their powers, were specific and registered for the healer.

The kids Fanny cared for were prepubescent and didn't have their skills yet. Once they did and could dream travel, then they were moved to a crew or performance role depending on their talent. But none really ever wanted to leave Fanny's care, although the luster of a job in the circus was intoxicating to them. All admitted that nothing was quite like the warmth of Fanny's hugs as she pressed a kid into her oversized bosom. And little was as comforting as the sound of her laughter, which was rich and warm and always full of approval. For kids who had so little there was no one they would ever adore more than the curly-headed caregiver.

Fanny currently had four children in her charge between the ages of four and eleven. They came from a life where no one wanted them and into a life where they were revered. To be the shining next generation of Vagabond Circus was a true privilege. Everyone was respected at Vagabond Circus. The crew was valued. The performers admired. But the children were honored. They, Dave said, brought the real magic. The magic of belief and wonder.

Chapter Eight

Finley watched from the wooded area bordering the circus, taking in the various characters as they drank and ate. He'd seen most of them working or performing, but to see people when they didn't know they were being watched revealed their true character. The only thing that revealed more was to watch people when they were alone, and he'd done enough of that last night.

Finley's meeting with Dave had gone extremely well. It half lightened his weighted heart to see the look on the older man's face when he unveiled his idea. At first the ringmaster had been surprised, but to Finley's relief he had never given him an ounce of skepticism. Dave Raydon, as Finley was learning, was a man who didn't greet the strangers and new experiences of the world with a critical perspective. He opened his arms wide to every experience as long as it promoted goodness and truth. Unfortunately for Dave, he was too open. Too trusting. And it was going to get him killed.

Finley had wanted to start right away, but Dave told him they would have to delay. He needed a day or two to get things in place. This left Finley restless to watch from the shadows and to observe those who didn't know he was watching. He scratched his scruffy jaw. Camping in the woods had taken a toll on his appearance, but it wasn't anything a few minutes in a gas station bathroom couldn't fix. And it hadn't deterred Dave's judgment of him. By tomorrow evening he'd look polished and clean.

Finley now fixed his gaze on the children dancing around a big-hipped woman. She was clapping and encouraging their play. Her smile was carefree, like the children she attended to. After watching this group Finley knew that his instinct had been right. He'd come to the right place and he was going to be successful.

Then his eyes swept from that group to the performers next to the children, all of them doing something to encourage the children's laughter. A group of telekinetic triplets juggled flaming marshmallows without touching them with their hands. A girl threw somersaults forward and backward over and over.

And then there was the girl with the platinum blonde hair and pink streak, sitting casually on the log doing nothing. Well, not nothing actually. She was enjoying the conversation of her companion, the other acrobat. He was the guy with the perfect blond highlights and a smile that always prompted a laugh from the girl. Jack. More revolting to Finley than how Jack made the girl react, was that he was the star of the show. His performance was the one that received applause which triggered car alarms. He was the one they came to see more than any other. Finley didn't like anything about Jack, but he realized it was only jealously fueling those thoughts. And soon it wouldn't matter. Soon he'd turn the tables. Soon he'd be the one everyone envied. All he had to do was wait one more day.

Chapter Nine

"What city are we in?" Jasmine asked, running her light brown hands through the grass where they sat, enjoying the way the soft blades caressed her palms.

Zuma smoothed out the map with her hand and eyed it with a speculative stare. "Seattle," she said after less than a few seconds.

"You didn't even hesitate before answering. How do you always know where we are? It's almost a different city every night," her friend said.

"How do you *not* know?" Zuma said with a low gaze, her tone disapproving. "And it's not a new city every night when there's a show. Just on the road."

"It feels like it," Jasmine said with a tired sigh.

Zuma traced the Pacific Coast Highway on the map with her fingertip down to Mexico.

"What's your deal with maps?" Jasmine asked, watching her.

She shrugged and flipped a strand of pink hair off her shoulder. "I think they're grand. It's so cool to see where you are, and where you could go and how vast the world is and all the possibilities."

"Yeah, so cool," Jasmine said with zero emotion. "Don't you ever get tired of traveling?"

Zuma flipped her head up with a look of astonishment. "You can't be serious?"

"Of course I am," the girl with the head full of fuzzy tight brown curls said.

"Jaz, don't tell me you're thinking of quitting?"

The older girl gave a guilty expression. "If I do then you'll have my spot in the show."

Zuma carefully folded up the map of California. "I don't want your spot. I want my friend to not abandon me for some steady job and fixed location."

Jasmine sighed. "Don't you want to meet people you can form lasting relationships with? No offense but I feel kind of limited with only seeing the same fifty people for the last three years."

"I do take offense. I'm the bestest of friends you could wish for and the other people here are the best you could meet anywhere," Zuma said.

"This is more than about having friends. It's about finding someone special," Jasmine said.

Zuma blinked at her friend in surprise. "But even if there wasn't the 'no dating each other' rule at Vagabond Circus, there isn't anyone here that's…"

"Gay. That's what you want to say," Jasmine said boldly. "Yeah, there's no girls here for me and that's exactly what I mean."

"Please don't leave, Jaz. There's ages to date and find Mrs. Right."

"Zuma, you can't tell me you don't think about dating?"

"I date," she said with offense.

"Oh, yeah, you meet a boy on opening night and go out with him once or twice before the caravan hits the road. Then you leave him heartbroken and wanting more of what only Zuma with her mysterious looks and sassy attitude can give."

Jasmine Reynolds-Underwood was referring to a situation with a boy that happened last year in San Diego. There was an undoubtable connection between Zuma and him, but she didn't look back as the caravan pulled away. The boy had begged her to stay after their three consecutive dates but Zuma hadn't even considered the option. She handed him back his bouquet of sunflowers and told him she'd see him another time.

"We will be back through San Diego this year," she said now, remorse in her voice.

"And he'll probably be in a happy relationship," Jasmine sang back.

"And have forgotten me, right?" Zuma said, a bit of snark in her voice.

"No. You're kind of unforgettable. And there won't be a 'we' going back to San Diego this year. I really can't keep this up much longer."

"Jaz," Zuma begged. She knew arguing with Jasmine was ridiculous. The girl was stubborn and if she was telling Zuma this now it was because she'd already considered and made up her mind. Still, Zuma plastered a pout on her face, but it had zero effect. Jasmine stared back with her soft brown eyes and shook her head.

The dark-haired girl patted the other's shoulder as she stood from her seated position in the soft grass. "Hey, and just think, in the top spot you'll have a lot more practice sessions with Jack," Jasmine said. "Dang, if I was straight, I'd totally rip that boy's clothes off him."

"What good does more time with Jack do for me? No dating rule, remember?" Zuma said.

"Oh, don't you know already that forbidden love is the best?" Jasmine said with a wink.

Chapter Ten

One hour before the Vagabond Circus begins, the gates open to the big top and the grounds. A line of booths borders the space directly opposite the concessions. Patrons can buy hot dogs and candy and get their faces painted or visit the various other booths set up. Dave didn't believe in selling crappy merchandise, but he did believe in selling a real service to patrons. Something that enriched their experiences.

Forty-five minutes before the start of tonight's show a girl of about seven stopped off at the first booth to get a horse and stars painted on her cheek and forehead. Her father, a middle-aged divorcé, was drawn to the second to the last booth. It was drenched in rich fabrics of neon green and teal blues, and firelight danced from the chandelier over a girl's head. She was actually what drew in the man's attention. Even with the light blue shawl draped over her head he knew she was beautiful, alluring. There was something of great interest about the girl, but the same could be said of everyone at the circus. He shook his head when he realized he'd been staring. It was just the combination of colors and the smell of popcorn that had him feeling nostalgic for the days when the circus meant something to him.

There's nothing really here, he thought. *Just crazy eccentrics who perform tricks.*

"Would you like your fortune read?" the girl asked, her voice soft and melodic.

"Excuse me?" he said, stepping close, not sure he heard her right.

"Your fortune," the girl repeated.

He shook his head and chuckled. "Oh, no, I'm just waiting for my daughter to get her face painted."

"What better way to wait?" the girl said, lowering her hood to reveal almost completely white hair streaked with a startling contrast of pink.

Freaks, the man thought. *Everyone in the circus is a freak, that's why they're so entertaining.*

The girl gave a clever smile like she just remembered something funny. "How about I not even charge you? I read your fortune and if afterwards you find the information of any use then you can offer me what you think is reasonable."

"And if I find what you say to be generic, like what most psychics spout?" the man said.

"Then you laugh and give me nothing," the girl said, flashing an irresistible smile.

The man nodded, already feeling victorious. He couldn't wait to tell his golf buddies about the pretty girl who failed to scam him. Most would probably fall for her act and sharp brown eyes, but Tony wasn't one of those softies.

"Go ahead and take a seat, Tony," Zuma said, pulling a silk scarf off the opaque orb sitting before her.

The man halted suddenly. "How did you know my name?"

She placed her hands on the ball and smiled into it. "Would you believe my magic ball told me?"

Tony laughed and took the seat in front of the fortuneteller. He had to give Vagabond Circus credit. They were strategic at their scams. He'd used a credit card to buy the tickets. All that information was probably fed straight to this loony girl.

Zuma glided her hand over the ball, not looking at it. It was indeed a prop, but a necessary one to allow her the time she needed. "Now I need you to clear your mind. Don't think of anything," she commanded. Those two sentences were also critical to her success. When told to not think of anything most people's thoughts flocked straight to their greatest worry before shoving it away.

"I'm getting something," she said, staring into the crystal orb.

"Nice script, honey," Tony said. "I've heard it before though."

"Shush," she said at once in a punishing voice. "I said to clear your mind."

He blinked at her in surprise, but tried to do as he was told, although it was nearly impossible. There were so many thoughts clouding his head lately. Well, always, but especially at the present. After ten long seconds Zuma raised her eyes at the stranger and leaned forward. "Your daughter…" she began in a breathless voice.

"Oh, sure, start with the one piece of information I fed to you. I told you I was here with her," Tony said, rolling his eyes.

Zuma smiled at him and took a long pause as the data flowed to her almost effortlessly. Middlings were exceptionally easy for her to read. Finally she said, "You don't think your daughter is yours. It's that fear that made you insecure, that made you cheat in retaliation and therefore land yourself divorced and with only partial custody," she said in one long flowing breath.

Tony dropped both his palms on the table in front of him half in disbelief and half in anger. "How?" he growled. "How did you know all that?"

"I'm a fortuneteller," Zuma said, her tone calm and nonchalant. "And that was only to get your attention, but here is your fortune."

Tony's hands shook and he pressed them into the tablecloth for support. No one knew his suspicions about Telly, his daughter. He'd been too mortified to speak about it even to his closest friends, unsure if he was paranoid over the whole thing.

"It shouldn't matter if she is your blood or not," Zuma said. "For these seven years she's been your daughter and you love her, right?"

"Yes, of course." His voice came out in a shaky croak.

"Then put the concern behind you and stop punishing her for what your ex-wife may or may not have done. Because if you don't then you *will* lose her, as you did your wife. Instead of being distant and withholding, love your daughter as your own." Zuma stopped abruptly. Blinked at Tony impassively.

He gulped, afraid his emotions were showing, making him look like a fool. It was only last year that he'd cheated. This year his wife had divorced him. And for all of his daughter's life he'd been like a yo-yo with his affection for her.

"Do you really see a future where I lose my daughter?" Tony asked, trying to keep his voice steady.

"I do," Zuma said with confidence. "I see one where she refuses to speak to you, tired of experiencing the heartbreak."

"Oh," Tony said, and lowered his chin, feeling almost unable to hold it up under the sudden weight of emotions.

"But..." Zuma continued. "I also see a possible future where you connect with your daughter like you've never done before.

Where you have a fulfilling relationship because you let go of the insecurities."

Tony dared to look up at the fortuneteller and it was her look of confidence that softened him slightly. "Really?"

Zuma nodded.

"Is that all?"

"No, one more thing," Zuma said. "Getting one's face painted is really more fun if there's someone to share in the experience with. If you hurry then you can enjoy that moment with Telly." Zuma pointed down to the end where the young girl had patiently been waiting in line and was now taking a seat to get her face painted.

"Yes, of course," Tony said, shuffling to a standing position. His throat was parched suddenly and his chest pinched. *Who was this girl? Had she actually read his fortune?* He nodded at Zuma before turning around and almost racing to stand beside his daughter. Telly was surprised when she saw her father there next to her, his face full of wonder and a brand new energy. Telly reached out and clasped his hand as the makeup artist brushed the first bit of paint across her freckled face.

Zuma smiled down at her crystal ball again. Her main role for the Vagabond Circus as a fortuneteller was a bit of trickery. She wasn't clairvoyant and couldn't see the future. But one didn't need to see the future to tell people what they needed to hear. All one required was to read their thoughts and give them sound advice. Lucky for Zuma she was excellent at both, a telepath and a girl with solid intuition.

Six minutes later Zuma startled suddenly when someone knocked on the surface of her table.

"Sorry to disturb you," Tony said, looking apologetic. His daughter stood next to him, her hand neatly tucked into his, a giant smile on her elaborately painted face. "I just wanted to give you this." He laid down a crisp one-hundred-dollar bill in front of Zuma. "It's all I have in cash, but what you foretold to me is worth more. Thank you."

Zuma allowed the bill to sit in front of her, unrushed to add it to her till. "You're most welcome and this is most generous of you."

Tony smiled, a real one, before allowing his daughter to tug him away, underneath the big top.

Chapter Eleven

The acrobats perform three separate acts in the two-hour show of Vagabond Circus. The first is right after the opening. While the crowd is still reeling from the disappearance of the six Arabian horses, Zuma and Jasmine are lowered from the ceiling on two hoops. They use them as a gymnast would the uneven bars, spiraling over and through them as the hoops make their descent from over forty feet in the air. Their silver hoops halt when they're ten feet off the ground. And then between them Jack is lowered, standing majestically on a large globe of the Earth. He begins walking at a slow pace and the Earth glides under him, like a gerbil on a ball. It spins from the axis through its middle that's suspended by two cables. The orb stops just above the girls. There are no nets or safety harnesses below them.

The six-minute act begins slowly. A series of twists and turns by the girls. The audience always stares mesmerized, as the music remains steady, a few harp notes. And then a sudden crescendo makes everyone jump and that is precisely when Jack jumps straight in the air and throws a series of flips and double-backs from atop the ball. Several times he descends nearly missing the globe, which makes the audience gasp with fear. This always produces a wide smile from Jack, who knows without a doubt that falling from twenty feet up would cause serious injury and knows that was never going to happen. It was also what he did after every flip that astonished the audience.

Jack seemed to pause in midair and hover a few inches over the spinning ball before landing on it in a sprint.

"He's floating," a girl screamed from the crowd.

"No, he must be suspended by wires we can't see," the guy in front of her said.

Finley, who sat in the back row, knew the truth. Jack was levitating. It's what granted him a brief moment to gain his footing before the next trick. And levitation was an impressive skill, but Finley guessed Jack could only do it for a few seconds at a time.

Again Finley found himself studying Zuma. It was one of the reasons he came to the show again. He wanted to know as much about the people as he could before tonight's meeting. Advantages were always gained by the person who sought covert information. He needed every advantage.

This was the sixth show Finley had watched and he knew what everyone's gift was but Zuma's. He knew she must be telepathic or clairvoyant since she did the fortune-telling before the show, but he couldn't figure out why she was an acrobat. She undeniably had a grace and speed that was breathtaking to watch, but she didn't appear to have a special skill during the performance like the others and yet he couldn't force himself to look away from her. He hardly noticed the girl who obviously had the second position in the act, Jasmine. Although she was irrefutably impossible to completely ignore. Whereas the girl with the pink hair was gorgeous, the other was unique with her slender shoulders and scrutinizing green eyes. And what she did was hard to miss.

Finley leaned forward just as the girls dismounted the hoops. Jack flipped backwards several times and on the last one he projected himself three feet back until he was off the ball. He then somersaulted four times in quick rotation, each one bringing him closer to the earth. The audience gasped in horror, sure Jack would crash to the ground. When he was three feet from the ground, he paused and hovered, his hands out flat, chin held high, and then slowly, like being lowered by a wire, he glided to the ground. When he was safely down he threw his hands into the air and received the second standing ovation of the night. The girls gracefully arrived at his side, presenting him like he was royalty.

The entire act was a series of flips and twirls and different holds until the finale. Everything had returned to the slow methodical rhythm that started the act. Then suddenly Jack took Jasmine's hand and just when the audience expected him to thrust her above his head in a shoulder hold as he'd done many times throughout the act, she lifted him above her head and held him there. A low moan of disbelief echoed from the audience as they watched a one-hundred-pound girl balance a one-hundred-forty-pound guy above her head. Their hands held on to each other's tightly as Jack was suspended in a handstand. They turned, the girl taking deliberate steps to show the audience all sides of them and that there were no wires supporting Jack.

And just when the audience digested this, Jack lowered both his legs forward and the girl with pink and blonde hair grabbed both his heels. With a concentration to impress, he lifted his legs as the girl pushed off the ground and extended her own legs upward. They worked together, Zuma and Jack, until he was straightened back into a handstand and she was in a similar position, her hands firmly planted on his feet. When she straightened all the way into a handstand the crowd erupted with deafening applause. Three people erected one on top of the other, two in handstands and the base of the tower a girl of only eighteen. Finley had never seen anything like it. He didn't know such a Dream Traveler gift existed. But there was no doubt about it. He was certain that if he challenged the dark-skinned girl to an arm-wrestling contest then he'd lose. Most anyone would lose to this girl who obviously had super strength.

Chapter Twelve

*A*fter the circus was over Finley didn't file out of the front gates with the rest of the patrons. Instead he lingered by the booths and concessions waiting until fifteen after the hour. Dave had told him to arrive five after, but being late would set the better standard. Finley checked his appearance in the mirror at the face painting booth, which was now abandoned. He'd spent his last bit of money on a new shirt and jeans. He could have gotten more money, but he didn't enjoy the means by which he would have to resort to do so. That was one of the reasons he was here. Only one of the reasons, though. Because for a guy like Finley there were multiple opportunities, but he only saw that now. He had cursed himself for being so blindfolded before. The blinders were off now, though, and his unlimited potential was stretching out in front of him.

Finley dared to smile at himself in the mirror. The white button-up shirt fit well. He'd never worn anything so nice. Never been allowed to. Only black T-shirts and black jeans. All hand-me-downs. He'd splurged and even gotten a haircut and shave. Now his dark brown hair almost looked tamed, parted on one side and making a spiky arc on the other.

"You got this," he said to his image, boosting the confidence he knew he needed. It wasn't the circus performers who intimidated him or even the crew. It was the one they all didn't suspect. The one he came to take down.

With his shoulders relaxed he headed straight for the back lot. Finley smelled the burning charcoal before he heard the voices and laughter. He'd watched, from the woods, this scene a few times, but now to willingly walk up to it produced a different feeling.

When Finley strolled straight into the Vagabond after-show festivities three things happened: Half the groups stopped conversing. Most of the groups regarded him with puzzled stares. And Finley realized he had finally entered this deadly game and it might cost him his life.

Chapter Thirteen

"*A*re you lost, son?" Titus, the creative director, asked Finley. He had stepped away from his conversation and approached the outsider as others stood curiously staring. "The circus is closed."

"Not lost," Finley said, deliberately not expanding on his statement.

Titus's forehead wrinkled. He was a tall lean man and constantly had an irritated look on his face, but more so after Finley's response.

"Are you looking for someone?" he asked.

"Yeah," Finley said, still keeping it brief.

"Well, I'm Titus," he said, extending his hand. "Who might you be and who might I fetch for you?"

Finley didn't take the older man's hand. Instead he roamed his eyes over the crowd at Titus's back. Several pairs of curious eyes stared at him, but politely pretended to be uninterested. Zuma was one of them. She sat between Jack and Jasmine, her eyes half on him, studying him. He smiled at her before returning his gaze to Titus.

"Dave Raydon is expecting me," Finley said to the man.

Titus's long face broke into a look of pity. "Thing is, son, Dave doesn't meet with the public after hours. And I'm sure you're excited to meet the ringmaster but he's quite bus—"

"Well, it's about time!" Dave's booming voice filled the air as he strolled forward. He clapped a gloved hand on Titus's shoulder, which stood even with Dave's head. "Thanks for welcoming my friend, Titus," he said and then turned his wide smile to Finley. Dave's face was round with an extra layer of fat, but he was undoubtedly attractive, especially in his youth. And the bushy mustache made him appear whimsical, and also sophisticated. "What kept you, dear boy? I had begun to think you'd had second thoughts about the job."

At this, everyone quieted down. No one even made a show of not eavesdropping now. All eyes were on Finley. He made note of where the different people of interest were to ensure he was a good distance from the most dangerous. For now he was safe.

"I just had some business to wrap up before I could devote my full attention to you and this meeting you've invited me to," Finley said.

"And do I have your full attention now? No other obligations from this point forward?" the ringmaster asked.

"None," Finley said, extending his hand to Dave, who immediately took it and shook it exuberantly.

"Very good," he said, shaking it for a few seconds more than necessary. "And this isn't a meeting, Finley. This here"—Dave turned to the crowd at his back, holding his arms wide—"is a celebration. We have one after every day of a show, and now we have more to celebrate."

"We do?" Titus said, his face growing a shade darker. His blond eyebrows reached up so high, like they wished to connect with his hairline. "Dave, what's going on? You haven't included me in any of this."

"I haven't," Dave admitted easily. "I wanted it to be a surprise."

"You know I don't like surprises, Dave," Titus said, his fingers pressing into his temples like he could feel the headache coming on from the news he hadn't yet received.

"Oh, but you'll like this one," Dave said, a laugh in his voice, like uncontrollable giggling was about to commence. "You're the one who's been encouraging me to do something to boost sales and help the circus be more prosperous."

Titus shook his head, his fingers still pinned on his temples. "Not make prosperous, but keep afloat."

Dave waved him off. "And that's what I'm doing." He then reached out and took Finley's hand and held it in the air above their heads, in front of Titus and the crowd of Vagabond Circus employees. The gesture was done easily between boy and older man. Although Finley was taller than Dave, they shared a similar grace. "I'd like you all to meet the newest performer for Vagabond Circus, Finley."

First there were several gasps of disbelief followed by a long sigh from Titus. Finley noticed someone in the crowd skirt to the back. Away. He suspected he knew who it was and they were already avoiding him, but not for long.

"No-no-no-no," Titus said, his head shaking. "We're mid-season. We aren't adding acts right now."

"Oh, but we are," Dave said, not looking at Titus but rather fondly at Finley, who was the picture of cool although everyone was now scrutinizing him.

"How can you think this will boost sales?" Titus asked. "This is suicide. Bringing in a new unrehearsed act when things are already running. Have you lost your mind?"

"My mind is as strong as ever. And after reflection I realized that you, Titus, were right and we needed to do something drastic," Dave said, that unrelenting spark always in his eyes, but magnified as he stared at the boy beside him, the one who was almost a man. Finley had a face full of subtle sharp angles, one that made him appear handsome and also discerning. His expression seemed to say, "I don't trust the world."

Titus sighed slightly. "I meant raise ticket prices or add furlough days."

At this the crowd groaned with disapproval.

"No worries, my lovelies," Dave said to the circus people. "And Titus, I realized what you meant, but I have done something that will benefit everyone. I've hired Finley to join us and I truly believe he will add great value to our show."

Finley didn't dare shift his flat expression, although his chest had swollen with pride. He didn't even change his expression when Dave slapped him fondly on the back. "This dear boy is the missing piece we all knew was lacking from the show. The part that will really wow the audience."

There was another round of disgruntled mutters from the crowd.

"Oh," Dave said calmly, "you all know you're spectacular, but here at Vagabond Circus we need to keep pushing the edge, and I think that's what we will do with Finley's help. Give them more of the unexplainable."

"Dave," Titus said, drawing out his name, irritation in his voice.

He held up a gloved finger. "Now Finley will begin rehearsal tomorrow and—"

"Dave! I'm the creative director," Titus barked. "How dare you make this decision without me?"

Looking unflustered, Dave smoothed down his dark brown hair in the front. "I told you already it was a surprise. You will, of course, have all the input on who he works with and how the acts are configured. Trust me on this, Titus. It will boost sales as you wanted."

Titus took in a long breath. He was quick to anger and quick to calm. And years of working with Dave Raydon had taught him to sometimes give the ringmaster a chance, because although spontaneous in nature, he also had good instincts. "Fine. What is this boy's skill?"

"He has a couple actually," Dave said proudly. "And I'd love for him to show you firsthand tomorrow morning. It really is quite fun to see rather than talk about."

"Fine, fine," Titus said, his face still red.

"And," Dave continued, "I'd like the acrobats to be there as well."

At this Jack and Zuma and Jasmine exchanged horrified looks.

"Why them?" Titus said, irritation flaring in his words again.

"Because Finley will be performing with them," Dave said casually, like this should have been obvious from the beginning.

Titus slammed his hand over his long forehead. "They're our best act though."

"And they're about to get even better," Dave said, and now the laugh did spring out, joining his words. "Like I said before, as the creative director, you have full authority in how the acts are changed, but…"

"But…" Titus said, having worked with Dave long enough to read the hint in his voice.

"But, I would have you consider pairing Zuma with Finley," Dave said, looking at the acrobat sitting beside Jack and winking at her. His affection for her went deep. She was more than like a daughter to him. Zuma also represented so much of his inspiration for the circus. The girl had fire and talent and mystery. He had loved her from the start, and had given her special treatment by providing her more than just one role in the circus. Now he wanted to reward her again by giving her a chance to be the star, alongside Finley.

"What?!" Zuma said, standing suddenly. She took hurried steps until she'd joined the ringmaster, the creative director and the stranger. "But I always work with Jack and Jaz!"

"And you still will, but I think your gifts will complement Finley's better in a duo," Dave said, clasping his hands behind his back and rocking up on his toes and then down again. He was thoroughly pleased with himself and it was oozing from every one of his pores.

"But I'm in a trio," she said stubbornly, her frustration evident.

"And I think we can all admit that they work, but duos are more compelling," Dave said, and then his face lit up with a clever grin. "They're more romantic to the audience."

Zuma rolled her eyes and then buried her head in her hands. She hadn't dared to look back at Finley, who stood stock-still, a stone expression on his face. Jack had joined Zuma at her side. He regarded Finley now with an analyzing stare, which the stranger pretended not to notice.

"Dave, I really—" Jack began but Dave simply held up his hand and he paused.

"Do you trust me?" Dave said.

"Well..." Jack blanched. "Yes, but—"

"Then indulge me in this," Dave said simply.

Jack nodded obediently and then looked at Zuma, who was just raising her head up to stare at Dave. She understood him better than most, maybe because she could get into his head if he allowed it, but also for the plain reason that she understood him. Looked up to him. Respected him more than any other. She stopped to study him, to try and piece this all together. When nothing of any help came to her, she revolved her gaze onto Jack. Where Finley's face was sharp angles, Jack's features were soft but still strong. It was his German heritage that was responsible for this as well as his blondish hair and wide shoulders. Jack had a look on his face that said he wanted to comfort Zuma, but he didn't know how. Knew he couldn't. Not like he wanted to.

"But Dave, I don't know the first thing about this person," Zuma finally said, haphazardly throwing her arm in Finley's direction, not looking at him. "How am I supposed to create an act when we are currently having shows?"

"Well, I suppose you'll spend extra time getting to know each other, dream travel time. It will be worth it," Dave said unconcernedly.

"Where did you find him?" Zuma asked, her eyes now roaming over Finley's face.

35

He allowed his expression to finally show some emotion. Anger. "I am right here, you know. You don't have to refer to me like I'm not," Finley said.

The ringmaster smiled, not put off by Finley's anger or Zuma's skepticism. "I think," Dave said, holding up a finger again, "if you, Zuma, want an answer to that question then you should ask Finley. It *is* his business."

She turned to the stranger and faced him with an odd confidence he hadn't witnessed before. Zuma was entitled, but not without right. She owned something about this world. And Finley couldn't figure it out. "Where did you come from?" she asked.

Finley didn't like the way she was looking at him. This wasn't the way this was supposed to go. "That is none of your business," he said with a defiant smile.

Zuma huffed with frustration, but also looked secretly happy to have received this reaction. It would make her case easier. "Dave, how am I supposed to work with someone so rude? You just bring this stranger in and split up our group?" The crowd around Zuma looked sympathetic.

"I didn't split up anyone. I'm making the circus more complete. And might I remind everyone of the first of my only two rules," Dave said, staring out at the people watching.

There was silence and then heads shook, but Finley looked around, confused. "These rules? What are they?"

"The first rule is to, above all else, respect each other," Dave recited.

"And the second?" Finley prompted.

"That we do not enter into romantic relationships with one another," Titus chimed in, his voice monotone.

"Oh," Finley said, having almost choked on his last breath. That hadn't even occurred to him as a possibility as far as rules. No stealing or no violence maybe, but no dating was a strange rule.

"And Zuma," Dave said in a sensitive voice, earning a softened expression from her, "the final decision will be up to Titus and I know you respect his creative judgment."

She nodded. "I do, as much as yours."

"Then we will see how everything unfolds tomorrow," Dave said, spreading his face wide with a smile again.

They all nodded. This was Dave's rule. It was hardly ever questioned and thoroughly respected. This was because he led through love and inspiration and Finley had never witnessed something so pure. Dave turned to Titus and he also forced a reluctant nod. "Okay, Dave. I'll keep an open mind to adding a new performer."

"Thank you, old friend," Dave said to the creative director. "Now would you do the honors?"

"Of course," Titus said and then turned to Finley. "Would you please follow me and I'll lead you to your trailer?" Titus said at once.

And after those words Finley's mask fully dropped, an excited smile popping on his face.

"My trailer?" he repeated quietly.

"Naturally," Titus said, marching off. "Follow me. We have one open on the far side, right next to the other performers."

Chapter Fourteen

*F*inley bolted upright when he awoke the next morning. The comfortable bed underneath him and the cozy surroundings weren't unwelcome, they were totally perplexing at first rising. It took him a few seconds of deliberation to piece together the parts of the night before that led him to this trailer and the queen-size bed that he was spread across. He was used to sleeping in the woods lately and the humid warehouse before that. He hadn't awoken in a soft bed with morning sunlight neatly streaming through paisley curtains in… well, forever.

Last night he was exhausted from the adrenaline of the weeks leading up to this part of the plan. After Titus showed him his trailer he collapsed into the bed and fell into dream-filled sleep the whole night. Now he wished he would have spent the night dream traveling to hone his skills or spy on these Vagabond Circus people. But even *he* needed good, old-fashioned sleep sometimes.

The trailer had a bathroom, kitchen, and living area. All were small, but they were more than adequate. He took a shower with real hot water and then found plush towels at the ready when he exited. He laughed when he realized he'd been ready to shake off the water as he was accustomed to doing. At every turn there seemed to be something new to amaze the almost adult boy and he quickly realized his shortcomings. If the people he was about to work with spied this awe in him then they'd ridicule it. Worst of all was that they'd wonder about him. They'd ask questions. Last night Finley had thrown off Zuma's questions about where he came from, but that wouldn't last. He had to be ready the next time. Not with an answer, but with something that would keep her or anyone from asking again. No one could know where he came from. Finley wasn't just ashamed of where he was from, he was incredibly appalled by it. Only one person at Vagabond Circus knew where he was from and they weren't going to talk about it, because they also shared this curse.

Upon exiting the bathroom, Finley found a box on the sofa. Titus must have put it there last night, although Finley didn't remember. Maybe he put it there this morning since Finley didn't care to lock his trailer last night before passing out. He shouldn't have been so careless. That mistake could have gotten him killed.

Too curious, Finley slid the lid off the box and there he stood, half naked in a towel, staring at what he suspected he'd find and still couldn't believe. It was so silly. Something everyone here had, and yet didn't appreciate. New clothes. He reached out and ran his hands over the smooth spandex of the workout suit. It was the colors of the Vagabond Circus, teal blue and neon green. He'd never performed in anything but threadbare street clothes.

Under the full-body leotard in the box was a jacket and pants for warming up. Everything was brand new and had a strange scent to it. They smelled clean and newly manufactured and also had an undertone of perfume to them.

It was upon pulling on the suit that Finley realized how revealing it was. He'd seen something similar on Jack in the ring. That guy wore it with pride and now Finley realized that was the only way. One can't walk out in front of thousands of people with a skin-tight suit on and not own it. And what was he supposed to be self-conscious of? Finley was all lean muscles. He had years of parkour to thank for that.

Finley pulled the jacket over his shoulders as he opened the door to his trailer. *His trailer.* The words still didn't seem right, and he didn't want to get used to them. This all wasn't supposed to last. He didn't belong here and neither did the person he'd come after. He'd take them out and then find a new life.

The smell of fried eggs and grilled flatbread was heavy in the air when Finley exited his trailer. He didn't know those smells well. Couldn't really identify them as anything more than "delicious." His stomach rumbled furiously when he made his way out to where many of the people of Vagabond Circus were chatting. They all stopped in their various spots and stared at him. Some were polite and smiled a little. Some pretended not to have seen him and looked away almost at once. Zuma, who was speaking rapidly to her friend Jasmine, locked eyes with him and seemed to be trying to pierce him with a single look.

"Z," Jasmine said, drilling her friend in the arm with loose knuckles. "We already discussed this. Just give him a chance."

Without laying her eyes on Jasmine, Zuma deflected her next assault almost before it came. "Keep your hands off me and your advice to yourself."

Finley brought his hand up to his mouth, kissed it, and blew it at Zuma, who was only two trailers away. "You know you want to catch this, so go ahead, sweetheart," he sang loud enough for her and everyone around to hear.

"Gah! He didn't just do that?" Zuma turned with revulsion and gaped at Jasmine, who appeared to be covering a look of amusement.

"I do believe our boy just did," she said, letting a giggle break through.

"Jaz," Zuma said and then trained the rest of her words into an inaudible whisper for only her friends' ears to hear.

Finley decided not to care and strolled dangerously close by the pair on the way to the trailer on the other side of them. In the common area, breakfast was being served from the food truck. And although Finley was half tempted to find out what real eggs actually tasted like, he decided that he had to stay focused.

The trailer on the other side of Zuma's was Fanny's. Four children of varying ages were kicking around a soccer ball when Finley approached. He'd gotten a strange look from most as he strolled through the trailer area, so he wasn't surprised when the oldest boy pulled a shorter one by the shirt collar at once. He seemed repulsed by Finley, like any association with him would ruin his chances in the future with the circus. They called after the two remaining girls, but only the older one ran after them into the open door of the trailer. The smallest, a girl of around four, stood staring up at Finley with ocean blue eyes. Her hair was braided back into two French braids. Fanny's handiwork.

Finley leaned down, almost too quickly for her eyes to register, and plucked the ball from the ground. He spun it around on the tip of his finger. "Do you like to play soccer?"

"I'm not very good," the girl, whose name was Emily, said.

Finley dropped the ball to the ground and sank down with it, now looking up at the girl with hair like spun sunlight. "Who told you that?"

She cocked her head at the trailer where the other children had disappeared. "Sebastian did. He said I am too young and mess up all their games."

Finley raised an eyebrow. "Do you know what I think?"

Emily shook her head, her long braids whipping against her face as she did.

"I think he's afraid that if you played, you might show him up," Finley said with a wink. And there was something in his almost hazel green eyes that even a four-year-old couldn't resist.

Emily picked up the ball and handed it to him at once. "So you'll play with me?"

"Of course I will, but you have to make me one solid promise…"

She was smart for her age, even though she'd had no real training from parents, and had been in a cluster of kids in a foster home most of her life. The little girl studied him and then said, "I have to hear the deal before I agree."

"Fair enough," Finley said, smiling at her, instantly feeling endeared to the little girl. She reminded him of a few of the kids he knew, but he didn't consider them friends. Not like he thought he could consider this girl. Back where he came from, no one was friends. It was easier that way. "You stay away from people like Sebastian who tell you you aren't good enough, and I'll spend as much time with you as I can, telling you that you are."

"What's the catch?" she asked.

"There's no catch," he said.

"Why would you tell me such a thing then? You don't even know me," Emily said.

Finley stood with the soccer ball and shot it between his hands several times, all with a blur of movement, and then tossed it up to his head, where it spun before rolling over his shoulder, down his arm, and landing in his hand. "Because it's true."

The girl's face burst bright with a smile and a giggle. "That was fantastic. Can you do more tricks like that?"

"I'm afraid he can't," Fanny cut in, stepping out of the trailer. She didn't look directly at Finley as she cleared the few steps to the young girl. There she kneeled down and looked straight into the four-year-old's eyes. "Dear Emily, would you mind popping into the trailer to fetch me my glasses? You can always find them and I've seemed to have misplaced the darn things again."

"But Ms. Fanny, why you say I can't—"

"Shhh. Shhh. Little Em, I just meant that I need you to wait before spending time with the new acrobat. In time, I'm sure," Fanny said, her Louisiana accent making her stern words sound sweet.

The little girl nodded solemnly and then turned without another look at Finley and ran to the trailer.

Finley was about to protest when Fanny rose to full height. She was the stature of the average man and had the shoulders to match. "Mr....?"

"Just Finley. No mister's necessary," Finley said, his eyes still pinned on the trailer door where Emily had disappeared.

"Mr. Finley, I'm sure you're a reputable gentleman with many qualities I'll come to admire," Fanny began, her eyes matching the sincerity in her voice. "But until I have the time and honor to appreciate you as a person, I ask that you kindly stay away from my children. It's nothing personal toward you, only that I don't personally know you and want to keep my kids protected from the unknown."

Finley hadn't been offended per se and yet he had been slightly banished. He didn't know what to make of this woman, who had perfect reason for her protection, but was taking her prejudice of the unknown and throwing it at him. He opened his mouth to argue and at that moment his ears were punished by the sound of laughter. A laughter he knew. Slowly he turned to catch Zuma giggling by the side of her friend. They, of course, had witnessed the whole thing. His good behavior and his humiliation. What they would remember would probably be the latter.

"Yes, of course," he said, bowing to the woman. "I completely understand, Mrs....?"

"Just miss and you can call me Fanny."

He arched a disbelieving eyebrow at the older woman. "Yes, Fanny. I look forward to getting to know you."

The caretaker then blushed and that's exactly what prompted the end of Zuma's laughter.

Chapter Fifteen

*I*t was strange to Finley to just walk up to a counter at a truck and order food. That was the first strange part and then the second, almost stranger part, was that a chipper man handed him a Styrofoam plate full of steaming food without asking for a cent. The man had turned away almost immediately, back to the grill, when Finley opened his mouth to ask questions. He shoved the disputes back in his mouth and turned to the many tables lining the common area. It felt odd to sit alone, making himself an outcast at once. Therefore he decided to be bold and plucked himself down at a table that was bristling with noise. It was a table of performers. Not the acrobats, who were two tables over, spying and dissecting his every move. The table Finley chose was the one with the illusionist, Oliver, and the triplets who juggled using telekinesis, and then another girl who he remembered had the fire act. They laughed and conversed adamantly and hardly noticed him when he sat down.

Finley was pretty certain they were making a show of pretending that him choosing their table was nothing of interest. They chatted about something foreign to Finley for a good minute before the girl with long black hair turned to him. She had the most discerning eyes he'd spied in a long time. She was undoubtedly from the streets based on her piercing judgmental stare, but she almost seemed to be trying to put him in the right light in her mind over and over again.

"So why *here*?" she finally said, revealing a row of tiny top teeth and a lot of pink gum. "Why did you choose to sit here?"

"Versus where?" he said, throwing his fork into a cushion of eggs. He almost smiled at the meeting of fork and eggs, but caught himself in time.

"Just seems you would want to be with your kind?" the girl with pale skin and cold green eyes said, indicating the table two over.

"I thought there wasn't a divide at this circus," Finley said, daring to look back at the acrobats two tables over, watching him.

"No matter how wonderful the leadership is, people will always do what they were born to do: create borders," she said, pushing her plate of mostly not eaten food away. "Don't get me wrong, I love my circus people, but I prefer to be with my 'nuclear family,'" she said, fanning her hand at the people at the table. "These are my immediate family and those people"—she pointed around at the rest of the circus members—"are the extended family. The cousins. The ones you take in small doses."

"Right," Finley said, staring at her plate of uneaten food. "I totally get it."

"No you don't, because you are about the newest newbie I've ever set eyes on. But don't worry, no one else knows that about you," she said with a wink.

Finley worked to corral the unsettling feeling in his chest. Before he could utter a rebuttal, the girl, named Sunshine, said, "I only know that because I'm empathic and have read all the various emotions you're experiencing right now. You hide and fake your emotions well."

The space between his eyebrows creased. "You've read my emotions…" He wanted to be angry about it, but there was something about the girl that garnered an unearned trust from him. She had this unbreakable sadness in her demeanor. Sunshine seemed to know emotion the way Finley understood survival. And he believed that her knowledge of his emotions wasn't something to be concerned about. There were other parts of him that posed a much bigger risk.

Sunshine nodded at him, a knowing in her solemn eyes. "Yes, I read your emotions, but they're safe with me. I won't tell another soul," she whispered for only him to hear. The other people at the table were talking to each other, ignoring them. "Really, I'd worry about Ms. Pink Streak over there," she said, pointing straight at Zuma, who noticed it right away and glared back at her. "She'll enter your brain and take all your secrets out if you're not careful."

"I'm careful," Finley said, pushing his full plate away too, not hungry all of a sudden. It had always been a mystery to him why his mind was a vault. But it was like that since he could remember, impenetrable. He had few worries that Zuma could trespass his thoughts. Finley knew how to do more than most should with their minds, but none of it was that useful now that he studied his list of attributes. The boy mostly knew how to take and shelter. What he needed to do now was perform and outmaneuver.

"I'm Sunshine," the girl said, extending a hand to him. The name was perfect for her and then also completely ironic. No one had less of a sunshine personality than this girl. Melancholy fell around her like a cloud over mountains.

"You already know my name," Finley said dryly.

Sunshine ignored this and the emotions brewing inside Finley that she read. "For the circus, I do the—"

"Pyrokinesis act," Finley said, completing her words. "I've seen the show. You're quite good and it's ever a wonder that Ripley's hasn't been called to observe you."

Blush showed up well on her pale cheeks. "Well, well, well, you're actually nice. What a surprise. I haven't met an acrobat who gave away compliments. You might do us well after all."

"I plan to save your very livelihood," Finley said with a wink. Everyone at Vagabond Circus knew the twenty-year venture was threatened by hard times, but most didn't speak about it. Finley's honesty and presence marked many things that brought both hope and fear to the troupe.

"So where are you from?" Sunshine asked, splaying out her black fingernails on the table. There wasn't much about the girl that wasn't black. Her eyes and skin weren't, but that was about all.

"All over," Finley said, rising from the table. He noticed just then that Zuma's eyes were still focused on him. Jack beside her was focused on Zuma. Jasmine didn't seem to care about anyone around her. Finley leaned back down, his face close to Sunshine's. "Maybe I haven't worn out my welcome and can come back here for lunch?"

She turned, putting her lips close by Finley's. "I think you'd be welcomed here. My friends welcome freaks and let's be honest, you're more freak than you are acrobat, but lucky for you, you pass for both."

He smiled at her before pulling himself upright and strolling by the acrobats' table. Finley then leaned over it and tapped the tabletop three times, startling Zuma. "Show starts in ten minutes. Get your judging hats on, because I'm going to give you a lot to stick your nose up at," he said and then left, the acrobats stared at his back as he did.

Chapter Sixteen

*T*he trapeze was set up when the acrobats entered the tent that morning.

"What in the world?" Jack said, staring up. He and Zuma arrived at Dave's side, who looked about as pleased as the night before. "I thought this newbie was showing us his skills," Jack commented in confusion at the sight in front of him.

"He is," Dave said, turning to Jack. He had his thumbs pressed into the folds of his jacket. "Finley has asked that we start with the flying trapeze act."

"He's a catcher on trapeze?" Jack said, looking around, still confused. Finley was in the middle of the ring, not stretching, but rather staring up at the wires with a satisfied smile.

"No, son," Dave said, slapping Jack's shoulder. Dave wasn't his father, but he was about the same age, and Jack respected him a great deal more. "You, Jack, are our catcher."

"Wait, you want him to demonstrate his skill with me?" Jack said, letting his disbelief take him a step back. "I don't even know the guy and you want me to catch him on trapeze?"

Dave nodded proudly. "Bingo. Now you better warm up. Finley looks to be ready."

"But Dave—"

"No buts," Dave interrupted, holding up a hand. "You said last night that you trust me. Let's stay with that thought for now."

"Yeah, fine." Jack looked to Zuma, whose eyes were beckoning him closer. He stepped nearer to her as Dave retreated. "What do you make of all this?" he asked her in a low whisper.

Over his shoulder she watched Finley, who was making no attempt to hide where his attention was, straight on her.

"I don't know," she said, refocusing on Jack. "But I trust Dave too, so let's see where this is going. We have to be willing to adapt. I don't like the idea of a new partner, but that guy joining the trapeze act is actually quite curious."

Jack leaned in close so only Zuma could hear him. His breath drifted down her neck. "I really don't like the idea of you partnering with him. I don't like the way he looks at you."

She pulled back so their eyes were locked. "Jack Fuller, are you jealous?"

He wanted to wrap his arms around her there, make it known to everyone under the big top who Zuma would belong to if such things were allowed in Vagabond Circus, but instead he smiled at her. "Yes, and more than a little bit."

She smiled, looking pleased. "You have nothing to worry about."

"One of these days, Z," Jack said, giving her a hungry look.

"You're going to what?" she said, flashing him a challenging expression. Dave was now conversing with Titus, who didn't look happy. Still, Jack and Zuma were running out of time for this intimate chat.

"One of these days I'm running away from the circus with you and then you'll find out," Jack said.

She stole another look at Dave before zipping up another inch between them. "I'm not ready to leave yet, but I do look forward to that."

Jack knew they had a tiny bit of privacy, since he still heard the director and ringmaster arguing at his back. That's why he glided his finger along Zuma's jawline. They never allowed themselves this type of moment but Finley's arrival was already changing things. "You should be *my* partner," he said. Zuma clasped her hand over his and then brought it to her mouth briefly.

"I wish that could be the case, but—"

"Giving our boy a pep talk, I see," Jasmine said, arriving at their side and winking at Zuma. She then knocked her hip into Zuma's and the three broke into an easy laugh. "Stop flirting already so I can see what this mystery man has in store," Jasmine said.

Zuma nodded to Jack, who backed away from her finally. When he turned he saw Finley standing, staring at her. His eyes seemed to be right on her, like she was all he saw in the gigantic tent.

She scowled at him and he returned her gesture with a disapproving head shake.

"Z, what is he shaking his head about?" Jasmine asked.

"I don't know, but he appears slightly deranged to me," Zuma said, not keeping her voice down.

"I'll show you deranged, sweetheart," Finley sang back to her as he climbed the trapeze ladder to the platform.

Zuma's face flushed red. Finley was bold and he did the unexpected. It was a beautiful combination, Zuma thought. And also an indication that he was a complete train wreck.

Jack had finished warming up by the time Dave and Titus joined the acrobats on the ground. Finley didn't take any practice swings but instead stood on the platform, his eyes always on Zuma. She worried something was wrong with him. He appeared distracted by her and she feared he'd get himself hurt. Jack would probably be fine since his levitation skill made it unlikely that he'd have a long fall. And there was the net. However, there were other things that could happen that were worse than falling. Flying trapeze needed complete concentration and she didn't like that this guy was about to swing straight into Jack.

"All right, Finley," Dave called from the ground, his gloved hand cupping his mouth. "Are you ready, my boy?"

Finley stood tall, staring down, his eyes still on Zuma. Jack had been right; there was something different in the way Finley looked at her, she admitted.

"Ready," he sang down, finally pulling his eyes up to focus across the net where Jack was now sitting on the bar swinging.

"What am I catching?" Jack called down.

Before Dave could answer Finley yelled, "The quadruple."

Zuma's mouth popped open.

Titus shook his head in disbelief.

Jack narrowed his eyes. "No way, man!"

"Way," Finley said, holding on to the bar, looking ready to disembark the platform.

"But I hardly ever catch the girls with a triple," Jack said, his tone sharp, disapproving.

"They aren't as good a flier as me," Finley said.

"I don't even know your skill," Jack yelled through the air.

"Just catch me," Finley said, sounding irritated. "I'll make the rotations. Just catch me."

Jack still sat seated on the bar, his position telling that he wasn't convinced.

"Jack, I believe Finley can do this," Dave yelled up from the ground. "Let's at least give him a chance. If he says he can do the quadruple in time for you to catch, then let's try it."

Jack eyes danced with both strange excitement and nervousness. He'd never caught a guy. Just the girls. And he'd never caught the quadruple. There were multiple things that could go wrong, especially catching a new flier. It wasn't like Dave to take these kinds of risks and maybe that's what finally convinced Jack. He consented with a nod and slid into position, the back of his legs hooked around the rope on either side of the bar. His head was angled down, arms helping him to gain momentum. Jack swung back and forth, gaining more speed, his upside down position almost more natural to him than being right side up.

A "hup" sound from Finley signaled the beginning of the trick. When Finley jumped into the air there was an incredible display of power. Zuma noticed his height was considerable compared to hers or Jasmine's. Her heart tightened watching him glide through the air. Finley swung back and then forward again, moving so fast he blurred slightly. And then at full swing he exploded into a tight somersault straight in the air. Her eyes could hardly register the rotations, but she counted them: one, two, three, and then four, and he was still a head over where Jack's hands were reaching out, ready to catch. They were moving fast though. Jack swung the opposite direction and then there was something like a pause and Finley flickered in the air and then suddenly, like she'd blinked and missed something, Finley's hands caught Jack's wrists. Jack's hands held onto Finley and the pair both completed the swing.

The scream of excitement that ripped from Zuma's mouth surprised her. She hadn't realized she'd been holding her breath or that her chest was beating wildly from adrenaline. Beside her, Jasmine, Titus, and the ringmaster clapped madly. Jasmine jumped up and down several times, the smile on her face infecting Zuma with even more excitement.

Jack let Finley down and he bounced on the net, not looking surprised that he'd made a nearly impossible trick look effortless. He flipped off the net and then shot a thumbs-up to Jack, who sat on his bar again, looking stunned.

"Thanks for the catch," Finley sang up at him.

Jack stared down at Zuma, who still wore the look of disbelief.

Dave clapped Titus on the shoulder. "He promised me he could do a quadruple and the boy doesn't lie. What do you think now, old friend?"

"Unbelievable," Titus said in a hoarse whisper.

Finley had his hands clasped above his head, gripping the net, pulling it down slightly from his weight. His eyes were pinned on the group discussing him on the other side of the ring, some forty feet away.

"I'm not sure I saw that clearly," Jasmine said. "It was almost too fast. What's that guy's skill anyway?"

And then Finley disappeared from their view and materialized right in between Jasmine and Zuma. Literally he popped up from the empty space, a clever grin on his face. "What do you mean? You miss something?"

Zuma screamed again, this time from the scare of having the stranger appear out of nowhere and drape his arm casually over her shoulder. Jasmine exploded with laughter.

"He can teleport?" Titus said with a shocked face. He looked straight at Dave. "But I haven't seen that since—"

"I know. It's pretty impressive," Dave said, cutting Titus off.

Jasmine was still laughing when Zuma pushed Finley's arm off her. "Get some manners, would you," she said, hiding her surprise and covering it with revulsion. Again she thought he was too bold.

"What just happened down here?" Jack asked, strolling urgently from where he had just dismounted the net. He shot a protective stare at Zuma, who was wiping Finley's sweat off her shoulder where he'd left it.

Finley stared at Zuma with a mischievous expression. "Some people are easily offended."

"And some people need to learn boundaries," she said, shooting an angry look at the new member of Vagabond Circus.

"Jack!" Jasmine said, still howling with laugher. "This guy just teleported."

Jack halted and gauged Finley. "That's how you closed the distance to complete the quadruple then," he stated rather than asked, seeming to piece the past events together in his mind. "I had thought I missed something, but it was all too fast."

"That's exactly how," Finley said.

"Wow, that *would* come in handy for acrobatic skills," Jack said, seeming to allow himself a moment to marvel in this new member's skill.

"And he also has super speed," Dave announced proudly. "That's another reason he could make those rotations fast enough to complete the quadruple."

Finley, who always seemed to be only half present even when the conversation concerned him, gazed impassively at the ground. Zuma was grateful that his eyes weren't focused on her. They did something to her. Affected her, although she wasn't sure how just yet.

"I want him to be my partner," Jasmine declared at once, taking the spot next to Finley and looping her arm through his.

He met her gaze with cool eyes and then shook his head at her. "No offense, but I don't work with anyone as a partner who could break my neck with the same effort it takes to snap their fingers."

She cinched him in closer. "I see you've watched the show."

"I have," he said, and swiveled his gaze on Zuma, a heat in his eyes that made her feel suddenly vulnerable. "It's already been decided who I'll partner with."

Zuma shivered, unsure why this guy had this chilling effect on her.

"I promise not to hurt you," Jasmine said, almost sounding to be begging. "And just imagine the act we could put together, your speed and my strength."

Dave seemed to be considering this, Zuma could see.

"But Jaz, I thought you were leaving the circus. You won't have time to put together a new act," Zuma said and quickly admonished herself for the announcement.

"Z!" Jasmine said in a hiss. "Would you be quiet?"

"Jasmine," Titus said in surprise. "I didn't know you were planning to leave."

"No one knew but my dear friend the blabbermouth," Jasmine said, glaring at Zuma.

Zuma wasn't sure why she'd divulged the secret. *Is it because I actually want to work with Finley?* she thought, the idea sending strange prickles down her spine. He was an amazing flier and the idea of pairing his skills with hers was inspiring. She understood

Jasmine's excitement, although she would never be showing it for Finley.

"Jasmine, you're not serious? You're not really thinking of leaving, are you?" the ringmaster asked, his tone filling the young girl's face with disappointment. No one wanted to disappoint Dave and usually no one ever wanted to leave him.

"I've just been throwing around the idea," she admitted.

No one said a word, they just stared between the ringmaster and Jasmine. Finally she said, "I'm wondering if I've outgrown the circus, that's all. I want more."

"Are you sure?" Dave said, staring at her, studying her.

"No, I'm not sure, which is why I'm still here," Jasmine said.

"My little Minnie," he said, using his sweet nickname for the girl, "stay the season through, will you? Give me that at least."

She nodded. "I'm not really ready anyway, just toying with the idea."

"Which is allowed," Dave said and then spun his gaze back to Finley, who still had his arm locked in Jasmine's.

"But my newest performer, I really feel is best suited as a partner with Zuma. And it's the deal Finley and I made," Dave said.

"You made a deal about who he'd perform with?" Jack asked incredulously.

"I did," Dave said casually. "He wanted to work with Zuma and I agreed because I think they will make a brilliant act. I can already see the chemistry."

Zuma dropped her eyes, her chest buzzing suddenly with anxiety. Dave hadn't just said what she thought she heard? *Chemistry?* Beside her she felt Jack tense. Zuma couldn't bear to witness the look of loathing she knew Jack wore right then.

"What about Zuma? Doesn't she get any say in this?" Jack asked, his voice growing unsteady.

All eyes turned to Zuma. She tried to make her face look like she was considering this ridiculous situation, rather than feeling confused by it. She wouldn't look weak, especially in front of Finley.

"Zuma," Dave called to her and she brought her calculating eyes up to meet his. "Are you, after seeing Finley's skill, amenable to be his partner? It's your choice, and I won't force you. You can have the job or I'll give it to Jasmine."

If Zuma declined working with Finley then she'd be assigned Jack as a partner. She knew that. Jack knew that. Zuma didn't need to be in Jack's head to know what he thought or wanted. She knew what most people in the ring were thinking right now. However, she didn't know what Finley actually thought. He was as much a mystery to her as she was to him. Nevertheless, his expression seemed to tell her enough. She didn't look back at Jack but instead allowed her eyes to lock on Finley's. They did something to her just then. Made her feel stronger than she was, although few were stronger than Zuma, even in Vagabond Circus. "I'm willing to give him a shot," she said, her voice even, stripped of emotion.

Dave erupted with applause. "Bravo! Then it's official. You two start practice after lunch. Let's convene now to discuss logistics, issues, and planning."

Zuma shifted her gaze to catch the dark expression in Jack's eyes before he turned and marched away.

Chapter Seventeen

Outside the big top, the circus was buzzing with commotion.
Everyone was busy discussing the newbie acrobat. Dave recruited
throughout the year, but new performers had to wait until the off-
season to be incorporated into the show. Never had an act been
added mid-season. The boy had to have an incredible talent to have
changed protocol so radically.

The triplets stood in a line, each only a foot from the other.
They were practicing outside their trailer, trying their best to ignore
the various conversations about Finley. Their act commanded full
concentration and without that, fatal injury was the result. Each had
six long daggers they were independently juggling from their
handles. The rotations sped up until it was a stream of blurs. Then
they began walking with measured steps until their line turned into a
triangle, each facing one another, still juggling. Before each act, they
always had an audience member authenticate that the blades were
real and deathly sharp.

The triplets were fifteen. Haady was the oldest by two minutes
according to their birth certificate and his brother, Nabhi, was the
youngest. Padmal, the middle sister, was only a minute older than
him. They knew this information because they broke into the
orphanage's main office and stole their file before they ran away at
the age of ten. Padmal cried for a whole day when she read that their
mother gave them up, unable to afford three babies. The file also said
that their mother confessed that splitting them up by only keeping
one would be heartless. So she had the orphanage take all three
infants two days after their birth. Moreover, their mother had been
adamant that the triplets stay together, which in actuality made it
even more difficult for them to ever be adopted.

Padmal hadn't thought that it would have been heartless for her
mother to keep only one of them. She selfishly wanted to have been
that one baby her mother kept. Her brothers took care of her, but she
had always wanted a mother. Always. Wanted to have a connection
to someone who wasn't her sibling. Or a boy.

The triplets only made it an hour outside the orphanage before a police officer brought them back. Three Indian children running through the streets of Sacramento at two in the morning were pretty easy to track down once the orphanage reported their disappearance. But a week later a man with a bushy mustache came to the orphanage and adopted them. He and his wife, Fanny, appeared to fall in love with the triplets at first sight. Of course, Dave and Fanny weren't married but pretended for such occasions. And the pair had quite the knack for convincing busy administrators that they were the perfect family for the children they wanted to adopt. The triplets were then raised under Fanny's care until at the age of twelve, when they all came into their dream travel gifts. Not only did they all share a birthday, but also the skill of telekinesis.

On cue the triplets widened their triangle and then began passing the daggers among each other. That was the part of the act that always earned gasps from the audience. The act didn't just depend on their telekinesis but also their unique connection to each other. They knew what one another thought without having Zuma's gift of telepathy. From that point in the act the handles of the knives didn't touch any of the six hands of the jugglers. That would have been insane since the blades were traveling at over forty miles per hour. However, that speed granted the illusion that the blades were being juggled from their hands when telekinesis was really the powerhouse of this act. Without a word, each of the triplets slowed the speed of the blades and caught them one at a time. During a show they would hold the blades high above their heads while receiving deafening applause.

The triplets wanted to do that part of the act with sharp, melting icicles, but Dave hadn't allowed it. Like most acts in the Vagabond Circus, they had to dial it down so it was mostly believable. Too much of the unexplainable earned the Vagabond Circus the wrong kind of attention. Dave didn't mind his performers being called freaks, but he didn't want them to be called fraudsters, which is a moniker all too often assigned unbelievable tricks and feats of grandeur.

"Let's move on to the second act," Nabhi said, gathering the daggers and putting them in their case.

Padmal consented, trudging over to the case of props, moving reluctantly, as she normally did. She wasn't just mad that Dave had disallowed them from using icicles in the act, but she was also still resentful that Dave had adopted her in the first place. To everyone's surprise she had protested the adoption. She wanted to stay at the orphanage, so sure that one day her mother would come for her, when she could afford her only daughter. Her brothers, the administrator, and Dave and Fanny were shocked. Everyone wanted a home.

Finally her brothers convinced Padmal to consent and all these years she'd stayed at Vagabond Circus for them. But there wasn't one day that she didn't plot her escape. She didn't enjoy performing and she made every excuse in her head for why what Dave did to create his circus was wrong. It was child labor. Enslavement. Exploitation. Some saw that he rescued the talented and brought out their potential, but she saw it as preying on the weak and manipulating them.

Chapter Eighteen

Sebastian and Benjamin, two of Fanny's kids, watched from the sidelines as the triplets practiced. They kept their voices down, knowing that the jugglers needed to concentrate to avoid injury.

"So what do you think the new guy's gift is?" Benjamin asked, his eyes trained on the knives spinning through the air, the shiny metal of the blades catching the sunlight as they flew.

"Probably mind control," Sebastian said, blowing out a long breath. "That's the only way I can imagine Dr. Raydon allowing him in the act."

"Oh, come on, man," Benjamin said, throwing a punch into the older boy's arm. "No one has the skill of mind control."

"If you know what's good for you, then you won't touch me again," Sebastian said, scowling at the younger boy before fixing his long-sleeved shirt.

Benjamin wasn't just afraid of Sebastian because he was older than him by a year. Benjamin was afraid of Sebastian because of the cold look the boy wore in his eyes. He'd noticed it when Sebastian arrived a few months ago. But since the girls Fanny also cared for were so much younger than him, he had no one to really play with. So he'd decided to befriend Sebastian. And since then he had been happy to have someone closer to his age in Fanny's trailer.

Sebastian was mostly all right as far as Benjamin thought. Everyone at Vagabond Circus was hard in their own way and Benjamin would probably have had that hostile look in his eyes too if he grew up on the streets like Sebastian. Benjamin was one of the fortunate ones who Dave found at an orphanage when he was just a toddler. He'd been under Fanny's care since he could remember and he firmly believed that no one could ever love her like he did. He loved Fanny more than the circus, which was an astronomical amount. Benjamin, unlike Padmal, was truly grateful Dave had adopted him. The circus was his life and one day he'd be like Jack, the star of the circus.

"What do you think your skill will be when you get it?" Benjamin asked.

"I have no idea," Sebastian said, sounding almost disinterested in the conversation. He watched the triplets as they brought out their props for their second act, bowling balls.

"Well, when do you think you'll get it? You'll be twelve sometime soon, eh?" Benjamin said.

"Beats me," Sebastian said, his eyes focused elsewhere. "I don't know when my birthday is really. I think it's in the winter, and I might not even get it when I turn twelve."

"True," Benjamin said, chewing on his lip for a second. "Ms. Fanny told me that boys mature slower than girls and sometimes don't hit puberty until they're fourteen."

"Yeah," Sebastian said, sounding as though he hadn't really been listening.

"Well, I hope that I don't have to wait that long. I hope I hit puberty on the early side."

"Huh?" Sebastian said, looking at Benjamin blankly.

"My gift," he said, looking at the other boy in surprise. "I hope I get it soon."

"Oh, dude, stop obsessing over that, would you? Just be a kid," he said and then walked off back toward the trailer they shared.

Benjamin blinked in surprise. Sebastian always said stuff like that, acting burdened like he had the weight of adult responsibilities on his shoulders. He was always lecturing Benjamin. After a moment, the boy shrugged the thought off and focused back on the triplets juggling bowling balls high above their heads.

Chapter Nineteen

Zuma spent all of lunch trying and failing to locate Jack. She wanted to explain. Explain her decision to him for choosing Finley over him as a partner. Zuma had been afraid to be Jack's partner in the act. And to avoid her fears she'd consented to be some strange guy's partner. And yet there was something so persuasive about Finley. She'd noticed it from the first moment she saw him. Little did she know then that she'd be seeing him again or that she would be his partner. And the more she thought about it, as she banged on Jack's trailer door and searched his usual spots, the more she was strangely excited to see what kind of act she and Finley could put together. His speed and teleporting were astonishing on their own, but paired with her skills they could do something incredible. It was when she started in the direction of the big top that she realized how brilliant Dave had been to pair them up. Their skills would completely complement each other's. But she was going to have to get past his challenging personality first.

Finley spent all of lunch trying to locate Fanny. He had the perfect way to gain her trust and he wouldn't even have to scheme to do it. Actually the situation might prove to be a win-win. However, she and her kids weren't anywhere he knew to look. He watched from the shadow of Fanny's trailer as Zuma pounded on Jack's door. Finley smiled to himself. He had hoped she'd choose him, but had his doubts about it. So when Zuma agreed to be his partner he realized he was finally in the right place and time in his life. For once things were looking up.

Neither Zuma nor Finley had eaten lunch by the time they were scheduled to meet in the big top. During this meeting, Titus had asked that they spend the time alone together getting to know each other's abilities before he joined them with ideas for their act. Knowing Titus, he already had a dozen ideas which were all good.

Zuma was lying on the practice mat, stretching, when Finley strolled into the tent. He walked by her without even acknowledging her presence. Zuma's head clouded with both frustration and disbelief. He hadn't even glanced in her direction. Behind her she could hear him taking off his warm-up suit. *Maybe he's just trying to get ready before talking to me. Maybe he's actually nervous,* she thought. There was no place with more ego and intimidation than the circus on your first day.

She leaned over her straddled legs to deepen the stretch as she focused on his thoughts. Zuma could feel thoughts like people did the wind. She could direct her mind to hone in on a particular person's thoughts and pull them to her, but she was hitting a wall with Finley. Nothing. Not a hint of a thought.

Most people at Vagabond Circus knew how to keep her out, as Dave taught Dream Travelers multiple shielding techniques for various reasons. He told them that there were people with the same skills as Zuma, but who shouldn't be trusted with private thoughts and that although he tried to protect them from leeches like that he couldn't ensure that he'd always be able to.

However, Zuma wasn't sensing a shield from Finley, but rather a void. It was like Finley didn't have any thoughts to shield. Whatever technique he was using to keep Zuma out, it was far more effective than the method Dave taught. She could usually find a back door if properly motivated, but there wasn't a back door to the invisible building of Finley's mind.

Unable to resist, she stood and turned around to spy Finley balancing on the slack line that was stretched out at the back of the practice tent. It hovered three feet off the ground. He pranced across it, not an ounce of unease in his steps. Finley moved like he was one with the line, and then she knew exactly four seconds before it happened what he was going to do. He flipped himself backwards in a back tuck and landed on the rope solidly. And then he took the momentum the line bounced back at him into a front flip and full twist and dismounted onto the mat. His back was to Zuma and he didn't turn to catch the look of amazement she was trying to cover up, but rather marched to the drink and towel station on the far tent wall.

He moved differently from Jack. Not like a gymnast. His flips were different from most too. There was a punchy power to them, less grace but still mesmerizing. And although she was incredibly impressed by this little show he'd just put on, she was growing more furious by the second that he was pretending she didn't exist. *What's this guy's problem?* He sipped water from a paper cup, disposed of it, and then toweled off before turning around and returning to the slack line.

Zuma managed to keep her frustrated sigh locked inside her, but that wouldn't last for long. With a firm determination she turned and stalked for the exit. She was almost to the door when Finley appeared out of nowhere two feet in front of her. She halted with a startled gasp. He'd teleported and had a half smile pulling up the corner on one side of his mouth.

"Where are you going?" he said, crossing his arms in front of his chest, a challenging look in his hazel eyes. *Were they green or brown?* Zuma wondered and then shook the stupid question out of her head.

"I'm going to tell Dave I changed my mind!" Zuma said, her frustration making her voice shake.

"Oh, about being in the circus?" Finley said, nodding like he understood. "Yeah, you're kind of in over your head."

She narrowed her eyes at him. "No, I changed my mind about giving an asshole a chance to be my partner."

Finley's smile widened. "You're only saying that because you can't get in my head. A valiant effort earlier though."

He could sense me trying to read his thoughts? Most never sensed her intrusion. Jack, Jasmine, Dave, and Titus did but that was because she'd formed an established link with their thoughts based on trust and seamless communication.

"Look I get that you're trying to overcompensate but we respect each other here," Zuma said.

"Right, rule number one," Finley said, that amused expression still on his face. "So based on rule number two I sense you and Jon are skirting a dangerous boundary."

"His name is Jack, and not that it's your business but there's nothing going on," Zuma said.

His eyes took their time running over the features of her face and then when they touched her mouth, they lit up with amusement. "Well, that's a relief." Finley took a step closer to Zuma and held out a hand. "Shall we get started?"

She knocked his hand out from in front of her and marched around him.

Again he teleported, appearing a few steps in front of her. "You really don't get how this works, do you? You leave. I'll stop you." He pointed at her and then him. "You and I *are* working together."

"You're not really giving me any incentives to *want* to work with you. I realize you're new to the circus but partners in an acrobat act have to actually get along and right now I can't stand you," Zuma said.

He bit down on the corner of his mouth and smiled. "But you don't despise me yet, right?"

She shook her head and sighed heavily. "You just don't get it."

He held up his hands as if in surrender. "You're right. Teach me?"

"Why is it that you asked to work with me? Why was that the deal you made with Dave?" Zuma said, scrutinizing.

"Because I'm new to the circus and obviously you are too, based on your skill, so I thought we'd relate," Finley said, not even daring to cover the mischief in his eyes.

"I'm not new to the circus," Zuma said through clenched teeth.

"Really?" Finley said in mock surprise. "Could have fooled me," he said and was proud of how he'd diverted her question. He could never confess the true reason he'd asked to work with Zuma...because she intrigued him.

She tapered her dark brown eyes at him. And then she made the decision to throw respect out the window and beat this guy at his own game. "Were you studying the circus, trying to find your in when you came to those six shows?" Zuma asked.

His smile faltered slightly.

Zuma stole his grin and plastered it on her own satisfied face. "Did you think that sitting in the back row would keep you hidden so you wouldn't be recognized when you invaded our circus?"

He studied her. "What's your other skill, besides telepathy?"

She tilted her head and batted her long eyelashes at him innocently. "Skills."

"What?"

"I have two other skills beside telepathy." She turned and made her way back into the center of the practice tent. This game was easier than she thought. And as Zuma suspected Finley teleported right in front of her again but this time only a foot away.

He leaned down. "What are your other skills?"

She looked up at him. "I think you'll earn that information by showing me more respect going forward."

Finley rolled his eyes. "That's not how respect works. It's something you earn by not treating me like a plague victim since the moment I took the job."

"What are you talking about? You didn't even acknowledge me when you came in here a little while ago," Zuma said.

"Oh, and it would have killed you to be the first one to say something?"

Zuma blinked blankly at Finley. "No, you're right. I could have. But I'm also not forgetting that you've insulted me multiple times during this conversation. Do you want to work with me or not?"

"I do," Finley said.

"Then why are you going out of your way to make me dislike you?" Zuma said.

It was Finley's turn to corral the emotion that tried to spring to his face. The last thing he wanted was Zuma to dislike him. Still, he had his reasons for treating her the way he had. But now looking at her disappointed eyes his reasons felt like fault lines underneath his feet. He stared at Zuma and she stared back, her unrelenting gaze twisting his doggedness into a fraying rope. "We've obviously started off on the wrong foot," Finley admitted after a pause. "Why don't we start over?"

She considered him and then nodded. "Fine. I'll give you one more shot."

"Thank you," he said, looking pleased. He stuck out his hand. "I'm Finley. I'm notorious for being an asshole, but I make up for it in other ways."

She couldn't help but smile slightly. "Nice to meet you, Finley. I'm Zuma and I have no shortcomings." And when she took his hand he pulled her in tight and leaned down and whispered close to ear.

"Nice to meet you, and I look forward to learning if that's true, Zuma." He parted with a satisfied smile when he spied the goose bumps surface on her neck. And just in time for Titus to enter the tent.

Chapter Twenty

*T*itus had spent the last two hours wisely before his meeting with Zuma and Finley. He didn't have a few ideas for their act, but rather one exceptionally solid one. Titus wasn't the excitable type. That was Dave's role at Vagabond Circus. Titus kept things calm and running in spite of the many distractions Dave created. But after brainstorming alone in his shared office, Titus couldn't wipe the eager grin off his face. Creating an act at this stage in the season was crazy, but based on the talent they now had, the possibilities were brilliant. Titus had to give Dave credit. This was a risk worth taking and would have people talking up and down the west coast.

"What we're going to do is create a new story that the circus tells," Titus said, sounding strangely breathless.

"Wait, we're changing the story? That's major," Zuma said in disbelief.

"Yes, but it's a great idea. It will be the most inspiring story the Vagabond Circus has ever told. And for you, Zuma, it's the break you've been waiting for," Titus said.

"Why does everyone think I want to be the star?" Zuma complained.

"Everyone wants to be the star," Finley said dryly before focusing on Titus. "What's this new story?"

"Well, the good news is that we don't have to change much to tell it. The narrator will take care of most of the changes and the acts won't be altered too much. But we will add a few acts with you, Finley, and of course, add your quadruple to the trapeze," Titus said.

"He can do high wire too," Zuma said, surprising herself with the sudden disclosure.

Titus arched an impressed eyebrow at Finley. "That will come in very handy." He coughed to clear his throat. "All right, so the show starts with you, Zuma, being imprisoned in a room. You're a girl whose father locks her up every night before dark, afraid of the creatures that prowl outside at night. However, you escape one night and meet the monsters, which will be our various existing acts.

Zuma, you will be in the ring most of the time. As the story progresses, you approach one of the monsters and duel him. During the battle you end up taming the monster and you two fall in love." Titus ends this with a triumphant smile. "What do you think?"

"The monsters I meet?" Zuma asked, looking skeptical.

"Well, they're the triplets, the acrobats, Sunshine, and Oliver. The cast," Titus said, like this should have been obvious.

"And the one I duel and fall in love with?" Zuma said, lowering her chin and giving him a measured glare.

"It's Finley, naturally."

"Naturally," she said dryly.

"What, don't you like it?" Titus asked. He was always sensitive when it came to his new ideas.

"No, I like it, it's just…" Zuma's face flushed although she couldn't figure out why. It wasn't like the story was really about her.

"I think," Titus began, "that pairing your skills to create a beautiful fight scene will really be impressive. We can even do part of it on the high wire." He stopped and smiled at the idea. "Yeah, two acrobats on a wire. It will be simply brilliant. Then the fight will morph into a dance and a series of flips and holds as you two fall in love."

Zuma tried three times to swallow the lump in her throat. She sought to cover up her nervousness with a compliment. "Titus, that's beautiful. You came up with all that over lunch?"

"Actually the whole idea popped into my head when I was in the john," he said with a guilty shrug.

"It is really beautiful," Finley admitted, his eyes not on Zuma for once. Then his face fell with a worry he quickly covered up. This act would put him much closer to Zuma than he had thought. And although he craved the idea of working with her, he also knew he needed to keep a boundary. Two parts of Finley battled. His deal to work with Zuma was his indulgent side, and the one that pushed her away was his pragmatic side. And currently the two parts were even.

"Then it's settled," Titus said, rubbing his hands together eagerly. "We have a new show!"

"I just have one more question though." Finley paused and then turned his pensive gaze on Zuma, putting her back under his spell. "What are these skills of Zuma's that complement mine?"

Chapter Twenty-One

*T*itus blinked in surprise. "Wait, you don't know?" He eyed his watch. "I realize I'm early, but what were you two doing before I arrived? You were supposed to be getting to know each other's skills."

"We didn't get to that," Finley said, his face turning dark. "Zuma was too busy going on about how much she didn't want to work with me."

Zuma shot Finley a startled look of fury. "I was not! He was the one acting like he didn't want to work with *me*!"

"Oh, right," Finley said with a huff. "By putting on a spectacular show for you," he said, throwing his arm at the high wire.

She tied her arms across her chest. "That's what you're calling spectacular? Ha!"

He matched her pose and tapped his foot, irritation heavy in the movement. "I did ask her what her skills were and she refused to tell me," he said to Titus, who looked confused. The creative director didn't do well when it came to conflicts between performers. Thankfully it happened rarely. He didn't have Dave's way with the circus family.

"Zuma, is that true?" Titus asked, growing more uncomfortable by the second.

"What happened to starting over?" she said, glaring at Finley.

He gave her a cold smile. "We did start over and this is where we are now," he said, hoping this was working, hoping she couldn't see through his act.

Titus slid his hand over his graying blond hair. "Okay," he said, drawing out the word. "You two obviously have some team-building opportunities here. I realize that you, Zuma, are used to being with Jasmine and Jack, but Dave is giving you an incredible chance." He turned to Finley. "And I'm going to be bold here and tell you that antagonizing Zuma is probably not going to work in your favor."

Finley smiled. "Oh, I don't know, I like the way she looks when she's angry. And she should be thanking me for provoking her," he said, staring straight at Zuma.

"Thank you? For what? For being a bipolar jerk?" she said.

"Exactly," Finley said, nodding. "Having strong emotions is great for performing."

"He's insane," she said, pointing to Finley and staring at Titus.

The creative director shrugged, looking defeated, and backed away.

"Titus!" Zuma yelled. "You can't just let him get away with disrespecting me."

He shook his head. "As far as I'm concerned, this is something you two need to get through on your own. And lucky for you there will be an ample opportunity. I want you creating an act based on my ideas for the rest of the day. I will review what you have tonight and then you will rehearse while dream traveling for all of the night. So, I'd advise you both to change your attitudes toward each other since you're spending the rest of the day and night together," Titus said.

"But it's my day off," Zuma argued.

Titus almost laughed at this, but controlled himself. "We all know there's no days off at Vagabond Circus. And besides I have high hopes for you two. I want to do a run-through tomorrow morning with the whole cast and then we will produce the new show tomorrow evening for Seattle before heading to Portland."

"This is crazy, Titus," Zuma said.

He nodded in agreement. "Yes, completely. But I think that it *will* boost sales and that means we all keep our jobs, so please do try your best to get along." Titus then turned to Finley. "Now, to answer your question, besides being telepathic Zuma also has combat sense and—"

"Wait," Finley said, swiveling his face to Zuma. "So…" He prepared to pivot on his back foot and before he did her eyes shot to his foot. He stopped. Smiled. "So if I go to kick you—"

"Then she will sense it seconds before you telegraph," Titus answered for her.

Finley nodded in approval. "That will make a fight between us quite interesting."

"Fight *scene*," Titus corrected. "You two will be creating a fight scene, and I agree. Most wouldn't be able to keep up with your super speed, Finley, but Zuma should have no trouble." He turned and nodded at Zuma proudly. "I had my doubts but Dave encouraging me to pair you with Finley was genius. The old man still has it, I'll admit."

Zuma couldn't help but nod with him in agreement, although her eyes were still narrowed with frustration.

"And what's your third skill?" Finley said, breaking in.

Zuma sighed, resigning slightly. "I have an eidetic memory, meaning I can recall images after only a brief exposure with a high degree of detail."

"Ahhh..." Finley said, piecing it all together. "So you can remember everyone in the crowd. And you know how many times they've been in the audience and where they sat. Is that right?"

"Yes," she said plainly. All her secrets were out now.

"That's a lot of information to catalogue," Finley said, looking impressed. "How does it help you in the circus?"

She shrugged. "I don't know, maybe it doesn't. But I see everything and with the right intention I can go back to memories and study them to learn more information. Reasons behind why someone would stalk the circus," she said, her tone filled with meaning.

For the first time that afternoon Finley's cool features shifted with stress.

"Well, I think at this point you two have everything you need from me to get started," Titus said, feeling the tension between the two and wanting to get away from it quickly. "No breaks until dinner and then I want to see what you've come up with." Titus turned and stalked for the exit, but halted just before. "Oh, and Finley?" he called back.

"What?" he said.

"Really I think your best advantage with Zuma is to allow her in your thoughts. If you do then you two can work together more seamlessly, the way she works with Jack and Jasmine," Titus said before leaving Zuma and Finley staring across the four feet separating them, a strange tension tethering them to each other.

68

Chapter Twenty-Two

*D*ave was almost skipping with a new exuberance as he crossed the grounds to his trailer. His meeting with Titus had been the best one in years. The creative director had a renewed energy. He was actually excited about the show. That hadn't happened in a long time. And they both knew changing the narrator script would take some work before the new show tomorrow, but it could be done. Everyone would be rehearsing during dream travel tonight. That was more than enough time for his circus to reconfigure the show.

The most important part of the show rested on Zuma's shoulders and there was no one he had more faith in. She was reliable, trustworthy, and she wanted the circus to be a success. Few loved the circus like he did, but Zuma was one of them. Sunshine had disclosed this to him one winter night when he questioned whether he had the support he needed to keep leading the circus. He knew Sunshine didn't much care for Zuma but she respected her and had been nice enough to share that information. She had said that Zuma's love for the circus was comparable to nothing else in her life.

Upon entering his trailer Dave's spirits dropped a degree.

"Again?" he said to the empty trailer. The space looked as it had when he left it this morning, except for three specific things: The mat in front of the sink was flipped up at the corner like someone tripped on it and didn't bother to fix it. Secondly, there were smudged fingerprints on the door handle. And lastly, the bottle of hand soap by the kitchen sink was turned at a thirty-degree angle. Dave would never leave a mat unfixed. Wore gloves and therefore made no smudges. And ensured everything was always facing forward, with the label showing.

This was the second time someone had broken into his trailer and he couldn't understand their purpose. They didn't take anything or seem to be looking for something. Actually it seemed to Dave that they touched everything like they were trying to give him a panic attack. Dave had been clinically diagnosed with obsessive compulsive disorder and couldn't stand the idea of foreign germs in his personal space. Maybe this person knew this and was trying to play a prank. He didn't think most people knew this about him though. Zuma and Sunshine knew due to their skill, and Titus, but no one else. Most people just thought that Dave wore his white ringmaster gloves most of the time out of habit. He had told the kids that they brought good luck when they asked one time.

Dave strode straight for the assorted chemicals he kept under the sink and went to cleaning his trailer. He didn't really have the time for such a chore, but he wouldn't be able to concentrate until it was thoroughly clean again. Dave was irritated that his disorder was making him lose time he could be devoting to the new show. But what he didn't realize was his OCD would keep him alive for another day.

Chapter Twenty-Three

"What was that about?" Zuma asked, pinning her hands on her hips. "One minute you're hot and the next you're cold."

Finley stroked his fingers through his brown hair, shrugged, then grabbed the pad of paper Titus left with his notes and tossed it at her. "You take notes," he said. The truth was he didn't know how to act around Zuma. She wasn't like most girls he met. She had a beautiful confidence. She had grace. And now that he knew what all her skills were, he was even more drawn to her. Drawn to her like the tide to the earth, like the birds to the trees, and like the predator to the prey. Her powers complemented his perfectly and all this was absolutely wrong. Finley couldn't allow himself this distraction. He looked at Zuma a few feet away, studying him. When he really allowed himself to look at her he saw himself failing. He saw himself turning weak and making decisions based on the wrong motivator.

"I really don't understand you," Zuma said, shaking her head and daring to take the seat next to him. She still couldn't get in his mind and there was no one's thoughts she'd ever wanted to read more than Finley's.

Chapter Twenty-Four

Jack knew the only way he could clear his head was to get away from the circus. It wasn't something he did often as he preferred the company of his friends. But the recent events had triggered an old anxiety. He borrowed Titus's car and drove to a park on the other side of town. He could have gone to one of the more interesting places in Seattle. The city was overflowing with places to dazzle the senses, but Jack's senses were currently on overload.

Actually, if Jack really wanted to get away then he could close his eyes and go to Egypt or Alaska or anywhere his mind intended by dream traveling. But Jack preferred to get away physically when his stress grew to this level. It was something about being away from everything that gave him hope that when he returned things would be better.

He should have been pleased with the recent events, not stressed. Dave was happier than he'd ever seen him and he was a man prone to happiness. Jack had caught the quadruple for the first time ever. And even he admitted that Finley's skills would add value to their show. Just advertising that they had a riskier trapeze act would earn them higher sales. And that's what they'd wanted as a circus. But Zuma... The way that she'd looked at Finley. The girl had caught herself. Rearranged her face into a grimace, but Jack had seen it. There was a connection between her and Finley and it brought up so many of his old insecurities.

Jack was the youngest of five boys. Four of those boys were famous, brilliant, regarded with prestige. And then there was Jack. From an early age he had been ordinary in his parents' eyes. He hadn't invented anything by age six, or scored a modeling contract, or graduated from high school by age ten. Those were things that his brothers had accomplished. He had failed his whole life to impress his parents, which was why he joined the circus at age fifteen. They hadn't cared. They had been happy for him and relieved that he was gone so they didn't have to hide their disappointment regularly. When the circus came through town, sometimes they came. Usually they didn't. But Jack didn't care because regardless, he was a star now. Maybe by his parents' standards he wasn't a real star, but in the eyes of the audience of Vagabond Circus he was famed. And now he felt his success being challenged. It made the anxiety begin its battle inside him. Making him feel vulnerable like his insides would burst. Like he needed to get out of his body. He took a few deep breaths as he sat on the top of the picnic table and watched various families in the distance.

Worst of all, what fueled the stress now was that Zuma, after given the choice, chose to perform with a stranger over Jack. She had to know that would hurt him. Hadn't she said she wanted to work with Jack? But she didn't choose him. This was its own stress, a new one, connected to Zuma. Since he met her three years prior, they were instantly endeared to one another. She arrived the same month he did, when she was also fifteen. From the beginning they were always together, finding that spending time with each other was easy and fun. For Jack there was no one who understood him like Zuma. She seemed to know he had a deep insecurity and never did anything to trigger his fears of lack. And maybe that's why he believed he was in love with her. Or maybe it was because he couldn't have her as long as they were at Vagabond Circus. Zuma was for sure his best friend, and yet he wasn't sure how he truly felt about her. And for the first time ever, she'd done something that she'd never done. She'd rejected him. She'd made him feel insecure.

Chapter Twenty-Five

*I*t took Finley and Zuma only thirty minutes to sketch out a full act.

Finley already had most of the act planned in his head, it seemed to Zuma. She jotted down his ideas, having to ask him to repeat things several times because he was speaking so fast. It was like a new person had stepped into him, one that was alive with creativity, all his bad attitude gone.

"You can really do all this stuff?" she asked, pointing at the page of notes she'd taken.

He didn't even glance at it, just puckered his lips and nodded.

The act they had created on paper was extraordinary, using their skills together to do more than the unexplainable. To Zuma the act sounded frightening and beautiful. She smiled, thinking of Dave's reaction.

Finley pretended not to notice the satisfied grin on the girl's face. He pretended it did nothing to him. Zuma's face was a series of slants that gave her an exotic look but also something relatable. He guessed she was at least half South American based on her dark brown eyes flecked with gold that complimented her blonde hair.

Finley pulled his eyes away from her face and stood, ready to practice. He extended a hand to Zuma, who eyed it before pushing herself up without his help.

"My question to you is, do you really think you can do all the choreography?" Finley asked with a skeptical look at Zuma.

She shook off his remark. "Of course I can."

He shrugged with a look of doubt.

"What?" she demanded.

"Just that you were the third-ranked acrobat in a three-person act," he said.

She almost laughed. He was trying to get under her skin again. It was working, but he couldn't know it. "Jack and Jasmine's skills work better together. But I'm still an incredible acrobat."

Finley actually couldn't argue this but he hoped his face communicated a different feeling. Watching Zuma perform was something he could do endlessly. He worried now whether he would be able to stay focused in the ring. "Okay, you can flip and all," Finley said, "but what about the martial arts in the act?"

"I wouldn't have put it in the act if I couldn't do it. I have been taking gymnastics and karate since I was five years old so wipe that look of doubt off your face," Zuma said.

He turned to the chalk station, covering his hands with powder and also hiding the expression on his face. *Of course she had professional training.* He wondered why he hadn't considered this before. *And why does it matter?*

"Actually," Zuma said, joining him at the chalk station, "Jack attended my gymnastics school too. And we went to the same high school, but we didn't meet each other until we joined Vagabond Circus. Isn't that crazy?"

Finley turned to her. "Not crazy in the least. Uninteresting maybe."

"I thought it was interesting," Zuma said, keeping her voice cool, unaffected.

"Why in the hell do you think I care how you and Jack met or that you went to the same school?" Finley said.

Zuma actually smiled at him, which made Finley furious. "Aw, you're jealous. I thought so," she said.

"I'm not jealous," Finley said.

"Then why the sudden attitude?" she asked, the smug look still on her face.

"I always have an attitude," he said.

"You know," she said in a sing-song voice, "being jealous kind of makes you a freak, since you hardly know me."

Finley had watched Zuma enough to feel he knew her. His knowledge of her felt intimate to him. And he hated the way she regarded him right now, like he was a diabolical jerk. But it was for the best.

"Let's get started," he said, turning and walking for the practice mat.

Chapter Twenty-Six

Oliver was one of the most recent performers to join Vagabond Circus; well, before Finley. His opening act, producing the Arabian horses, had given the circus a new reputation. And Dave would have loved for him to perform more than the two acts in the circus, but it was beyond the young illusionist's capacity. Creating illusions in the physical realm was extremely draining and complicated.

His second act involved a magic show with Padmal as his assistant. He'd begged her to take on the extra act and she'd finally agreed. Oliver didn't pull rabbits out of hats and saw Padmal in half. He pulled a rattlesnake from an audience member's small purse and threw it out in the middle of the ring, where it appeared to slide under the back curtain. And he made Padmal disappear and reappear in multiple places around the ring.

"We could really add to the act if we combined your telekinesis with my skill," he said to Padmal across the lunch table. Almost everyone had left to enjoy their free afternoon. Her older brother, Haady, had tapped Oliver on the shoulder and given him a sympathetic look as he left. He knew the uphill battle Oliver suffered working with Padmal.

"I don't want to do more for Vagabond Circus. I want to do less," she said, making her plate fly to the bin on the cleaning station using her telekinesis.

"Then let's leave," Oliver said, his scratchy voice low. "Haady and Nabhi's performance won't be as good without you but it will still be fantastic."

"I can't," she said through clenched, crooked teeth.

"But if we left then we could really be together. No more stupid rules" he said.

She stared at his black Mohawk. Oliver had a look she never thought she'd find attractive, but it paired with his soft personality perfectly. Most thought he'd have a bad-ass personality to match his look, but he didn't. He was sweet. Considerate. And utterly amazing with his illusions. She stared into his eyes. They were what she liked most about him more than anything else. One green and one brown.

"You know I want to leave," she finally said. "I hate being Dave's puppet, but let's be honest, you wouldn't be happy then. Even if we were really together."

She was right and they both knew it. Where she hated performing, only tolerating it, Oliver loved it. There was nothing like making kids gasp with disbelief. People had thought he was a freak before he came to Vagabond Circus but here he was treated like a star. People stared mesmerized at his two different colored eyes when he signed autographs. Girls gave him their number. Girls who would never have given him a chance before. But that just fed his ego because he didn't want anyone but Padmal. And whereas she resented Dave Raydon because she hadn't wanted to be adopted, Oliver loathed the man because of his no dating rule. If he could just love Padmal openly then maybe she'd be happy at the circus. And he'd be a star and have everything he wanted.

"And you know I can't abandon my brothers," she said, staring off with an irritated expression.

"I know," he said and checked to ensure they were alone before reaching across the table and covering her hand with his.

Chapter Twenty-Seven

Sweat trickled down Zuma's back. They had been practicing for over two hours without a break. Finley's endurance was incredible. She had demanded a water break and fumed when Finley stayed on the mat practicing. He had more focus than any performer she'd ever seen. It was fascinating to watch him work, like he was a born acrobat, although she sensed his newness to the art. It was like he was fueled by something based on survival. And working with him in the ring was actually quite exhilarating. He wasn't careful with her like Jack. He threw his kicks straight at her head knowing she would sense and deflect. And his speed tightened her chest every time he moved. And yet he wasn't too fast for her combat sense. After numerous perfectly timed blocks Finley had flashed an expression at her that almost looked like he was impressed. It was the first one and he covered it quickly with a fierce fighter's face. Zuma wanted to know what he was fighting inside. She wanted to dip into his thoughts and know one thing about this enigma of a guy.

When she returned from quenching her thirst, Finley had pulled off his shirt. He used it to wipe the sweat from his face. Zuma strained to keep her eyes up, away from studying the lines of his chest. He turned and when he did she noticed three long scars running down the length of his back.

Maybe he was finally wearing down because he startled a bit when Zuma said, "How did you get those scars?"

He hadn't expected her back yet. That's what his face said when he looked up. Finley turned at once, putting his back toward the wall. "I don't remember," he said too fast.

"It looks like you were whipped," she said, and couldn't believe the tone of her voice. She sounded sympathetic. *For Finley.*

He shook his head, but didn't say anything.

"You don't remember how you received three giant scars?" she asked in disbelief.

"That's the answer I'm going with," he said, his voice light, almost playful.

"Well, then tell me something about you. Like tell me where you learned that stuff you do, your acrobatics," she said, which earned her a smile from Finley. Again her chest tightened. He had the look of a rebel embedded in every feature of his face.

"It's called parkour," he said.

"You mean that stuff that people do in urban settings, like jumping between buildings and doing handstands on top of skyscrapers?" Zuma said.

He sighed. She made it sound unprofessional, like something hoodlums did. "Sure," he said.

The way he moved, his flips, they weren't graceful, they were robust and powerful. Zuma imagined that her movements and his contrasted greatly, which made the story in their act even more compelling.

"How did you learn parkour?" she asked, intensely intrigued by the idea of doing flips and tricks in such a dangerous environment.

Finley shrugged. "I just picked it up."

"All right, never mind," she said, taking her position and preparing to do another run-through of the part they were working on. "Don't share. It's not like I care."

Finley took his place, ready to start. "Oh, you care."

And without saying a word Finley turned on his back toe and spun around, throwing a round house kick at Zuma. He was unsurprised when she spun to the side, missing it. No one had ever been able to stand up in a fight against him. His super speed prevented it. His teleporting made it impossible. Again he threw a punch and Zuma ducked. Then she grabbed his arm and spun it around so it was locked behind his back where she stood. She felt his heart racing in his chest. His bare back pressed up against her. The scars an inch from her face.

On cue he teleported so he replaced her position, holding her from behind. She dropped to her knees and used the momentum to pull him down and throw him over her head in a somersault. Finley landed on his back and popped up at the same second. Zuma crouched low and when he tried to slide a low kick to take out her legs she flipped backward twice. When she landed, Finley had already teleported to right behind where she stood. He grabbed her hand and spun her around. A beautiful blur of movements. And then the act turned more into a dance as the scene shifted into a story of love. The characters they were playing had fallen for the person they couldn't defeat. They moved as figure skaters did, like they were gliding, every one of their movements complementing the others.

It felt natural to Zuma, as if she'd always performed like this, although this was the first time. For Finley, there had never been a more freeing feeling than to move beside Zuma. Finley picked Zuma up by the waist and rapidly twirled her around before tossing her in the air and then racing fast enough to catch her on the other side of the ring where she landed. He let her slide down until her feet touched the ground and then when she turned to end the act he spun her around in an impromptu move. She'd expected it and hadn't moved away, too curious to see what he was doing. He tucked his leg behind one of hers, encouraging her back, dipping her low. Zuma leaned backwards, her back arching as Finley leaned over her, his arms supporting from behind. They looked like a beautiful statue of a couple finishing the tango. He slipped down further. Whispered close to her. "I just thought we needed a more powerful ending."

"I like it," Zuma said through a rattled breath. She was dipped back low but felt secure in Finley's arms.

Finley's breath collided with her cheek. The sensation prickled her skin and pulled at an unhealthy desire. His eyes tampered with satisfaction and he leaned in closer, spying the sudden movements of Zuma's chest as she fought for oxygen. His lips almost grazed her ear when he whispered, "You know, I'm close enough to kiss you right now. You want to add that to the act?" He looked amused, and unlike Zuma, completely unflustered.

Her hands around his neck tightened. Zuma cocked her head to the side and looked at him straight on. "And I'm near enough to punch you in the face. Maybe we should add that instead," she said.

Finley stood straight, pulling Zuma to an upright standing position, and instantly yanked his hands away from her. He wore a jokester's smile. "You actually need some distance to throw a punch and just now you weren't far enough from me. It sounds like you're as awful a fighter as you are an acrobat."

Intent on not looking rattled, Zuma rolled her eyes as if only irritated by the statement. "I'm a fantastic acrobat and fighter, *and* not only that but I'm the fortuneteller for the circus. I have more than just the skill to dance and flip around like you. Sounds like you're jealous that I have more talents than you," she said.

"Right, and your telepathy, go ahead and use it on me. Read my fortune, would you?" Finley said.

Zuma narrowed her brown eyes at him. He knew she couldn't. That he could effectively shield her. "Titus said it would be to the act's advantage for you to take down that barrier. Jack and I perform better together because we communicate telepathically," she said.

"I can outperform Jack with my eyes closed, mind shielded, and a broken toe. I don't need the advantage of letting you in my head."

Zuma was now the one who trespassed the space between them, putting only two inches from her face to his. "Sounds like you're afraid to let me in your head. What are you scared of?"

He patted her on the shoulder with a mock look of sympathy. "Just trying to protect your ego. Wouldn't want you to find out how badly I think of you."

Zuma threw his hand off her and shook her head at him. "Well, if you could read minds then you'd know the same is true for me."

Chapter Twenty-Eight

Zuma was exhausted after working with Finley. Still, she had to find Jack. She raced to her trailer, intent on taking the world's fastest shower before she hunted him down. He would know she wanted to see him. Jack always knew these things about Zuma. Just as she knew he was currently punishing himself and would until she explained. And all he had to hear was the truth and then they'd be back to normal. Well, after her confession, not normal, but at least Jack would feel better.

She grabbed a protein bar as she ran out of her place. Zuma crammed a few bites into her mouth as she raced to Jack's trailer. Missing lunch had been a mistake. She wondered again how Finley had stayed so strong throughout the practice, never even taking a break to rehydrate.

With the protein bar clutched in her hand she rapped at Jack's door, loud this time. The smell of grilled vegetables was already wafting through the air. Bill, the circus chef, would be grilling up crates of organic vegetables and steaming pots of rice for tonight's meal. Dave provided only the best food for the people of Vagabond Circus. It was all organic and completely vegetarian since that was the optimal diet for Dream Travelers.

Jack opened his door with a tired expression. His blondish hair was a mess, lying down flat on his head like he'd been sleeping. "Zuma, I don't really feel like discussing this right now." Then he looked at her beet red face and her hair still wet. "Are you all right?"

"I'm fine. Just flushed from running over here after the longest and most irritating practice of my life." She stepped past Jack, giving him little opportunity to keep her out of his trailer. She turned around, tossing the half-eaten protein bar on his dining table. "And yes, we need to talk right now. I tried to find you at lunch."

"I left," Jack said simply.

"And you stormed out of the tent right after our meeting," she said.

"That wasn't me storming."

"Jack…" she said, a warning in her voice.

"What?" he said, throwing his hands up in surrender. "What do you want me to say right now?" There was a pain in his eyes that she'd seen but never when it had been caused by her.

"I don't want you to say anything. I'm the one who needs to talk," she said, pointing her finger to her chest. "You've been punishing yourself all afternoon because you think Finley is going to steal your stardom."

"That's not why," Jack said and then clenched his mouth shut, wishing he would have thought before speaking.

"Well, regardless, you'll always be a star. The people love you." She paused and watched him visibly soften. Her combat sense made it incredibly easy for her to notice the micro-expressions most people didn't even know they gave off as they became stressed or let stress slip away. Zuma could read people better than anyone because of this. "So what you're saying is that you've been mostly sulking all day because I didn't choose you to be my partner," she stated and watched Jack's shoulders tense a degree. "If you wouldn't have run off," she continued, "then I could have explained and you wouldn't have wasted a day feeling sorry for yourself."

"Zuma, I wasn't—"

"Yes you were," she interrupted. "And with every right, but what I'm trying to tell you is that you're wrong. I didn't choose to work with Finley over you because I wanted to. Believe me, I can't stand that jerk. He's one of the last people I want to work with."

"Then why?"

"It's not that I don't *want* to work with you. It's because I *can't*, Jack."

He blinked at Zuma like he misheard her. "What?"

"Look, I never told you, but Dave gave me the option of being your main partner when we started the acrobat act together. Jaz had already been at the circus awhile and she didn't have a preference in her role," Zuma said.

"Wait, *you* chose to have the third position in the act? And you made the choice *not* to be my partner in the other acts?" Jack asked, a crease between his brown eyes.

"Right," Zuma said through a strained breath. This wasn't how she wanted to disclose this information to Jack. She always pictured that it would feel different, romantic. Instead it felt contrived, like it wasn't real.

Jack's eyes bulged slightly as he gave her a look that begged for her to elaborate.

"I made that choice because I knew I couldn't spend that kind of time alone with you," she said, in one long rushed sentence. Jasmine and Jack were required to practice together more often and alone due to their roles in the circus.

If Zuma was Jack's partner then they'd be together almost all the time, based on how much they already saw each other.

As Zuma's explanation sunk in, Jack's expression went from confusion to one of relief and then nervousness.

Zuma nodded at him, realizing he understood. "You and I both know there's nothing more important than being a part of Vagabond Circus. And I knew that if we had to work that closely together, that there was a chance that…"

"We'd act on our feelings," Jack said, completing her words.

"Right," she said.

"But you gave up a chance to have a central role?"

"It was fine," Zuma said, with a shrug. "The important thing was that I stayed at Vagabond Circus. Us not being partners was the better option for everyone. Less stress. And you're safe with Jasmine so it was kind of a no-brainer, because we both know how intimately you get to know your partner."

At this Jack's face darkened. "And you've just made the decision to spend that intimate time with Finley."

"Jack, did you hear me when I told you I can't stand the guy? He infuriates me," she said, her face flushing with anger thinking of how many times he insulted her that afternoon.

Jack nodded. "Yeah, I guess," he said, wondering why Zuma couldn't see that Finley was doing what some boys do to the girl they like on the playground: push them down to get their attention. "So that's really why you didn't choose me?" he asked, knowing Zuma wouldn't mind the ego-filled question.

"Yes. And that's another reason Jaz can't leave. You and I are able to keep things professional and I think that balance is important," Zuma said.

"You're right," he said, nodding. He watched her watching him, knowing she was studying him as only she could do. He never minded it. "You're undoubtedly my closest friend here and sometimes I wonder…" Jack trailed off, looking flustered by what he wanted to say, so he didn't and instead invited Zuma in his head. Due to her telepathic link with him she could feel him pushing the thoughts across the space at her.

She smiled after her brief intrusion. "You think that we just want to be together because we can't?" she said with a laugh. "Yeah, I've wondered that before too. Forbidden fruit."

Jack smiled with relief. It was always so easy with Zuma. He just let her in his mind and she understood everything he didn't want to say. "It's so hard to know what we truly feel for each other. And as long as we're here we aren't finding out," he said. And it had never occurred to Jack that he and Zuma could have had a relationship behind Dave's back. It had occurred to Zuma, but she figured Jack respected Dave too much to consider the idea. Dave treated Jack as a son, giving him the attention and praise his own father never did. Zuma knew Jack needed that. He needed that more than he needed her and she understood this. Everyone at Vagabond Circus was there for a reason and most of them were not financial ones.

Chapter Twenty-Nine

$\mathcal{R}$elief swept over Finley when he finally found Fanny sitting between Emily and the other little girl, who was older. He leaned down over Fanny's shoulder, making eye contact with Sebastian and then Benjamin on the other side of the table. Benjamin watched Finley, his eyes wide with disbelief. Sebastian pretended he hardly noticed the new acrobat. He ducked his head low and dug into his rice.

"Can I have a private word with you?" he said in a low voice to Fanny.

The older woman turned over her shoulder and smiled wide at Finley. "I'd hoped I hadn't seen the last of that handsome face."

"I promised you wouldn't," he said with a wink. She was about his mother's age, he guessed. Maybe if his mother had him on the older side. He didn't know. Had no idea how old his mother was. Had no idea who she was. Finley wasn't raised in an orphanage, it was more like a factory, and children the products. "Anyway, I apologize for interrupting your meal, but I need to ask you something. Can we talk in private?"

Fanny wiped the corners of her mouth with a napkin. "Of course we *may*," she said, putting the emphasis on the last word to show the contrast in hers and his statement. Fanny taught by example. "You *may* always have the attention I can afford," she said before turning to the older boys across the table. "Sebastian, you're in charge while I'm gone."

He nodded his head, his long black hair falling into his face as he did.

"Sebastian," Finley said to the boy. "That's an interesting name."

"Is it?" Sebastian said, an edge in his voice.

"Yes," Finley said and his eyes lingered on Sebastian's cold stare.

"Well, it's nice to meet you Mr...?"

"Just Finley," he said.

"Don't you have a last name, mister?" Sebastian asked.

"I do, but I don't think such formalities are necessary," he said. Finley, in fact, had no last name. Not one he knew of. He had actually picked his first name when he was a kid.

"Formalities?" Sebastian said, an icy grin on his face. "That's a big word. You're a kid from the streets, like most of us, right?"

"Yeah, I'm a runaway," Finley said, his voice even.

"Wherever did you pick up such a large vocabulary, mister?" Sebastian asked, looking curious, but also cunning, like he was playing a game with Finley.

"The world offers many opportunities for learning. And dream travel is a great way to observe," Finley said.

"Oh, dream travel…that makes sense," Sebastian said, his chin low.

"One day you'll see what I mean. When you're older," Finley said, an emphasis on the last word.

"Right, one day," he said, his words slow, deliberate. "Well, nice to meet you, Mr. Finley." Then Sebastian extended his hand to Finley, a clever grin on his face.

Finley shook his head. "I'd shake your hand, but I'm totally gross from my practice session."

"Next time then," Sebastian said, pulling his hand away.

Finley gave a slow nod. "Yeah, next time." He turned to Fanny, who watched the whole display with a pleasant smile.

"Shall we?" she said, holding out her arm, directing the way.

"Yes," Finley said, and followed her out to the recreational yard which was empty since it was meal time.

Chapter Thirty

Zuma pulled Jack to the food truck after their conversation. She hadn't stopped complaining about her growling stomach until she shoved the first bite of rice dripping with teriyaki sauce into her mouth.

"Mmmm," she said, filling her fork again. "That almost makes me feel normal once more."

"You really practiced hard," Jack said, watching her.

"I did," she said through a full bite.

"And besides from Finley being a jerk, how did it go?"

Zuma sighed, stuffed more food into her mouth and shrugged.

"Well, do you two have an act?" Jack asked.

"Yeah, but working with him is probably going to kill me," she said.

"I hope it doesn't," Jack said, giving her that look, the one that meant something.

Zuma hadn't noticed the look. She hardly noticed anything that wasn't on her plate. "I just don't understand what his problem is. It's like he goes to great lengths to make me hate him."

"What's going on in his head?" Jack said.

"Beats me. He's got his thoughts locked down."

Jack shot one eyebrow up at this. Most couldn't keep a determined Zuma all the way out of their head. "That's a true surprise. He's a mystery for sure. And I'm curious what he's up to now."

Zuma brought her eyes up to Jack's but he was staring at the table two over where Fanny and her kids ate. Finley was speaking to the new kid, Sebastian. Fanny was behind Finley, looking to be waiting.

"Oh, great, that's all we need is for him to spread his bad attitude to our kids," Zuma said. And the sight of Finley turned her stomach suddenly, making the food she'd just swallowed churn with unease. She pushed her plate away. Jack eyed her with concern.

"Are you all right?" he asked.

"No, he makes me sick." But Zuma was confusing her true feelings for sickness; they were actually something quite different.

Whereas Jack was concerned before, now he was sincerely baffled. Zuma was affected by this guy and nothing affected her. Not her distant family or the crowds or her clients with their problems. She was always stone. Zuma knew the thoughts of the world and it didn't disturb her. But Finley...

Fanny and Finley then turned and strolled through the tables. When they passed their table Jack slid his hand around Zuma and pulled her over so her head rested on his shoulder. He didn't like to think that someone was hurting Zuma. Making her vulnerable. *But is it such a bad thing actually?* he suddenly thought. He sometimes worried Zuma was too hard. Too unaffected.

Finley's gaze connected with Jack's as he passed. There was much communicated in the one look.

Zuma didn't notice this. She was too surprised by Jack's display of affection. It was nothing to get them in trouble. They *were* friends. And then she was even more curious how Finley wasn't shoving a plateful of food into his mouth right now. How could he not be starving after that practice? How was he just casually strolling by with Fanny?

Chapter Thirty-One

*H*ow old are you?" Fanny asked, her voice low.

"Seventeen?" Finley said, his voice cracking.

"You really don't know how old you are, do you?" she said her voice warm, accepting, and richly coated in her southern accent.

"It's a guess," he said, pushing his hands into his pockets, his nervousness showing. He couldn't help but be who he was with Fanny. It must be her gift.

"And you still can't—"

He shook his head quickly, almost as if begging her not to say it again.

"Not even a little bit?" she asked skeptically.

He shrugged and the look of self-loathing on his face made Fanny grab her chest with emotion. "No you don't," she said, and then reached out and clasped his hand. "Don't you feel bad about this. Actually I'm not that surprised. Kids come to me in all different states. I'm just impressed you've gotten by so long. Your skills must be very good."

Again Finley shrugged, not bearing to fake confidence with this woman. "Yeah, I guess."

"Well, I simply can't wait to see what your skills are and watch you perform. I'm going to be in the front row for your first show," Fanny said proudly.

At this Finley smiled, something raw opening up in his chest.

"And yes, darling, I'll help. We will find time when the kids are sleeping or at a lesson with their phys ed instructors."

"Thank you," he said and squeezed the woman's hand again.

Chapter Thirty-Two

*F*inley hadn't been starving after his long practice with Zuma for two reasons. The first was he was used to going without food. He could survive on very little. The second reason was that he was full on adrenaline and the emotions rolling around inside him. He wanted to believe they were the result of the creative process, but he knew Zuma had something to do with it. He fed off the looks she gave him, and was strangely fulfilled by her attention. It was such a foreign feeling to Finley. To feel nourished by another person.

Again it seemed so weird to just walk by the food truck and grab food. Finley felt like he was stealing, but he wasn't. Never again did he want to steal.

Zuma was still seated at her table when he turned with the plate of rice and vegetables. To Finley's relief her head wasn't resting on Jack's shoulder. It had taken everything he had to walk by them and not say something earlier when he and Fanny passed them. But he didn't even know what he would have said. Why in such a short period of time did he feel possessive of Zuma? This consumed his thoughts. She wasn't his. Actually Zuma was one of those people who seemed she would never belong to someone. She would always be her own person, never relying fully on the support of another. But she had laid her head on Jack's shoulder like she was in need of comforting. *Why did she need comforting?* Finley questioned.

He slowed as he passed Zuma's table, hoping she'd look up. He'd had her attention all day and it wasn't enough. When she didn't look up at him, Finley picked up his pace and took the spot next to Sunshine. The girl was speaking to the boy with a black Mohawk.

Sunshine paused in mid-sentence and checked out Finley as he sat down. "Well, well, well. Look who has picked us over the royalty over there," she said, pointing at Zuma's table. "I saw you slow at the acrobats' table and almost thought you were going to sit there, with them."

"Didn't realize you were watching me," Finley said, looking creeped out. "That's kind of bordering on stalking, you know?"

"Yeah, it's something I do," Sunshine said without guilt. "My own life is fairly boring, so I entertain myself by watching other people. I invite myself into everyone's affairs secretly."

"You really shouldn't say that out loud," Finley said, poking at a mushroom with his fork. He'd never had half the stuff on this plate. And although he was grateful for the food he was nervous to try it in fear that he wouldn't like real food. He also feared he'd eat the food the wrong way. Like the bud-looking thing he was pushing around with his fork. It looked so foreign.

"That's an artichoke heart," Sunshine said, pointing at the food beside his fork.

Finley shot her a frustrated glare. *How specific of information does her empathesis give her?* he wondered. "I know that," he said, rolling his eyes. "Why do you feel it necessary to educate me, huh?"

"Just sensed that you were a little unsure about some of the food on your plate," she said, that glum tone always present in her voice. It was like an undercurrent in the girl.

"Don't worry," Oliver said from across the table. He had a rough voice of someone three times his age, like he spent years smoking. In truth, the boy's voice was a result of years living on the streets, hunched over barrels of fire to stay warm. "Sunny does that to all of us. It means she likes you."

"I don't like him," she protested at once.

"Well, not like that," Oliver admitted. He turned his eyes on Finley. One was green, the other brown. "Sunshine here doesn't really like anyone. It's kind of what makes her so endearing to our group. She likes me, the triplets, Dave, and on occasion, Titus. And now it appears she likes you, so get used to her rummaging through your emotions and making observations and giving advice. It gets really old, really fast."

"Oliver, why don't you go make out with Padmal," Sunshine said and then playfully threw her hands to her cheeks, looking suddenly melodramatic. "Oh, dear me, I totally forgot. You can't."

From the other side of the table the girl with hair the color of dark chocolate and eyes to match swiveled her eyes to them. Finley recognized her from the juggling and magician's act. Her eyes were large and almond-shaped and she was incredibly petite, especially sitting next to both her tall, lanky brothers.

Oliver smiled back at the girl, a smile that transformed his face into something soft, taking away the sharpness it had before. Then he returned his focus to Sunshine. "I see you're abusing your powers again," he said to her.

"Only with the ones I love," she said, raking her fork through her rice like it was a meditation garden.

The boy stood. "Can I be deselected from that list of people?"

"I'm afraid not," Sunshine said, making a pattern in her rice. "Your emotions are extremely complex and make my own feel normal. I need to surround myself with people who are more warped than me."

He shook his head at his friend and then looked at Finley. "Welcome to the circus, Finley. I'm Oliver, and I won't be the least bit offended if you choose not to sit here again. Sunny has a way of scaring people away."

"Is that my cue to light your Mohawk on fire?" she said, with a fake sweet smile that made her face look peculiar.

Oliver didn't grant the girl a response, but instead just turned and left, glancing once at Padmal on his way.

"So…" Sunshine said, her eyes still on her plate of rice as she traced one of the tines of the fork through it. "How did it go with Ms. Pink Streak?"

Finley finished his bite before saying, "I prefer to call her Ms. Entitled Witch. And not so good."

Sunshine brought her eyes up to meet his, but didn't say a word. She was waiting for him to elaborate.

"I told her she was an awful acrobat and apparently that offended her," he said like the whole thing actually baffled him.

Sunshine studied him and Finley realized at once what she was doing. She was using her empathesis on him. It was different from how he'd been taught to sense telepaths in his head. And the shielding technique he knew so well didn't seem to keep Sunshine's pilfering all the way out. "Would you stop that?" he said, irritated.

"Why?" Sunshine said simply. "Because you don't want me to know that you don't actually think she's an evil witch or because you're in denial about how fascinated you are by her?"

"I'm not," Finley said in a hush.

Sunshine went back to her meditation with the pilaf of rice. "And we both know she's an amazing acrobat. I won't even argue that. However, Pinky's ego is fragile, although less so than most at the circus, but still, telling her she's awful would have hurt her. Has." She teetered her head back and forth like weighing something in her head. "So all in all, I'd say you were successful."

"Successful at what?" Finley said.

"At pushing her away. At protecting yourself," Sunshine said in ho-hum voice.

Finley was grateful that Sunshine had kept her voice down. And he strangely desired to talk to her more about this. He had never had anyone to talk to and Sunshine made it easy by diving in and stealing a read on his emotions. This was a jumble of desires for him: to want to shield himself and also have help with his emotions. Everything about the circus was complicated.

"You have a lot of secrets, Finley," Sunshine said after a long pause. "Most of you is hard to read, but I do feel that you have many contradictory emotions. That must be difficult." And when Sunshine said this last statement she actually sounded sympathetic.

"I'm not fascinated with her," Finley finally argued, thinking he could find a way to stand his ground on that one. "I just find her interesting."

"Hmmm…" Sunshine said, studying him again. "No, that's not what I'm getting. You find this food interesting. You find Pinky hypnotic."

Finley noticed again the disdain in Sunshine's voice at the mention of Zuma. He tried his best to ignore what she'd said and changed the subject slightly. "Why don't you like Zuma?"

Sunshine almost smiled, but caught herself. "Is it that obvious?"

Finley didn't care to answer, just waited for her reply, which came a few seconds later.

"To my judgmental eyes, Pink Streak has everything she wants and still she's not completely happy. She has Dave's unwavering admiration, friends, a great spot in the circus, beauty, talent, a wholesome upbringing, money and still she chooses every day to be unsatisfied with her life. There's a lot of people here with less who are happier than her," Sunshine said.

"Maybe you're wrong and she can't have what she wants. Maybe she really wants to be with Jack, like Oliver wants Padmal, and therefore she's unhappy," Finley said.

"You know," Sunshine said, something shifting on her face like she had a small epiphany, "I think you might be right. Newbies always help me see things clearly and cut through my own biased readings of emotions."

"So she is unhappy because she can't have who she wants...Jack?" Finley said.

"It's close to that," Sunshine said, seeming to reflect internally for a moment. "But I think it's more that she hasn't found what she really wants in life." Her green eyes lifted from the table, a spookiness to them. "Maybe it's you."

Finley's own eyes slid over to find Zuma's seat empty. "I'm not sure if you realize this since you seem to live in an alternate universe, but Ms. Entitlement and I *have* met."

"Yes, and since you have come here her emotions have turned into a storm cloud, brewing with many new feelings. It appears that you, Fin, have an effect on her." Sunshine whistled through her teeth. "Good thing, because I was starting to think she was a one-trick pony when it came to feelings. I was beginning to think she was the queen of indifference."

Chapter Thirty-Three

The lights shone bright overhead in the big top. Zuma and Finley had been rehearsing in the practice tent before, but Titus wanted to see the act in the big top to ensure it used the whole ring adequately. Zuma pretended to be paying extra attention to chalking her hands when Finley entered. He was five minutes late and Dave and Titus were sitting discussing all the changes.

"Well, there's my newest star," Dave said, waving Finley eagerly over to him. Finley strode over and shook the ringmaster's gloved hand.

"Are you finding your way around the circus all right?" Dave asked, his eyes twinkling bright with his new enthusiasm.

"I am," Finley said, his eyes skirting to Zuma's back facing him.

"Then you might want to work on being on time on occasion," Titus said, eyeing his watch. His excitement had waned as the stress of making all the changes took over.

Dave puckered his lips and shook his head. "Don't listen to him," Dave said, throwing a thumb in Titus's direction. "He's unrelenting about things like time and schedules."

"I just don't want to set the wrong expectation," Titus said, pulling his reading glasses up on his nose and glancing at the notebook in his hand. "Now I need to know how you want your name spelled for the press release. It's Finley with an 'e' right?"

The acrobat's eyes dropped to the ground and he seemed to deliberate on it. "Yeah, with an 'e.'"

"And I didn't catch your last name," Titus said, scribbling on the notebook.

"Uh…" Finley said. "Right. I'm not sure I gave it. It's…uhhh." Obvious hesitation covered Finley's face.

Titus dropped his pad down in his lap. "Oh, great, Dave, you brought a convict to our circus, haven't you? Are you wanted by the authorities, son?"

Finley spied Zuma turn around, her attention piqued by the recent questions.

"No, I'm not wanted. And I'm not a convict. It's just that…well, I don't have a last name," Finley said, his eyes dropping to the ground. He didn't look nervous, and yet all his confidence had disappeared rapidly.

Dave playfully slapped Titus's bicep. "Gosh, Titus, how many times are you going to offend the new talent? Seriously, can you lay off the boy?" The ringmaster turned his attention back to Finley, a sympathetic look in his light blue eyes. "Don't worry, I've recruited many a kid like you. You're not alone. Kids from the streets don't know their birthday, let alone their last name. Most make one up. It's actually a lot of fun. What do you want your last name to be?"

Zuma had arrived beside Finley, a rude smile on her mouth. "I've got a few suggestions if you want them," she said.

Finley shot her a piercing glare that was supposed to punish her, but instead made her feel rewarded. There was something so beautiful in every one of his looks.

"That's very helpful of you, Zuma, but I think Finley should choose his own last name," Dave said, a smile in his voice.

"I'm not sure any of your suggestions will be that complimentary," Finley said to Zuma.

Dave shot a confused look at Zuma and then at Finley.

"These two," Titus said to Dave, pointing at the acrobats, "are having some challenges working together. They'll get through it."

"Oh," Dave said with a nod, and sat back in his seat. "Sure, sure. This has been very abrupt. So last name, what would you like it to be?"

Finley smiled, a glint in his eyes. "Zuma."

"What?" she said in response.

"Zuma," he repeated. "I want my last name to be Zuma." He turned and gave her a devious look. "That way when you marry me you'll be Zuma Zuma."

Dave howled with sudden laughter. "Oh, that's funny. Good one, my boy. I see what you mean, Titus," he said, tears in his eyes. "He knows how to get under her skin."

Zuma narrowed her gaze at Finley. "Very funny," she said, not amused.

Dave corralled his laughter. "Okay, okay. That's enough. Remember the rules."

They both nodded, staring at each other with sharp eyes.

"Seriously this time, Finley," Dave said. "What's it going to be?"

"I've always liked the name Anders," he said.

Dave erupted again. "How do you come up with this stuff?" he said through the laughter.

Finley's face went slack with confusion. "What? I don't know what's so funny this time."

"It's your choice of last names," Zuma said through clenched teeth.

Titus was almost laughing too. "I like it actually. Anders and Zanders, the newest act of the Vagabond Circus," he said, scribbling it on his notepad.

Finley's face lit up as he turned to Zuma. "Your last name is Zanders?"

"Don't pretend you didn't know that," she said.

"I didn't. I had a guy named Mr. Anders who helped me out once," he admitted honestly. His name was George Anders. He'd helped Finley just recently. Had found him lost walking down Sunset Boulevard. George must have sensed Finley's confusion and also his fear. He gave him directions without Finley asking and also told him where a safe hiding spot was for those trying to get away from people. He then shook his hand and told him his name. If it wasn't for Mr. Anders then Finley never would have gotten away. He wouldn't be at Vagabond Circus. And he still didn't know how George knew he needed help. He just seemed to sense so much about Finley. His fear, his confusion, his need to hide away. It kind of reminded him of the things Sunshine knew about Finley without him telling her.

"Whatever," Zuma said, rolling her eyes at him.

"Your parents named you Zuma Zanders?" Finley asked, suppressing a laugh.

"Yeah, they thought it was amusing," she said, not sounding amused.

"Well, I really didn't know that was your last name, so it's a nice choice on my part and a bit uncanny," Finley said.

"Revolting, more like it," Zuma said.

Dave stopped laughing. "Okay, that's enough, Zuma. I think Finley Anders has a great ring to it."

"Thank you," Finley said, taking a bow. He then turned and held out a hand to Zuma. "Ms. Zanders, shall we put on a show for these two?"

She turned, not taking his hand, and marched to her starting position.

Chapter Thirty-Four

*W*hen Finley dipped Zuma low at the end of the act Dave jumped to his feet, clapping so fast that Zuma whipped her head up at a strange angle, banging her forehead into Finley's. He pulled her upright and she rubbed the place on her head where they hit.

"You all right?" Finley asked, rubbing his own head.

She ignored him and turned her attention to the ringmaster and creative director. Dave was still clapping and Titus sat behind him, legs crossed and a satisfied look on his face.

"Simply brilliant," Dave said, bouncing over to Zuma. He then wrapped his arms around her, squeezing the girl in tight and patting her back. He pulled back and cupped her chin. "You, my dear, made me want to cry. That was an unbelievable display of your talent. Never seen you move in quite that way."

Zuma smiled back at him. A genuine one. It made Finley instantly envy Dave, for he'd caused that smile and therefore had been rewarded with it.

"And you," Dave said, turning and slapping Finley on the shoulder. "Well, I don't think you were just the secret ingredient Vagabond Circus needed to do better but you were also what Zuma needed to unlock her true talent. You two are perfection together," he said, puffing up his chest and walking back to his seat.

Zuma leaned over to Finley. "I love Dave, but he's going senile if he thinks you unlock any of my talent," she said in a whisper.

Finley shrugged like he didn't care. "Well, you unlocked something in me," he admitted freely.

"The true jerk inside you?" she said, looking interested in his answer.

Finley ignored her and turned his attention to Titus, who was shuffling through notes. "Yes, I totally agree with Dave. That's going to be our best act." He stacked a few pages together. "Maybe it's better for the circus if you two don't get along," he said with a snicker. He then stood and handed the pages to Finley. "Here's my notes on things I want you two to work on. There's also notes on the other acts you'll be incorporated into. Read through them and you two rehearse during dream travel time tonight. We have a dress rehearsal first thing tomorrow. Which reminds me, stop off at the costume trailer, Finley, before heading to your own trailer tonight." Titus then turned to Dave, who had a huge grin plastered on his face.

"Yeah, yeah, Dave," Titus said, walking past him, having read the expression on his old friend's face. "You were right. This will be great," he said dryly.

Chapter Thirty-Five

Stars were poking out one at a time through the darkening sky when Dave entered the miniature big top. He froze. Someone had been in there. Someone who wasn't Titus. He and Titus had shared an office space since the beginning and it worked because the creative director respected Dave's obsessive compulsive disorder. His friend ensured that all papers were stacked straight. Titus was careful to put back writing utensils with their tips down. And he never touched Dave's laptop, which the ringmaster constantly cleaned with toothpicks and condensed air.

Dave knew instantly that someone had been rummaging through papers, using the pens, and touching his laptop. The greasy fingerprints on the screen were proof enough that someone was snooping around. Dave's head swam with dizziness. His gloved hand steadied himself on the table. The germs had voices in Dave's head. They spoke to him, antagonized him. Yelled his name. The germs of this foreign person were like heat marks on an infrared screen inside his mind. He could sense every one of their marks and it stretched his tolerance to a deadly limit. The chaos this person created by making things slightly askew made Dave scratch, first at his elbows, then his arms, then his sides. He could hardly stand being locked inside this space that felt like the aftermath of a battlefield.

Dave reached for the cabinet of chemicals he kept beside his table, his hand shaking. *I don't have time for this,* he thought. And because his OCD was so overwhelming his first thoughts had been dedicated to how he'd have to clean the office quickly before the creepy crawling sensation on his skin sent him into one of his panic attacks. Dave could only manage his life at the circus, being around germs constantly, because he had two private, sacred places.

The thought that someone was again rummaging through his personal belongings was a secondary thought. It hardly took up much of his attention until well after the tent was mostly back to normal. He stood back, eyeing the space for anything that needed another wipe down.

Why? Why was someone sneaking around his trailer and now his office? And who? He thought he knew everyone at Vagabond Circus. Dave had personally recruited every single person. And he was an exceptional judge of character. But even he admitted there were people he didn't know as well as others. *Also, people change,* he reasoned. Maybe the ones he used to know weren't who he thought they were anymore. And then there were fairly new recruits whom he hardly knew at all. Was it his imagination or had these attempts increased in frequency since Finley arrived? And why? What would the boy have to do with it? Dave shook the suspicion out of his head as he wiped the laptop down again with a towel drenched in rubbing alcohol.

Chapter Thirty-Six

*T*he bed was soft under Zuma's sore muscles. She was relieved that the next eight hours of practice would be in consciousness form only, giving her muscles a break. Through dream traveling muscle memory was affected, but it didn't impact the actual body. Workouts in the dream travel realm built no muscle and strained it very little. However, injury was still possible while dream traveling. This was an unavoidable rule. Whatever happened in the body's mind, happened to the body. It was similar to the experience of a Middling dreaming they were stabbed and awakening with a sharp pain in their ribs. However, a Dream Traveler would awake with an actual laceration.

What Zuma wasn't relieved about was spending the next eight hours alone with Finley. She didn't know how to be around him, and Zuma was the kind of girl who always knew how to be. Her role in the circus had exposed her to all sorts of people. And the circus's reputation had given her the opportunity to meet fans with various statuses. She had been introduced to princes and movie stars and never had she felt uncomfortable. The girl shook hands with ease, always a confident smile on her face. But with Finley she didn't know how to behave or react. Should she be nice to him? Or should she have a threatening demeanor? She'd already tried multiple approaches and it didn't seem to matter. No matter what, Finley affected her. He made her feel that her very heart lay on the outside of her chest, exposed. But he was just a boy. A stranger. A performer.

Zuma smiled as she closed her eyes. *Yes, he is just a boy,* she thought. That single idea seemed to make him smaller in her mind, less intimidating. She then turned her thoughts to the place she intended to dream travel to, the practice tent. Finley and she would practice there the entire night, their consciousness working on honing every detail of their acts until they were perfect. The rest of the circus was performing in the big top, ensuring that all the changes would be ready for the run-through in the morning.

The metallic tunnel wrapped around Zuma's mind as her consciousness relaxed into the dream travel. This was her transport to any place and any time. This was the device that connected her with every Dream Traveler on Earth. Only they had access to these tunnels of consciousness, which bonded them as a race.

It always felt so strange to Zuma that she belonged to this race that most of the world was unaware of. She had often asked her parents why Dream Travelers were not well-known. They had said the same thing that Dave said about magic: People forget that which is fantastic. This was one of Dave's other reasons for owning Vagabond Circus. He firmly believed if he didn't take his show up and down the west coast every year, then people would forget that magic existed. He had said that people needed to be reminded because life was inundated with the mundane. And Zuma's parents had said something similar about Dream Travelers, except no one regularly reminded the world that they existed. And as a race, most thought it was better that they keep a low profile. The rich shouldn't publish their bank statements, the brilliant shouldn't tout their IQ scores, and Dream Travelers should live amongst themselves quietly. That was for the best, most thought.

The tunnel disappeared around Zuma, as her conscious mind entered the practice tent. She was really there, her mind seeing it in real time. However, she was invisible to the physical eye. The tent was empty beside her, but only for a minute. Finley's ethereal body flickered briefly before becoming almost solid. In the dream travel form, bodies have a whitish glow and are solid only to other Dream Travelers, but not to anyone in the physical realm. And to Zuma's disappointment, looking at Finley in this form still made her feel outside her usual self. *Just a boy*, she thought.

"You're late," she said to him when he approached her, a speculative look in his eyes. He was studying her, like she'd changed somehow.

"I'm always late," he said. She actually didn't look any different to him. In dream travel form she was as beautiful as ever, except she glowed even brighter and he hadn't thought that possible. She would make the brightest light look dull in dream travel form. Zuma was a star, through and through.

"Don't you own a watch?" she said, trying to keep herself steady under his scrutinizing stare.

At this question, he dropped his eyes. She hated that she instantly longed for his gaze on her. Finley hardly owned anything. The clothes he wore to Vagabond Circus. The things they had given him since he arrived. But other than that he had nothing. He swallowed. "No I don't."

"Never mind then," Zuma said, scooping Titus's notes into her hands. "Did you read through these?"

He flicked his eyes at the papers. "No."

"Well, you should," she said, scanning the page. "A lot of these notes pertain to you."

"I'm good," Finley said indifferently.

Zuma looked up with offense. "What? You can't just ignore Titus's input. He's the creative director."

"I can though," Finley said dryly. "I don't work for him."

"If you're in this show then you do. And if you don't incorporate his feedback into the act then you're not going to work here for long," she said.

"Do you forget that he said this was the show's best act?" Finley said with an unruly smile.

She gave a tired sigh. "This bad boy act isn't always entertaining."

"But the act is entertaining *some* of the time?" he asked, amused.

"So you admit that it's an act? What are you faking, and why?"

Finley lifted his hand. Zuma had known he was about to reach out for her, but she froze, interested in what he was doing. He tugged gently on a stray piece of her pink hair. "You're one to talk about fake, aren't you?"

Zuma slapped his hand away. "Actually, it's totally real," she said, stepping backward.

"What? That's impossible," Finley laughed.

"Not impossible. A tragedy can cause all sorts of crazy things to happen. People have been known to have white hair after something shocking occurred," she said.

Finley measured up Zuma before he said, "That's true. But pink?" After studying her, he thought her hair was slightly reddish, but it might also be the lighting. "What sort of accident?"

"My mother died, if you *must* know. I watched it happen," she said, turning around to hide the guilty expression that would reveal her lie.

"Oh, I'm sorry." Finley had thought Zuma had a family. Maybe she was more like him, he realized. In that instant he felt a brand new draw to her. One to tether him to her more completely. He stepped around her, preparing to apologize, to comfort her, but instead he paused. He spied the tiniest crack in Zuma's tough exterior. Not a painful emotion, like he'd think from an intimate admission like that, but rather a mischievous grin. A jokester's smile. Heat flared across his cheeks. "Wait. Are you lying?"

Zuma burst out with an indulgent laugh. "You really think a tragedy could cause a streak of pink hair? Oh my god."

He shrugged, turning around to hide his embarrassment. "I haven't been out much to be honest. And I also didn't realize people lied for their own entertainment."

"You don't seem like the honest kind," she said playfully, not realizing how mad she'd made him.

He spun around and sharpened his eyes at Zuma. "So your mother isn't dead, is she?"

Zuma tilted her head with a confident smirk that said "what do you think?"

He'd been played. A tool used for her amusement. He felt scorned somehow, although he realized Zuma was making it easier for him to push her away. He should have been grateful for that, but he wasn't completely. "Do you like to lie about your parent's death? About brutal things you witnessed?" Finley asked, his words sharp and growing hostile.

"Like it matters," Zuma said flippantly.

"It would matter to you if they were actually dead," Finley said and just then Zuma caught a haunting look in him.

"I'm sorry," she said, shifting suddenly, her mind catching up with her unsympathetic heart. "Oh gosh, are your parents dead? Did you lose them?"

He wheeled around and marched off. "Hell, I don't know. I'd love to. But you won't find me pretending they're dead to mortify a stranger."

He'd almost cleared the practice tent when Zuma called out to him. "Finley! I'm sorry. I didn't know. You're right, I shouldn't be so offhanded about my parents."

He turned and looked at her with a pointed stare. Sunshine had mentioned that Zuma had a wholesome upbringing; the idea twisted around Finley's brain like a noxious weed. "You *have* a family, don't you?"

She nodded. "Yeah, a good one," Zuma said in a hush.

"And you just left them to come to the circus? Who does that?"

A sound of frustration fell out of her mouth. "It's not how you think. Dave is friends with my parents. I made the decision to leave them. And they don't care."

It wasn't that Zuma's family didn't care, they didn't feel it mattered if they did. She often thought they forgot about her, and the thought was just a thought, not something that plagued her. But Zuma's family hadn't forgotten her; that was impossible for anyone to do with Zuma. The truth was that Zuma's family felt they couldn't handle her. And Zuma's parents, who craved little attention, always felt worn out when around her. It wasn't the girl exactly, but rather the things that happened around her. It had been like that since she was born. People were magnetized to the girl. And as with everything, the attention of people at restaurants, at school, and at parks had no real effect on Zuma. But to her family it was exhausting. They couldn't go anywhere without Zuma being the center of unwanted attention. There was just something about the girl. She didn't know what it was and hadn't much cared. Her parents and siblings didn't know either. But Dave Raydon had seemed to know. He told her parents, his childhood friends, that the girl had the mystery of the circus buried within her. Dave offered her the opportunity to join Vagabond Circus if and whenever she wanted. When Zuma turned fifteen she decided that she'd join the circus, her parents exhaustedly agreed, and so she did.

"And so you just make jokes about them being dead for fun?" Finley said, trying and failing to understand the girl who stood before him. She was beautiful, and yet had a dangerousness about her.

Zuma wore a toughened look in her eyes, one he hadn't seen in her before, but realized it was always there. That look was a part of her.

"They wouldn't care if I made those kind of jokes, at least I'm pretty sure they wouldn't," Zuma said.

Finley studied her with sharp eyes. He could dissect a frog with that glare. And Zuma felt that if she was an amphibian then he'd have split her in two. "You're one of those types who doesn't feel, aren't you? You didn't look back after you left, did you?" He paused, like waiting for her answer.

Zuma shrugged, mostly trying to dispel his cold words and the guilt they created, rather than actually provide an answer.

"And let me guess," Finley said, his tone growing more challenging, "You don't think about them now, do you?"

Another pause.

"You have a family who loves you and you came here for what? The love of strangers in an audience?" He said, and the idea was unfathomable to him. Why would anyone leave a good home? He shook his head at her, and it was that one movement that made her regret everything she'd done leading up to that moment. Finley looked absolutely repulsed by Zuma. "Yeah, I lost my parents but who knows how or when. I don't remember much, but I remember enough to know I wouldn't lie about the people who brought me into this world."

"Finley—"

"No, Zuma, why don't we count this as a failed interaction and promise not to have another one willingly? Let's just perform together and leave it to that."

She nodded to the dirt floor. "Yeah, sure," she said and strode past him, almost breaking into a run. It was only when Zuma was on the other side of the tent that she allowed herself to pick up her pace, racing out of the exit. Once in the open air her face broke into one that revealed her anger. And then she was moving too haphazardly until she collided with another person. Zuma was appalled, but arms wrapped around her at once and she realized she'd rushed straight into Jack. His arms did something to her. They softened her, making hot tears full of her humiliation spill over. Jack startled at the sound of her cries. Then he pulled her into his chest. Zuma *didn't* cry; at least he'd never seen it happen.

Never had she felt him this close in this way. They'd been close before, bodies arched together for a stunt in the act, but never like this and for the intention to comfort. They'd never allowed themselves this closeness, afraid of what it would lead to, both reading the desire in the other one's eyes. Jack's arms now tightened, pressing Zuma so firmly into him she gasped from the gesture. He patted her back and whispered, "It's okay," into her ear although he didn't know what was wrong and that it wasn't okay.

And then she forgot her momentary distraction related to Jack's arms and Zuma's mind flashed to Finley. He was right and it made her all the angrier. She was a deserter. She'd been doing it easily her whole life. Leaving people behind. She'd dropped so many people like they were disposable parts of her life, meant to be discarded and replaced by someone with a fun new personality. And circus life was easy for her, whereas it should have been difficult, at least at times. Most kids had trouble adjusting when coming to Vagabond Circus, but Zuma had no problems. It was like she had been hatched rather than born to a loving family.

Jack pulled back, pushing Zuma's hair out of her face. "What has my girl of stone so worked up?"

"It's nothing, Jack," she said, already corralling her emotions, pushing them inside the vault. The tears dried up as quickly as they came. And then Zuma sensed Finley approaching, before his movements registered any sound. His footsteps on dirt and hay grabbed Jack's attention, but Zuma knew Finley had no intention of stopping where they stood.

Jack's eyes diverted to Finley's and then back to Zuma. He pinned both hands on her shoulders and stared into her eyes. "What did he do to you?"

"I told her she was calloused," Finley said as he passed by.

Jack tilted his head in confusion. He wanted to question why something like that would bother Zuma. People had said much worse things about her. She never cared. And yet, Finley casually stating the obvious had the girl shedding what seemed like her first tears.

Jack flicked his eyes at Finley, who continued to march away from the tent. "He made you *this* upset?"

Zuma raked her hands through her hair. "I don't know. No, not him," she said, injecting conviction into the last statement. "I'm just feeling the pressure of the new show."

Jack eyed her suspiciously and then nodded. "Why don't we practice together, since it appears your rehearsal with Finley has been cut short?"

Finley walked until he now stood in the place he'd hid before officially coming to Vagabond Circus, right outside Dave's office. What had just happened had been too easy. Finley had planned to pick a fight with Zuma so he could have an excuse for not practicing with her. However, he didn't realize that the fight would actually make her upset. Pissed, yes. That was the goal. But Zuma had seemed to be hurt. Like he struck something in her. And hadn't that been the goal? However, when he passed her in Jack's arms and saw the expression in her eyes, one filled with raw pain, he instantly regretted everything. Why did being hostile to her have to be a part of the plan? It felt wrong to him. But he was here now, as he intended, standing outside Dave's office, watching the ringmaster through a crack in the tent. This was where he would spend the rest of the night. And although he could have used the extra practice with Zuma, being here was his very reason for being at Vagabond Circus. He wouldn't fail this mission.

Chapter Thirty-Seven

Zuma had the intention of working with Jack. She knew she needed to rehearse. But who she needed to practice with was Finley. Her head clouded with frustration each time she tried to focus. His eyes, haunted with his mysterious pain, kept swimming into her vision. Finally she acquiesced to the distraction and threw herself down on the mat.

"I need a break," she said to Jack, lying on her back and throwing her arm over her eyes.

"Yeah, I was going to suggest that, since you keep losing your balance," Jack said and she sensed him take the seat next to her. "What can I do to help?"

"Distract me from this maddening chatter going on inside my head," Zuma said.

"Oh," Jack said, disappointment in his tone. He had half hoped that Zuma was going to want to talk about it. Maybe it wouldn't help her, but he thought if he could understand what was going on between Finley and Zuma then he might feel better. Jack half wanted to believe that they really despised each other, but he couldn't bring himself to accept this. There was something in the way they stared at each other. It wasn't a rehearsed look like how most people do, where they see people without really *seeing* them. Zuma and Finley looked at each other every time like that was the first time they had met and they hardly believed the other person was standing in front of them. At least that's how it appeared to Jack.

"So…" Jack sang, searching for a topic that would pull Zuma's thoughts away from her troubles. "Jaz joined a dating site."

"Has she met any nice girls?" Zuma asked, her words muffled from her arm draped across her face.

"I don't think so, but she's trying."

"That's admirable," Zuma said absentmindedly and then rolled over on her stomach and looked up at Jack. "Finley called me out for leaving a good family. That's what you really want to know, isn't it?"

Jack gave her a half smile. He hadn't realized she'd dipped into his thoughts.

"I just skimmed them," she said, returning the smile.

"Okay, you can get out now," he said with a grin that contradicted his request.

"And there's no connection between Finley and me," Zuma said, then her hand propped up her head. It looked strained, like it also held up all her burdens.

"There is," Jack argued, "and it's not like I thought it was entirely a bad thing. Kind of intriguing. Kind of frustrating."

"You ever get tired of me being in your head?" Zuma said.

"Not at all," Jack said honestly. "You and I don't keep secrets. Well, maybe you keep them from me, but I think most of the time you're straight with me. It's relieving that the one person who can read my thoughts is someone I trust."

"Well, there is Sunshine too," Zuma reminded him. "She can read all sorts of stuff about you."

"I don't mind her either. There's something about that girl that earns trust, not sure what it is," Jack said.

"It's that you feel sorry for her," Zuma said, almost laughing.

Jack shrugged. That wasn't it, but he wasn't arguing the point when there were other things more important to discuss. "So, your family…"

"Right," Zuma said, sitting up because her hand had fallen asleep under her weight. "Am I heartless not to think about them more often?"

"I don't really think about my family," Jack said, his tone commiserating.

"Yes, you do. You despise them every chance you get, as you should. They're all a bunch of haughty jerks who can't see how amazing you are in your own right," she said.

"Don't ever change, Zuma," Jack said with a wink.

"So you have a reason to not want to be around your family, but I don't. My parents are great people. My brother and sisters are lovely. And still…"

"Well, when we pass through there do you want to stop by for a visit?" Jack asked.

"Honestly?"

"I hope you never give me anything but that," Jack said.

"Well, honestly I don't want to stop by when we pass through," Zuma said with a sigh. "I know I should, but I'd rather stick around the circus."

"That's the thing I've noticed about you, Zuma," Jack said, his voice introspective. "You never get enough of the circus. Some people need a break from it. They get away when they can. You don't tire of these trailers and the big top. You're like Dave in that way."

"Yeah, it's like I'm a homebody," Zuma said.

"And this is your home," Jack smiled in agreement. "So it's not that you don't love your family, it's that you prefer this one."

The tension that had been in Zuma's chest since her argument with Finley dissipated, like a tight knot was unraveled by Jack's words. "You're right," she said. "There's just something about the chaos of the circus and the constant adrenaline that calms me somehow."

Jack laughed. "Pandemonium makes you feel at peace," he said, marveling at her. "You really are one of a kind, Zuma."

"Thanks," she said, her voice softening. "And Jack?" Zuma waited until he pulled his eyes from the mat and met hers. "If you want me to, I'll go with you if you want to visit your family."

"You know, Zuma, I think if I showed up with you on my arm then I'd actually get some admiration from my family." Jack laughed suddenly, his eyes imagining the scene. "My brothers would envy me for once."

Zuma wasn't one to blush, so she just smiled wide at Jack. "So that's a yes?"

He shook his head. "No, but thanks for the offer. You're not *really* mine, so the attention I'd get wouldn't *really* be genuine."

Zuma agreed with a solemn nod. It hurt her to see the look that plagued Jack's eyes when he reminisced over his family. Whereas she needed none of her family's approval, Jack would never be complete without it. She hoped one day they saw him for who he was, extraordinary in his own way.

Chapter Thirty-Eight

$\mathcal{F}$inley stared at his image in the full-length mirror. The skin-tight suit was decorated with the colors of Vagabond Circus, teal blue and neon green. They alternated around the suit, the blue specked with wisps of smoke and the green arranged like flames. It wasn't a distracting suit like in some acts, it was complementary to the performance. Finley almost felt like a real performer now.

After the dress rehearsal he'd have a break before his first show. *His first show.*

At the circus.

The idea seemed strange running through his head.

"I'm in the circus," he said out loud and smiled at himself in the mirror. "You got this," he said and gave himself a cheesy thumbs-up and then promptly laughed at himself. The sound seemed strange coming out of his mouth. Finley didn't laugh. He hadn't really been given any opportunities to do so. There was nothing fun or funny in his life. But this was his new life.

He exited his trailer to find Zuma leaning against the RV, one foot propped up behind her. He hadn't felt nervous thinking about his first show, but staring at her made his throat prickle with tension. Everything about her demeanor was casual: the way she leaned against the white trailer, the way her arms were crossed in front of her, and the way she lifted her eyes to look at him. She was wearing a white gown. It was her costume for the first part of the show where she'd be locked up in a clear orb that was lifted to the top of the tent and then filled with colored gas before night came in the story.

The nightgown wasn't loose like most, although it flowed at the bottom. It was tight at the bodice with a low neckline. Pieces of chiffon formed the bottom of the dress and the long train she had tucked under her arm. She seemed unconcerned about the potential of getting the white dress dirty by leaning on the trailer or messing up the intimate series of braids her hair was arranged into. The pink in her hair threaded through various braids, solitary diamonds pinned in multiples places.

Finley struggled to swallow and the attempt produced a startled cough from him. If Zuma noticed his nervous reaction then she covered it.

"What were you laughing about?" she asked, pointing to his trailer. "I heard you in there."

He arched a disapproving eyebrow at her before turning around and stalking off a few feet. Finley was glad he could avoid Zuma's question by pretending to still be angry with her.

"We need to talk," she said.

He halted. Turned and appraised her.

And then quite deliberately Zuma checked out his suit and looked away, feigning boredom.

"I thought I made myself clear that we should refrain from talking in the future," he said, trying to match her casual stance. "It gets us nowhere."

"Thing is, Finley," Zuma said, her voice dull, "that communication between acrobats is kind of key to their performance."

"Oh sure, we can talk about the act," Finley said. "We can discuss timing, arrangements, and whatever else. But let's limit it to that."

She kicked off the trailer and stood tall. "Look, I'm sorry if I offended you. It appears I'm good at it. But you and I are in this act together and the show rests on our performance. You may be able to wall off your emotions but I can't go out there and put on show after show with a guy who hates me. Acrobats don't just need to communicate about logistics, they need to communicate in other ways. They need to know each other and you're not even trying on that front."

The idea of knowing Zuma was exhilarating. It was the other part that created a chorus of no's in Finley's head. Zuma couldn't know him, not who he really was. "I think we've proved that we work just fine with the way things are. Dave and Titus loved our act."

"Damn it, Finley. There are several times in this show that I'm trusting you with my safety and I'm not sure why I'm doing that since you're a complete jerk to me half the time. And why should I trust you at all when you won't even tell me the first thing about you? You aren't even trying to meet me in the middle here!" Zuma's voice rose until she was yelling, her face flushed pink as her hair.

"I won't ever drop you," he said through clenched teeth, a heat in his eyes.

"What?" she said, her voice low again.

"That's what you're worried about, right? That I can't be trusted? That I'm going to hurt you in the act? You're worried that I might drop you because of what you don't know about me. And you're afraid of me because of what you do know about my attitude toward you."

"No," she said quickly, then took it back with a slight nod. "I mean, maybe. But more than anything I worry how I'm going to maintain focus working with a partner who won't communicate with me."

"Is this another attempt to get in my head?" he said.

"Well, that's part of it," she urged. "If I just knew you were okay up there," she said, pointing to her own head, "If I could get a glimpse, then maybe I'd understand you. Maybe I could trust you. And also, don't you see that we would be able to communicate throughout the act without saying a word to each other? It's very efficient."

Finley hid the shiver that transpired through his body at the idea of Zuma in his head. There would be nothing worse. He shook his head roughly. "It's just not necessary."

"Damn it, Finley—"

"You know, maybe I should have made my last name Finley and changed my first name to Damn It, since that's what you prefer to call me," he said, grateful for the opportunity to divert the conversation.

"Seriously though—"

"Seriously though," he said cutting her off again, "I do find your attempts to try and get along with me kind of cute." He also found it was threatening his resolve to push Zuma away.

"Well, we really have a lot of people counting on us and the last thing I'm going to allow is for something to make this circus fail," she said, stomping her foot into the earth, a frustrated determination on her face.

He saw in her right then a passion that froze his heart and injected it with its drug. Zuma was in love with Vagabond Circus. It was so clear in the way her eyes changed talking about it. He took a step toward her. "I will not fail the circus. There's little more important to me than ensuring that Dave's circus is a success."

Zuma studied him. Her eyes made Finley realize how vulnerable she made him. In that moment, Finley was dangerously close to his determination crumbling. "And Zuma, you may not know me but you can trust me. I would never let something happen to you."

She gave him a sideways skeptical look.

"It's true," he said, a new lightness in his voice. "If the big top implodes I'll throw my body over yours to keep you safe."

She laughed and it brought a carefree smile to his mouth. There were few things that sounded as attractive as her laughter. And now he'd been the one to bring it out of her.

"Okay, well then I guess that means we are getting along yet again."

"Well, yeah," Finley said, "how could we not after you totally just groveled at my feet with that apology?"

Her mouth popped open. "I did not."

"That's not how I'm remembering it," he said, hooking his arm around her shoulder and heading them in the direction of the big top.

Zuma's face flushed from the contact. She'd hoped to smooth things out with Finley but to have his arm casually draped over her was unexpected. It unsettled her in all the right ways, stirring a cluster of butterflies in her stomach. She kept her eyes trained on the tent as they walked. Finley was a tornado, changing every second, beautiful and dangerous and unpredictable. But Zuma loved storms. Always had.

Chapter Thirty-Nine

*F*rom the moment Dr. Raydon introduced the circus to the finale, which was Zuma and Finley's big act, the entire show was seamless. Fanny's kids sat in the front row, Emily and Benjamin both jumping up and down in their seats several times. The employees of Vagabond Circus were people who took an insurmountable challenge like rearranging and changing an entire two-hour circus and made it look easy. Middlings would never be able to pull off such a feat. The success of the circus wasn't just because the performers had super powers, but because they could spend sleep hours training. All things take time and Dream Travelers have more of it than anyone.

Finley and Zuma took their final bows as the lights dimmed overhead. They stayed in the ring, ready for the dress-rehearsal after-meeting. The performers all spilled out of the backstage area and stadium, wide grins on most everyone's faces. Fanny was still clapping, unabashed tears swimming down her cheeks.

"That was marvelous," she said in her warm voice so everyone in the ring or nearby could hear.

Zuma gave Finley a slight smile, not meeting his eyes entirely. He leaned over and whispered into her ear. "I told you. I won't let down this circus."

"I want to believe you," she said through her smiling teeth as she waved at various crew people in the bleachers, who were throwing her kisses and thumbs-ups.

Finley was about to say something else when something poked him in the leg. He looked down to see little Emily standing beside him, a smile lighting up her blue eyes. He kneeled down. "Well, hey there, Emily," he said.

"Would you come over here?" the young girl said, pointing to where she'd been seated. "Benny wants to meet you but he's too nervous." Finley looked up to see the three other kids sitting next to Fanny, who was now wiping tears away from her cheeks. Between the older girl and Sebastian was a boy of about ten. He had short brown hair and a nervous smile. Finley's eyes slid over to Sebastian and the boy got up at once and left the tent, looking to be rushed like he just forgot something.

"You bet I will," Finley said, throwing a glance back at Zuma, who was watching the whole thing with a new interest. Emily slid her tiny hand into Finley's and urgently pulled him over to the group.

"He says that you're the new star of Vagabond Circus, and that he wants to be you when he grows up," she said, her words rushed with excitement.

Jack arrived at Zuma's side without a word. He was watching her watch Finley. She turned her eyes to him. There was a group of performers behind him who looked eager to relay their compliments to Zuma. It was unspoken but everyone knew Jack got her attention first.

"Great catch," she said to him. "That's going to wow the audience more than anything."

Jack's eyes were still on Finley, who was signing an autograph for Benjamin. "It is Finley who you should be complimenting. I only catch the quadruple because he teleports."

"Jack, that's not true," she said, a little deflated by his bad attitude, which was oozing off him like bad cologne.

He slid his eyes to hers, a quiet anger in them. "So it appears you and Finley made up after last night."

"We kind of had to. We are in a ton of the show together and then there's the last act."

"Yeah, about that," Jack said and he could feel the resentment in him building. It was petty and he knew it but he didn't know how else to feel. Not when it came to Zuma.

"You didn't like it?" she said, turning to him, half mad and half sad.

"No, of course I did. How could I not like it?" He said, his voice lower than hers, his eyes scanning the curious faces around them. They weren't being loud but everyone could sense the tension. "The act was breathtaking. You were more gorgeous than I've ever seen you. The way you moved, it made me hurt from the force of emotions you unearthed."

"Then why do you look disappointed?"

Jack stole a glance at Finley, who was talking to the kids, but his eyes kept finding Zuma.

"Because you've never moved like that when performing with me," he said, his shoulders slumped in defeat.

Chapter Forty

𝒟ave and Titus didn't want Zuma doing fortunetelling before the show now that she had more responsibility. Ian replaced her. He was in charge of the rig crew members and preferred the labor of putting up and maintaining the big top. However, Ian also had the gift of divination and clairvoyance. Dave had asked that along with his responsibility on crew, he run Zuma's booth for an undeterminable amount of time.

Since her conversation with Jack after the rehearsal that morning, Zuma had felt lost. And she also had trouble staying away from the preshow activities. She loved watching the patrons arrive at Vagabond Circus. Some had faces full of anticipation and others only tolerated the experience for their kids. Zuma loved watching them before and then after as they left, transformed.

With a fond gaze she ran her eyes over the blue and green fabric bathing her booth. This was one of her favorite parts of Vagabond Circus. She loved the ring, but her interaction there was impersonal. As the fortuneteller she connected with patrons and helped them, or at least she hoped she did. Most came back year after year to visit the fortuneteller who advised them and therefore saved their business, strengthened their ties with their family, or helped them with a major decision.

Zuma's black hooded cloak mostly hid her face and entirely covered her white gown. Still, to some she was always recognizable. It was her energy.

"Hey, lovely," Ian said, pulling his round face up from a deck of cards. "Are you checking up on me?"

"No, I know you're doing an excellent job. I bet you'll want to keep the booth after a few shows," she said, drawing closer, her cloak taking pieces of hay strewn on the ground with her.

"It is fun," he agreed, "but I don't know. I prefer the backstage. Dave was right where he cast me, just as he was right with your casting."

Ian was Zuma's older brother's age. Twenty-four. He looked odd in the velvet robe with his broad shoulders and barrel chest. Most would say that he didn't look like the average fortuneteller, but there was probably no one more accurate than Ian. He had what Zuma only pretended to have when doing the job. Ian could actually see the future and with a precision that most would kill for.

"So, then what brings you here? I thought you were supposed to be resting before each show," Ian said, his round chin tucked into his chest, eyes discerning.

She cast a sideways look around. "I am resting…"

"Are you?" he said, a challenge in his words, although he wasn't trying to intimidate the girl.

"Well, I'm trying," she said, taking another step forward, keeping her voice low, her eyes constantly scanning.

"Is it that you can't rest because of the stress weighing on your heart?" Ian said, sliding the deck of tarot cards, used only as a prop, to the side and clearing the space in front of him.

"Do you know that because you're a fantastic observer or because of your abilities?" Zuma asked, her eyes ablaze with curiosity.

"Well, psychics are great because of their attention to detail, so call it both."

They both laughed easily. "True," Zuma said, taking a seat in the chair across from him. "Ian, can I get a reading?"

He gave her a look of concern. "You know where your expectations need to be if I do, right?"

She nodded. "None of it is true. It's all potential truths. Potential realities depending on which way the wind blows, what someone else does, and what I have to eat for breakfast tomorrow."

He smiled, showing a mouthful of braces. "I see you've played this little game before."

Ian's parents hadn't wanted him to have braces growing up because it was a cosmetic thing. They also didn't want to shell out the money for the expense. After he came to Vagabond Circus he saved up enough money for orthodontics to fix his buckteeth. His parents ridiculed him about it every time he visited and also about the fact that he'd turned down the opportunity to go into banking like his father.

"All right, you know how this works," he said, holding out his calloused hands.

Zuma nodded and offered both her hands to Ian. It was when he touched another person that things about their future were sparked in his mind. It had been like this since he was thirteen and tried to hold Molly's hand. They had synagogue together and spent most of that time giggling in the back. He grabbed the young girl's hand one morning and had been assaulted by a vision of Molly stepping out onto the road without looking. A car swerved, missing Molly, but it still hit a tree, killing the driver in the vehicle. However, because of what Ian told Molly about his vision, that never happened and that driver was still alive to this day.

Ian wrapped both his hands around Zuma's, which were hardened like his but from the flying trapeze. Zuma's hands were long and slender in contrast to his. He sucked in a breath. Zuma watched as Ian's eyes roamed around under his closed lids, like he was watching a movie inside his head. After only ten seconds his eyes sprung open. With a jerk he pulled his hands from her, a new stress in his eyes.

"What?" she said, sensing his concern.

"It's nothing. I mean…you know how this stuff goes?" Ian said.

"But you have information for me, don't you?" she said, leaning forward, careful to keep herself hidden inside the cloak.

He nodded, his shoulders slumping a little. "You have to trust Finley enough…"

"What? *Enough* for what?"

"You have to trust him enough that…he drops you."

"What?" Zuma straightened suddenly, a cold chill zipping down her back. "He's going to drop me? Like during a show?"

"No," Ian said, looking to the side like examining the vision in his head. "I think this is during a rehearsal."

"Why would I want him to drop me?"

"Because it changes everything," Ian said.

"I don't understand. I have to trust him enough and then he ends up dropping me and that changes everything?"

"Yes," Ian said, a strange weight in his eyes now. "It puts things in motion that *have* to occur."

"But we don't know what has to occur. We're always guessing," Zuma said.

"I feel strongly that this is important," he said with a new conviction in his voice. "It's not ideal, it's not pretty, but it's an important catalyst."

"You realize it's going to be hard for me to rehearse now?" Zuma said, a shudder vibrating across her shoulders.

"You aren't hurt physically," he said, and the implications hung between them.

"But his mistake of dropping me, it sets something in motion?" she asked, needing to confirm every detail of this.

"It is no mistake," Ian said in a hush.

"He drops me on purpose?" she said too loud.

"Just put this out of your mind and trust him. It's imperative that you do, that he drops you," Ian said with that too-wise look in his eyes. His vision was a burden and it made him look older than he was.

Zuma was certain there would be no forgetting this information. There was already too much mystery surrounding Finley and now this potential reality made her heart palpitate. She offered her hands to Ian. "Will you look again? Maybe you missed something."

He shook his head roughly. "I didn't," he said, turning his gaze away from her hands like they made him ill suddenly.

"Ian, what is it?"

"It's a future that has to come to pass, Zuma. And it brings you much sorrow before giving you the opposite."

"Then why do you look so sad?"

"Because the things that affect you at Vagabond Circus tend to affect us all," he said, his voice eerie.

Zuma rose slowly from her seat and gave Ian a look he saw too often: reluctant acceptance. It was difficult for people to hear their future and have the tools to shape it. This was mainly because the tools involved doing the last thing they wanted and Ian knew that for Zuma to trust Finley was almost impossible. Still, it was critical. The future of Vagabond Circus rested on the well-sculpted shoulders of the two acrobats.

Chapter Forty-One

The warm spotlight glowed down on Zuma. She stood on the side of the ring playing the character of the sheltered girl who had escaped the cage she'd been locked into almost every night. She'd already met many creatures of the night, all proving to be entertaining rather than dangerous, as her father had warned. The girl was searching quite melodramatically for a new animal who would enchant her as the others had done. She turned in one direction and a loud drum sounded, making her jump and retreat two steps. Then she turned in the other direction and another bang of a drum stopped her. The acrobat crouched down low, the orchestra playing a spooky arrangement that flowed perfectly with her jumpy movements.

She ran, a series of graceful steps, and stopped suddenly. A curious look lit up her face. With a tentative hand she glided her palm over something. Zuma pressed down on what appeared to be invisible and her hand sprang back. With a look of delight the acrobat placed her hand on the invisible thing again and then hopped up onto it. It was then that the lights shone fully on the wire that the audience couldn't see before. Like a kid exploring a toy for the first time she practiced a few steps on top of the tight wire, which was only three feet off the ground. Zuma played with the bounce. Shuffled forward and back and then spun herself around. She was elegant on the wire, moving like she would through water. Her arms flowed, her legs swam across the wire, never losing balance.

But in the shadows something appeared. The girl Zuma was playing didn't see the presence watching, but the audience did. A few in the audience pointed. A kid in the crowd tapped his mom. "Look!" he said, his voice too loud.

Finley moved to the side of the wire, his suit a dark blue, an elegant contrast to Zuma's pale green costume. His was the color of a darkening sky, hers the color of grass coated in morning dew. Zuma now overflowed with confidence on the wire and leapt along it, sashaying after the move and then jumping straight in the air, one leg coming up behind her and her arms reaching behind her head to grab it before landing again with perfect precision. She didn't see Finley at her back, crouched down on the end platform where the wire was tethered. He reached down and grabbed the wire and shook it. Zuma startled, almost losing her balance.

Whipping around she fumbled on the wire backwards at the sight of the monster. She played the character so well, acting frightened at just the perfect time. This was what the girl's father had protected her from. She held out a hand at the beast and it hissed in return. Then it jumped onto the wire, sending her straight into the air. But she landed back on it in a crouch, her hand reaching down between her bent legs to grab the wire, tethering her to it. On the monster's next bounce she grabbed the wire with both hands and her hips came down on it as she spun around the wire, before coming off it in a flip like a gymnast dismounting the uneven bar.

Finley jumped straight in the air then flew down on the wire and bounced high before throwing himself into a full twist with a front flip also dismounting from the apparatus. He landed just before Zuma, who played the terrified girl. He bowed to her, offering his outstretched hand. Zuma paused, searching him by trying to look at his shielded face. Finally she reached for his hand and once their grips clasped he wrestled her to the ground, and that's when the fight scene of their act officially began.

Chapter Forty-Two

The audience was silent when Finley and Zuma's act morphed into a dance of two lovers' hearts united. Every eye was trained on them, hypnotized by the pair who moved like water flowed. Only Sunshine was aware of how many audience members were close to tears, feeling the overwhelming emotion under the big top. She watched with Dave and Jack from the side of the curtain. Dave had asked her to scan the emotions of patrons throughout the night to get a barometer of how the new show was working. And the girl would soon report to the ringmaster that never before had the audience had such heightened emotions. And during the finale every emotion was hanging on a hinge, ready to burst open.

Sunshine prepared herself for the cacophony of feelings that would assault her when the act ended. She pulled her eyes to Finley, who had just caught Zuma in his arms, completing the last trick of their act. The audience seemed to suck in a collective breath all at once. Finley slid his leg around Zuma's leg, encouraging her back as he had done during every practice. She arched her spine as he dipped her down low. The pair slid together, Finley in a deep lunge, Zuma's arms tied around his neck.

They held the pose for a three count as Titus had asked. Three seconds where Finley allowed the adrenaline of finishing his first show to rocket through his veins. Three long seconds where the applause he'd earned during the show reverberated in his chest. Three seconds where he stared down at Zuma and realized she made him feel more emotion than the adrenaline and the applause combined. She owned him. And automatically he wrenched her to him and covered her mouth with his. She sensed the kiss coming but didn't know how to react with over a thousand eyes watching her, so she just gasped against his lips, sucking him in.

Zuma tightened her arms around his neck, assaulted by the tremor that ran down her body. All this happened inside of a few seconds and then Finley pulled away, drawing Zuma to a standing position. Their hands were clasped in each other's as they bowed low to the loudest and longest applause the Vagabond Circus had ever earned. Then they turned in unison, hands still connected, and took another bow to the other side of the ring. Kids jumped up and down. Women pushed glistening tears from their cheeks. Zuma scanned the crowd, taking in the faces of every patron, all smiling, cheering, and overflowing with excitement. The lights faded on them and Finley dropped her hand as they ran in complete darkness to the back curtain. When they were through it the houselights dawned on a crowd who would never forget the show they just watched.

Chapter Forty-Three

*F*inley wasn't even completely on the other side of the curtain before Zuma twisted around and shoved him in the chest, knocking him lightly into the blue velvet behind him.

"What in the hell was that?" she said and her voice wasn't as angry as she tried to make it. She sounded curious. Zuma wanted to feel violated, but she couldn't make herself. That kiss had a pureness to it.

He stared down at her, his mouth pinched together, a weight in his eyes. He was battling something inside himself that didn't exist in most. A torture of overpowering emotions.

"Well?" she said when he didn't respond, didn't look like he could. Finley's eyes just stayed tight on her, which was why he didn't see the blur of movements that Zuma saw. From the side, Jack bolted through the space and raised his hand and punched Finley across the face. Finley should have moved fast enough to deflect it, but his focus was overwhelmed by the angry expression on Zuma's face. She appeared to be mad at him; however, she had kissed him back, cinched her arms around his neck and pulled him into her. Breathed him in. He didn't understand. He also didn't know why he did it in the first place. Everything was unexplainable when it came to Zuma.

Finley hardly stumbled back from Jack's punch, although it had incredible force behind it. Finley was used to being punched. Assaulted. He knew how to take it with little effect.

Frantically Zuma grabbed one of Jack's arms and pulled him away. Jack stared at Finley with a look of complete disdain. Another abuse Finley was used to.

"Where do you get off doing something like that? You know Zuma can't stand you. Why would you take advantage of her in front of the audience?" Jack said, his voice a hush but his words hot.

Finley hardly heard all that Jack said. His eyes were on Zuma, who had her hands wrapped around Jack's arm still, encouraging him to calm down.

"That's not true. You don't despise me," Finley said to Zuma.

She dropped her gaze, unable to stomach the brutal pain in Finley's eyes. Still, she felt echoes of the tremor his kiss caused deep inside her. Never before had an experience produced that reaction. Not even the flying trapeze, which gave her a high like no other.

"Jack," Dave said from behind him, a caution in his voice. "Why don't you leave the big top and cool down."

Jack turned, Zuma letting his arm drop. There behind them stood Dave, who was only a few inches taller than Zuma. He wasn't wearing his normal jovial smile but rather under his frayed top hat he had a serious expression. It looked all wrong on his face, like a dog with cat ears.

"But—" Jack said.

"I understand you're angry, but we do not conduct ourselves in that way," Dave said and even Zuma flinched from the sternness in his voice. There had to be nothing worse than to earn the ringmaster's disapproval, she thought. And for Jack, this would be a curse. "Go to your trailer and I don't want you at tonight's festivities. We will discuss this in Portland, you and me," Dave said, his voice full of authority.

"Dave, you can't let this go—" Jack began.

"And Jack, I don't intend to. But this is *my* circus, and *my* issue to handle. This matter concerns you no longer, is that clear?"

Jack closed his eyes and nodded.

"Now please leave me to discuss this matter," Dave said, his voice lightening an octave. "Zuma, you are free to go as well."

Jack turned and walked a few paces, but he paused as soon as he realized Zuma wasn't by his side. She was standing still. She hadn't gone with him. He gave her a confused look.

Zuma turned her gaze to Dave. "I'm staying."

Dave nodded his consent. "Very well." He swiveled his head to Jack, who was watching dumbfounded. "Go on now. Go cool off," Dave said, his voice calm but insistent.

Jack's last look was at Zuma, who was staring at him with consoling eyes. Then he whipped around and stormed off. And this time he wouldn't argue with Zuma if she called it "storming off."

Jack was furious. Everything during the first new show had gone perfectly and it put an unbearable weight on his chest. To watch the crowd respond to Finley the way they did, with more surprise and amazement than he ever received, was a knife right under his breast bone. It created a searing pain and he pressed his hand there, rubbing on the ache. And now Finley had kissed Zuma, in front of the circus and its patrons. Finley knew what her lips felt like. Knew what she tasted like. Two things Jack had wanted to know since he set his eyes on her over three years ago. What burned Jack up wasn't that Finley was taking what had belonged to him. Finley was taking that which Jack never had and always wanted.

Chapter Forty-Four

"The rules were made clear to you when you came to Vagabond Circus," Dave said to Finley, his voice firm.

Behind him Titus was clearing the back area of performers, encouraging them to change and toddle off to the after-party. He was grateful that Dave was intervening and not him. How uncomfortable this tense situation must be for someone to deal with. People kissing. People hitting each other. Relationships. Titus shivered with unease. "No thanks," he said under his breath. The memories of the relationships that tore the circus apart almost twenty years ago were still fresh in his mind. Nothing was a bigger motivator than love. It made people happy. It made them depressed. It made people challenge themselves. It made them different people. It made them kill. *There's a reason domestic violence is the most frequent,* Titus thought. *Love makes people insane.*

In the main big top area patrons were filing out of the exit. Excited voices discussed the various acts, Zuma and Finley the topic of most people's conversations. They were undoubtedly the favorite act. Girls twirled as they exited, pretending to be jumping into the arms of a waiting Finley.

"Mom, can I put a pink streak in my hair?" a girl asked, skipping beside her mother.

Another child heard the request and soon every little girl was asking for a new hairdo. Someone would have made a fortune selling pink hair dye by the gates of Vagabond Circus.

"You made the rules implicitly clear," Finley finally said to Dave's question.

"And is it also clear to you that when I said no relationships among circus members that that meant no necking?" Dave said, holding his gloved hands out, exasperated.

Zuma's stomach turned over from the use of the word "necking." *Is there a worse word,* she thought with a grimace. There definitely wasn't a more humiliating way to describe a simple kiss.

"Yes, I'm aware that's implied," Finley said, his chin held high, eyes mostly on Dave, although he caught Zuma's look of revulsion.

Dave dropped his hands to his side and they clapped on his legs. "I'm a bit overwhelmed by this one, Finley. You've broken both my rules in one setting and I don't really know how to handle it. This was our best show ever and you're mostly responsible for that, but that doesn't mean I can excuse such behavior."

"Sir," Finley said, his eyes confused. "How did I break both rules by what I did?"

"Well, it was hugely disrespectful to force yourself onto Zuma," Dave said, matter-of-factly. "And then there's Jack's feelings to consider, which I'm certain you did not do."

"Wait, I didn't force myself on Zuma," Finley said. "She didn't push me away."

At this Zuma buried her head in her hands. Now she doubted her reasons for staying. Why had she stayed? Didn't she know this would be a humiliating conversation to be a part of with Dave present and leading the questioning?

However, when she looked up the ringmaster had turned to her, a fond glint twinkling his light blue eyes. "Well, of course not, that would have ruined the show. My Zuma is a brilliant actress." And then he gave her a wink. "Nice cover-up, Zuma. It almost seemed planned. You incorporated the surprise kiss seamlessly."

She gulped. Nodded. Tried to keep an unsurprised look on her face.

"Right." Finley bit on the word watching Zuma, whose passive stance was actually quite commendable to him, if it hadn't also been infuriating. "And Jack? How was I disrespecting him?" Finley asked.

"Well, my boy, Jack, is obviously very protective of Zuma, as you would be too if you two grew up together. They have a special bond. That was a very disrespectful thing to do to a girl he loves."

"Wait! What!?" It was Zuma who voiced the question.

Dave looked at her and said, "Zuma, I did ask you to leave. I thought it might be easier if Finley and I discussed the relationships at Vagabond Circus in private, but you made the decision to stay and I respected it. And you must know I'm aware of Jack's feelings for you."

"Dave, there's nothing going—"

Dave stopped Zuma's speech by holding up a single white-gloved hand. Dr. Raydon was an intelligent man. He knew people were hardwired to mate. He didn't have any disillusions about this. Most were like Jasmine and stayed at the circus until the urge to have a relationship was too much and then left him. During their time with him he fed them with nutritious food and intoxicating memories. In return, he asked that the staff not have romantic relationships amongst each other during their time at Vagabond Circus. But he saw the way Jack looked after Zuma and knew he had feelings for her. What Jack didn't realize was that everyone had feelings for Zuma. She captured the attention of anyone whose eyes tripped over her. If Jack realized this then he'd know that Zuma's true love was the person who did to her what she did to everyone else, steal their focus.

Dave knew this, and knew how it would affect Zuma one day. Not yet, but one day. If what he learned from having a reading with Ian was going to come to pass then Jack would figure out one day soon that Zuma wasn't his true love. It would be both a disappointment and a relief for him. And if the crew member with the braces could be believed then Jack would figure this out very soon.

Dave also knew that he never had to worry about Jack because he observed rule number one as did Zuma. And both acrobats respected the ringmaster enough not to have a relationship behind his back. And although Finley wasn't as endeared to Dave yet, he still trusted the boy.

Dave finally turned to Zuma. "Jack does love you," he said, a consternation on his face. And then he added, "Zuma, most everyone at Vagabond Circus loves you in their own way. Jack may have a bit more of a connection than the rest though," he said, his face light again. Zuma was glad since she didn't like that serious expression Dave had worn before. "Anyway, I only mean that Jack loves you dearly, as a friend. And what Finley did made Jack feel you were threatened, so of course he would try to protect you. Although I think he was too aggressive in his approach."

"Yeah, I guess," Zuma said, sensing the shield in Dave's head. She didn't even bump against it once she knew it was in place. He was trying to keep her out and she wouldn't fight it.

"Don't look so heavy, Zuma," Dave said, reaching out and cupping her shoulder. "I know it's a platonic love. Jack needs you as a friend. I don't worry about you two betraying me."

The ringmaster then turned to Finley. "But honestly, I have to admit that although I know little of you, my instinct tells me you're good. But do please tell me why you kissed Zuma at the end of the show."

"Well…" Finley said, his eyes falling on Zuma before he forced himself to rip them away. "It was a sudden decision. I was swept away by the energy of the audience and truthfully I thought that it's what *they* wanted. It is a love story and I felt they wanted a tender and touching ending. So I just improvised."

Dave looked at Finley and then at Zuma, who had a flat expression. If Dr. Raydon was Zuma and could read the tiny expressions in people, he'd know Finley was lying. But Dave was a trusting man. "Fine, fine. First show. I get making such a decision," Dave said, his cheeks tightening like he was on the verge of smiling. He seemed to always be on the verge of a smile or ending one. "You'll get used to the audience and realize they don't get what they want, but rather what we've rehearsed." The ringmaster then stepped forward, leaving Zuma a foot behind him. "People make mistakes. I understand that. But don't ever consider forcing yourself on Zuma while in my circus. I'm not a man prone to anger but next time I won't let this go unpunished. Next time you won't be a member of Vagabond Circus for such mistakes. Is that clear?"

Finley nodded, forcing himself to meet Dave's eyes.

Dave then clapped Finley on the shoulder, loosening him up with his infectious good nature. "And may I be the first to tell you that you and Zuma just put on the best show I've ever seen. You two were unmistakably the stars." Dave could shift suddenly and Finley had just witnessed his high after a low.

He choked out a forced laugh. "Thank you."

Dave turned and then offered an arm to Zuma. "My lady, you were more spectacular than I ever dreamed."

Zuma knew Dave didn't dream. For some reason unknown to her, he didn't allow himself to have dreams directed by his unconscious. Still she nodded, accepting the compliment. "It's all thanks to your support, Dave," she said.

"Would you accompany me to the festivities?"

She nodded obediently and took his arm. They walked to where the cast and crew were already starting the bonfire, Finley a few feet behind them.

Chapter Forty-Five

Drinking wasn't against the rules, but it was frowned upon at Vagabond Circus and things that were frowned upon were as good as rules. Still, it would have appeared to an outsider that the employees of Vagabond Circus were drunk based on their infectious laughter and chatty voices. There were no borders in the crowd at that night's after-party. Everyone was congratulating each other on putting together such a challenging new show in such a short period of time. And a breathtaking one at that. Each person took turns telling one of their favorite parts. And for most the ultimate favorite part was the ending, where the two lovers, torn by circumstances, celebrated their love with a kiss.

Everywhere Zuma turned someone was waiting to talk to her. The guys from the crew lined up, ready to greet her by laying a kiss on the back of her hand. She scanned their thoughts and knew this at once. And then a quick scan of the people's minds at the party told her she was the center of most people's thoughts. Well, not Finley's. As always, she didn't know what he was thinking, although from the way he kept directing his attention at her, she suspected she was also on his mind.

Even the freak performers had split up for that night's celebration and were commingling with crew members. Padmal was quietly picking Fanny's brain about alchemy, a side hobby of the nurse and caregiver. Oliver was having Ian read his fortune, and looked quite grave about the news. And Haady, one of the triplets, was giving Bill, the circus chef, tips of things he'd like added to the menu. Sunshine was sulking alone, but not all things can change at once.

Zuma couldn't bear the company of her circus family for very long. She'd had enough attention for one night. As the festivities went on she knew the obligation to speak to everyone who wanted her attention would be too much to resist. Passing the line of patiently waiting crew members she gave a quick wave. "I'd love to chat, but I've got to pack for our trip to Portland tomorrow," she said in a rush.

One guy reached out for her hand as she cruised by, but sensing this before he did it, she sped up and hurried away. She then ran to get as far from the people she loved like a family, and who were also her biggest fans.

Finley followed Zuma out when she left. He had broken away from Dave and Nabhi, saying he owed her a real apology. Dave consented with a nod. Finley was about to turn on his speed to catch up with her when Zuma made an early turn and headed straight in the direction of Jack's trailer.

Chapter Forty-Six

*F*inley halted, watching Zuma hurry in the opposite direction. Then he opened his mouth and was powerless to the word that fell out of him. "Zuma," he said, too loudly.

She stopped and turned to him, her face trying not to look startled. He sped up just a little, so he crossed the thirty yards in only a second. She blinked rapidly at him. "In a hurry?"

"Just to talk to you," he said and found his fingers reaching out for her. But Finley covered the move by pulling his hands all the way up and stroking them through his hair. The kiss had broken a latch he had locked. It had created a deadly possibility. He needed to reinforce his guard and remember why he was here, which had nothing to do with Zuma. "You headed to see Jack?" Finley said, pointing at the trailer behind her.

"Yeah," Zuma said, her expression would have been hard to read in the dark, but Finley had excellent night vision.

"I wanted to apologize," Finley said.

"For kissing me and potentially getting me fired?" Zuma said. With this, Finley noticed her eyes narrow some.

"For some of that," he said, a rebellious smile on his face. It was easy for Zuma to spy since the light from Jack's trailer was shining on his face. "But we both know Dave would never fire you."

She couldn't argue with this, although she still never wanted to let him down. Of all the people at Vagabond Circus, Zuma could have gotten away with the most. But it was the fact that she knew this and didn't take advantage of it that continued to endear Dave to her. "You were lying," she said in a whisper.

Finley pushed his chin to the side. He had considered that her combat sense might make her a human lie detector. Now he wondered if he'd been right. "About what?"

"How many lies are you telling around this place?" she shot back at him.

"How many do you think?" he said.

"I was referring to what you said to Dave, your reasons for kissing me."

And now it was confirmed. She had such confidence in her voice. Zuma spied his lie and that meant she could spy all the other ones he'd have to tell to remain here. She was indeed dangerous to him in more ways than one.

"So what was your reason for kissing me?" she asked.

He stepped back, out of the light streaming from the trailer, into the dark. "Let's call it a social experiment."

Zuma squinted at him through the dark. "Hmmm…I'm not sure I buy that."

"So you're headed to see Jack?" he said again, ignoring her statement and pointing at the trailer behind her for a second time. It was the only way he could think to derail the conversation.

"He'll be upset and need to talk." She paused and then took a step forward, angling her eyes at his jaw, wondering if it had bruised. "I'm kind of sorry he punched you," she said.

"As Dave said, he loves you," Finley said, staring down at Zuma, his tone uniform. "He was protecting you from who he thinks is a monster."

"I don't think you're a monster," she said.

"You don't?"

"No, and Jack and I are just friends."

"As are you and I, right?" he said.

"No," she said. "We're partners."

"Right, like business partners," Finley said, wanting to agree and then hating the idea.

"Exactly."

"Fine," he said, "great show tonight, partner."

"Same to you," she said. And there was so much not being said that the unspoken words felt like they would suffocate Zuma.

Finley took a step backward as he gave a half wave. "Tell Jack what you always tell him about me, that I'm a jerk who can't be helped."

"I'd planned on it," she said as he moved farther away. She turned and forced herself in the opposite direction.

"Zuma?" he called back at her.

She stopped. "Yeah?"

For the second time that night he used his super speed to race up right next to her. It made her hold her breath. Finley leaned down low, his breath making a presence on her cheeks. "When I kissed you tonight, I did it for the sole reason that I forgot who I am." Finley slid back an inch and that was enough to catch the startled look in Zuma's eyes. This time he'd told the truth.

"What does that mean?" she said, her hands shaking by her sides.

"It means that you won't have to worry about it happening again. That's not who I am and that's not why I'm here," Finley said and then turned so swiftly that the movement was lost on Zuma's eyes. He strode like a person moving in fast-forward, away. Away from Zuma and her troubled thoughts.

Chapter Forty-Seven

Zuma's knock was soft on Jack's door.

"Come in," he said in reply.

She was unsurprised to find him with his head in his hands, hunched over with his elbows on his knees. This was often referred to as the "Jack's frustrated" stance. It was more his trademark than the globe act. She knew at once that he didn't want to talk, but they didn't need to speak in order to communicate.

Zuma, why did he kiss you? Jack thought in his mind.

It was just a stunt to add drama to the show, she said to him, sending the message over their telepathic link. It took complete concentration for her to send information this way, but it felt fitting right then.

Jack pulled his head out of his hands. His eyes held a sobering look.

"Do you believe him?" he said out loud.

"Yes," she lied.

"He is a really strange person, isn't he?" Jack said, and he didn't sound angry, but rather perplexed, like Finley was a complex riddle he was trying to figure out.

"A complete mystery to me," she said.

"You know, the thing is that I actually like the guy."

"You do?" Zuma said, not having expected this.

"Well, I'm furious at Finley right now, but yeah, I do. There's something compelling about him, something undefinable," Jack said, thinking of how Finley had a way about him that should be admired to an extent. "But then I don't understand his motives and that worries me."

Jack was a person who wanted to see the best in people. He believed people were inherently good. And in Finley he saw something he didn't understand, but it made him feel the stranger was trustworthy somehow. He'd felt it since he first caught Finley on the flying trapeze. The guy had trusted Jack, and when he grabbed his wrist Finley looked back at him with relief like his confidence in

Jack had been reaffirmed. It was hard for Jack to understand, but the way acrobats feel about each other is often complex. Few occupations rely on another person so completely.

"I don't really know what to make of him honestly," Zuma said, and this was the sincere truth. Like Jack, she kind of wanted to like the guy, but he was hiding so much. She'd actually never felt a stronger draw to a person while her instinct told her to be on guard. And even that wasn't clear, because her instincts told her to pull the guy closer to her and unravel the mystery. *How could one person create such confusion in her, when she was a master at reading people?* she wondered.

"Well, I think we need to try to put this whole thing behind us as quickly as possible," Jack said.

Zuma was surprised by this. She figured Jack would sulk, especially since it was the first time he'd ever been in trouble with Dave. "Really, you do?"

"Yeah," he said with a heavy sigh. "Because I don't want to think about it and also because it's what's best for you."

"How's that?" Zuma asked, although she didn't disagree.

"Zuma, your performance wasn't just your best one ever, it was the best act I've ever seen, period. You were more than stunning. I don't want anything to detract from your ability to do that over and over again."

Jack never ceased to surprise her with his affection for her, his unconditional love. "Thank you, Jack," she said, mesmerized by his thoughtfulness.

They were quiet for a long moment before Jack said, "I'm sorry I punched him."

"Because Dave saw it?" she said.

"Yes, but also because it didn't make me feel better. The way Finley looked at me afterwards, it was kind of heartbreaking. That guy can make you feel strong emotions with a single look," Jack said, suppressing a shiver.

You have no idea, Zuma thought, keeping it to herself. Then she was glad that she hadn't taken a seat and instead stayed standing in the room. Of all things, she was certain she needed to be alone with her own thoughts for the rest of the night.

"Don't worry about this any longer," she said, her hand on the doorknob. "Things will be better tomorrow. We leave this in Seattle and start fresh when we hit the state border."

Jack brought his eyes to meet hers. "Sounds good," he said.

Then she was gone, leaving Jack's trailer hollow from her absence. That was Zuma's curse; she never left people or places the way she found them. She changed them. And when she was gone, Jack knew something was different about her. Had it been the show, her new role, or the kiss? Something had unlocked a new power in her and she was glowing, way more than usual.

Chapter Forty-Eight

*T*he after-party was still happening when the crew left early.

Tonight the big top would have to be disassembled and packed away for transporting. The Vagabond Circus crew would drive to Portland first thing tomorrow morning and set up the tent in a new location. Tonight they'd do the first half of the work in the physical realm, taking down reinforcement beams and deflating the four-mast tent from top to bottom. Then when fatigue set in, the crew would go to sleeper row and dream travel back to the big top area. In the dream travel realm they'd finish up the work and have it all done in half the time than most circuses.

Ian watched from the side as the big top shrunk. This was always a poetically sad part of every location to him. The big top deflating symbolized death to him. The end of another round of shows. The last part of the life of this big top. The same big top would be reborn in another city. It would rise into the air, like the phoenix, but it would never be like this tent, with its backdrop and its smells and its winds.

A tear peeked out at the corner of his eyes as he scanned through the vision he'd gotten from Zuma. He hadn't told her all of it. He couldn't. And although he realized he owned the information to stop something tragic from happening, he couldn't. Bad things had to happen. People had to die. Sometimes he told people enough to change things, but he'd learned how to filter the information. He'd used his instincts to direct him. And he knew that Zuma needed to allow something to happen so that other things would occur. He was navigating a future by telling her part of her fortune, but not the rest. It wasn't that he didn't want to intervene, it was that other visions of the future told him that it was time for this brutal reality to take place. And that night Dave and Ian had discussed it and made a decision. The ringmaster had asked him to follow his instinct, allowing the visions to direct his decisions from here on out.

He'd felt that same instinct eleven years ago and ignored it. He told Molly about the accident she caused. And she didn't step into the street the next day. And the driver of the car didn't die; instead, he went home that evening and murdered his wife. Sometimes fortunes need to be told and sometimes they don't, and sometimes only part of them. And sometimes they need to be told to one person and not another. Ian didn't feel like a God shelling out this information, intervening in lives and futures. He felt burdened and wished that he would have been born like his Middling father, with only the gift to manage money. His real mother, not his stepmother, had been a Dream Traveler and she'd still be alive if she hadn't taken her own life because she was like Ian, so burdened by the visions.

Chapter Forty-Nine

The Seattle Times

"The Vagabond Circus has changed, and for the better. This reporter didn't think it could improve but it was like real fairy dust was sprinkled on every part of the circus. I left the show with a firm thought in my head: I'll never see anything more spectacular than what I witnessed in these two hours. I'm not sure how, but last night's show changed me. I feel like I've had an out-of-body experience, a soulful experience. I type this article at two in the morning. I can't sleep. I'm too inspired. I'm too touched by the images I was gifted with tonight. It feels like I have new eyes. My life feels brand new. And I'm afraid to go to sleep right now, afraid I'll miss something magical. I've been transported by this show and I'm frightened of touching back down in my old life."

Seattle Post

"The star of the show, a beautiful acrobat, must be a hunter because she captured my attention. And she's definitely a thief because she stole my heart. The Vagabond Circus, without a doubt, delivers the most fantastic show in the universe."

Chapter Fifty

*W*hen the Vagabond Circus stirred from their dream travels the next morning the big top was completely down and loaded into trucks. An urgent knock sounded at Dave's door before the sun had even broken through the fog. Usually he liked his mornings quiet, reserved for meditation. Everyone knew that. He still would never allow a knock at his door to go unanswered. He was always available to Vagabond Circus. He pulled on his white gloves and opened the door to find Titus, who looked to be vibrating with excitement.

"All the shows in Portland are sold out!" he shouted at once.

Dave paused, tilted his head to the side. And then as Titus's statement sunk in he slowly released a billowing laugh. It grew in intensity second by second until it became contagious and Titus joined in laughing too.

"That's great!" Dave finally said, almost hopping down the stairs as he joined Titus on the grass.

Titus, who rarely smiled, looked like he might permanently have a grin on his face. At least as long as they were in Portland. "'Great' doesn't even begin to describe it," he said, his voice trembling with excitement. "Dave, with the profits we have on tickets alone we'll be able to pull ourselves out of debt. By the time we reach California we are going to be running a billion-dollar venture. Venues are already asking that we add shows, which will undoubtedly sell out too."

At this, the smile on Dave's face faltered. "Well, you tell them we're honored, but no."

Titus's face fell too. "What?! No. I told them yes."

"Call them back. The answer is no," Dave said, finality in his tone.

"But, Dave, don't you see this is what we need to do to pull ourselves out of debt? And also this is key to how we're going to make serious profits for once. We have to add more shows," Titus said. His long forehead was creased and resembled open blinds in a window.

"I don't want to make serious profits, Titus. I want to put on an extraordinary show and provide a happy environment for my circus family. Both of those goals are compromised if we add shows."

"Dave, I think your judgment is clouded by your good intentions," Titus said, careful to keep his voice down, although he was growing furious.

"There's no such thing," Dave said, a pure conviction in his voice. "My employees serve me with faith that I'll make the best decisions for them. And that means I won't put too much stress on everyone. They will perform no more than what is scheduled."

"But Dave—"

The ringmaster held up a white glove. "My circus. My decision," he said, and turned back to his trailer, leaving Titus tight-lipped and angry.

Chapter Fifty-One

*D*ave's RV was the first to pull out, followed by the long caravan of Vagabond Circus. He always led the circus to the new locations. Portland was one of his favorites so it made sense that it was the place where they had their first sold-out shows. Vagabond Circus always had a full house because of its reputation, but it had never had a slew of sold-out shows. This was undoubtedly due to Finley being added to the acts. He was the missing ingredient. Dave had been searching for twenty long years and now he finally had it. The perfect circus. Vagabond Circus was complete. He knew one day he'd create a flawless show. He knew that one day all the talent would come together, complementing one another as only Dream Traveler gifts can do for one another. Dave smiled at the road, clear ahead of him. Then he fondly looked at the rearview mirror. The long caravan of trailers followed him. He'd finally done it. He could die now, a happy man. And he was prepared to do just that, if it brought about a better future for all.

Part II

Chapter Fifty-Two

*F*inley kept his promise. At the end of the next three shows in Portland he didn't kiss Zuma. His gaze always locked on her brown eyes, his body attuned to the frequency of hers, like he read her from the inside out. And Zuma didn't rip her eyes from his until he pulled her out of the dip, to a standing position.

Still, without the kiss at the end of the show, the audience erupted with applause to be heard blocks away. The reviews flowed in about the new show, and the upcoming performances in Beaverton, Salem, Eugene, and Medford all sold out while the Vagabond Circus was still in Portland.

Dave had never been happier, but Titus was still holding a grudge over their last argument. The creative director wasn't the only one walking about with tense shoulders and a pinched face. It could have been their new success but everyone's emotions were heightened at Vagabond Circus. Padmal was moodier, Fanny's kids more restless, and Sunshine extra glum.

Most would have thought that Sunshine would find a way to be happy. She'd received her first standing ovation in Portland. The weird people of the city really appreciated her fire act, which usually left the audience breathless with fear.

"Let's figure out what you did differently during that show and try and replicate it," Dave said to her during rehearsal one afternoon.

She'd only gotten that one standing ovation and then none again for the last two shows. Dave was encouraging her to tweak her act for tonight's performance.

"I don't need the extra attention," she said, a fiery look in her eyes.

"Oh, did the applause bring the forbidden emotion of happiness to your black heart?" Jasmine said from the sidelines underneath the big top.

Sunshine zipped her gaze in the direction of where the four acrobats were stretching. She then shot a beam of fire from her hand and it landed in the dirt just beside where Jasmine sat.

"What the hell?" the girl said, rolling to the side, although the fire disappeared into the dirt almost at once. "What's your problem, Sunshine? It was just a joke."

"I don't like your jokes," the pyrokinetic said. Sunshine felt the emotions in Dave building and then on cue they erupted.

"What has gotten into everyone?" he said, his voice bordering on yelling. He stared at Sunshine with a confused expression. Then he turned and shot the same look at Jasmine. "Rule number one," he said with such severity. "Never, ever forget rule number one."

Both girls nodded in unison.

Zuma widened her eyes at Jack, and then at Finley, both of whom had curious expressions. Jack and Finley hadn't said a word about what happened after that first show and both seemed to have moved past it easily. Actually Zuma noticed that Finley and Jack got along without incident. She thought it was good for Jack to have a male acrobat on the team.

"I can't do it any faster," Padmal said on the other side of the tent, gaining the acrobats' attention. She was practicing with Oliver, who looked taken aback by her sudden flare of anger.

"I'm sorry," he said softly. "I just meant—"

"I know what you meant and you're pushing me and I'm tired of it. You're doing what Dave is doing to Sunshine right now and I won't put up with it." Padmal had no idea that everyone had stopped to watch the fit she was throwing. She was too consumed by the fury she'd harbored for too long. It shot out like Sunshine's fire flew out of her. "I don't want to be in your act anymore!" she yelled at Oliver, who looked instantly heartbroken.

"But Padmal, I need you," he said.

"No, you don't," she said through gritted teeth.

"Hey, my lovelies," Dave said, striding over, "what seems to be the issue over here?"

Padmal turned to Dave, her brown eyes seeming to try to curse him. "Everything is the issue," she said.

"Well, let's talk about it," Dave said in an encouraging voice.

Oliver looked from Padmal to Dave, his face a mixture of anger and embarrassment. "I think, Dave," he said in a restrained voice, "that Padmal and I can sort this out on our own."

Dave again gave that look of confusion. He was sincerely baffled by his performers. They had never acted with such diabolical emotions and it was bringing back a waking nightmare. Things needed to be scaled back a notch. He had to decelerate whatever was causing this tension. He cast his eyes to Finley. He wasn't sure why he thought he had something to do with it. *It was just strange timing*, he told himself. But he wasn't sure he believed that. There was something askew at the Vagabond Circus and he felt blinded to it. He knew because of Ian that dark days were ahead for the circus, but not yet. He still had time. Time to offer his support.

"Can I have everyone's attention," he said to the tent of performers. Everyone paused and turned their attention to the ringmaster. "We are all going to take a mandatory five-minute break. No working. No talking about work. Just put your mind at ease. It starts now."

Around the tent various performers laid down props or abandoned their practice areas, trailing off to the refreshment table.

Dave strolled over to the mat where the acrobats were still lounging. They hadn't needed a break since they rarely practiced between shows at Dave's order. Their acts were perfect and he didn't want Finley and Zuma overexerting themselves.

"What's everyone's problem?" Zuma said to him when he stopped by their area. He had set up his workstation beside them.

Dave grabbed his notebook with a heavy sigh. "I haven't gotten a clue," he said, studying Finley, who was the only one of the acrobats who didn't have his eyes on Dave. He looked distracted by something in the crowd behind Dave. The ringmaster turned, but only found an assortment of performers chatting.

"Well, I apologize for my joke," Jasmine said, grabbing the water bottle beside her and unscrewing the lid.

Dave noticed that the side of the bottle had "DR" written on it in black marker. His initials. His bottle of water. He was about to say something but Jasmine already had it pressed to her lips. *I'll just get a new drink,* he thought. He didn't want to embarrass her.

"You know, who you really need to apologize to is Sunny," he said.

Jasmine nodded. "I will," she said, scooting to her feet before trotting toward the pyrokinetic who was still sulking on the other side of the tent.

Dave watched, with curious eyes, the brief interaction between the two girls. It appeared to him that they were at least making a show of looking amenable to each other. *Things will settle down,* he told himself, *once the excitement of the success wears off.* That's all it was.

Jasmine strode back through the crowd, something in her hands.

"Minnie, you are a sweetheart," Dave said to her when she was close. "Always trying, aren't you?"

"I admit that I'm pretty fabulous," she said with a sideways smile. "And I'm helpful too. I intercepted a message from Titus. That older kid was looking for you so he could hand it off." Jasmine then handed a crisp, folded piece of paper to Dave, who took it with a raised eyebrow. It wasn't like Titus to send him notes. They both preferred to talk in person.

Finley stood suddenly, each of his movements a blur. No one really caught the look of fear that surfaced in his eyes before he sprinted through the tent. He had raced in the direction of Oliver and Padmal, who still looked to be arguing, although quietly. And only Zuma saw this, as everyone else was studying Dave's confused face. Zuma knew a myriad of stressful thoughts were pouring through the ringmaster's head, but she couldn't help but keep her attention on Finley as he darted around the crowd, trying to find his way through the tent. Her attention was always inadvertently on Finley. His on her as well, most of the time. But now he was searching and then he was gone from her sight. Disappeared.

Dave brought his gaze back to Jasmine. "Thank you," he said absentmindedly in Jasmine's direction as he broke the seal on the paper. He opened it with a tight look and then scanned the contents, his face growing heavy with concern.

Zuma stood at once, reading the look in his eyes and the thoughts in his mind.

"What is it?" Jack said, standing too.

Dave shook his head with disbelief, dropped his hand to his leg, the letter with it. "It's Titus's letter of resignation."

"What? That's impossible," Jack said, reaching for the letter, but he never got to it because in that moment Jasmine swayed, unsteady on her feet, and then fell to the mat, completely passed out.

Chapter Fifty-Three

"Jaz!" Zuma yelled, dropping to her knees beside her friend. Her fingertips went straight to Jasmine's pulse on her wrist.

"What's happened to her?" Jack said behind Zuma.

Dave leaned down, dropping the resignation letter on the ground, forgetting it at once. "Is she…?" he asked to Zuma, who had her ear down by Jasmine's lips.

"She's breathing, but it's faint," Zuma said and then she brought her shocked eyes up to find Finley returning, looking defeated. His gaze flashed to Jasmine and then to Zuma's face.

"Go get Fanny," she yelled to him. "As fast as you can."

He nodded, a startled expression blanketing his face, and then disappeared in a blur of movement.

There was nothing for Jack, Zuma, and Dave to do except sit next to Jasmine. They'd need to wait for Fanny to examine her. She had a medical degree and also the skill of healing. Performers were now turning their attention on the scene, but stayed back, sensing the seriousness of it.

Dave thought the wait would make him pass out as well, and then his eyes drifted to the water bottle lying on its side next to Jasmine. The initials on it burned like a branding on his heart: DR.

Chapter Fifty-Four

Zuma paced outside Jasmine's trailer. Dave and Jack stood under a nearby tree sheltering themselves from the unrelenting July heat. Finley took turns watching Zuma and then Dave. He had left to fetch Fanny and returned faster than what for most would be humanly possible. He was a blur until he stopped beside Zuma. She hadn't left Jasmine's side until Fanny arrived and ordered the girl to be transported to her trailer. Finley and Jack had been elected for the job and to everyone's astonishment Finley was hesitant to perform the duty. Finally Jack picked up the girl and tossed her over his shoulder. She hung limp in his arms. Zuma shot a confused look at Finley as they followed to Jasmine's trailer.

"I can explain," he mouthed.

"Are you going to?" she asked at his side.

"Not right now," he deflected and hoped that she'd forget the whole thing and not bring it back up. He could explain but he really didn't want to. There was so much Finley could explain, like why Jasmine was passed out in the first place. However, he didn't dare. He was too far into this now. There was no going back. No changing plans. His eyes flicked up to Jasmine's lifeless form. If she woke up she'd live. If she didn't then she'd stay locked away in a coma forever or die immediately. Finley was certain there was nothing Fanny could do and so there was no point in telling anyone what he knew.

As he sat on the doorstep of Jasmine's trailer, the newbie's eyes studied Dave under the nearby tree. It was obvious why the ringmaster was stressed right now. One of his performers was sick. But Finley saw the nervous stress under that. Dave wasn't just worried, he was on edge. And Finley had studied the ringmaster while they waited in the big top for Fanny to arrive. The ringmaster's eyes swiveled from Jasmine's lifeless body to the water bottle a few feet away. The one with his initials on it and also Jasmine's lip gloss around the mouth of the bottle. The ringmaster may have been wrong in his suspicions, but he was suspicious now. He'd be more careful.

He'd be vigilant. Finley wasn't certain if that was going to work in his favor or not. People make mistakes when motivated by fear.

The newbie's eyes then swiveled on Zuma. She hadn't stopped moving since they were told to wait outside for a prognosis. Her concern drained her face of her normal spark. She was still beautiful, but now it was a poetic beauty, like a sad but elegantly written poem.

Finley stood in one fluid movement and reached out for Zuma as she passed. She sensed this and pulled herself away at once.

"Don't," she said, halting. Her frantic eyes covered Finley in a way that broke him a little.

Why had he reached for her? Did he think he had the right to comfort her? That she'd allow it? He wondered all of this as he watched her watching him. So many unspoken messages transpiring between the pair.

And yet Zuma's quick rejection confounded all Finley's reason. He instinctively knew he could make her feel better. He didn't know how he knew that but with everything inside him he knew what Zuma needed. And now after staring at her face he knew she knew too and didn't want it. Zuma wanted to be alone with her pain.

"I was just going to—"

She closed her eyes and nodded, cutting him off. When she looked back at him she almost appeared apologetic. "Yeah, I know." She wrapped her arms around herself. Then her gaze shot to the side. She noticed Titus approaching before the rest of them. The man ran in their direction, worry blanketing his face. Dave caught sight of him and strode forward, meeting him.

"What's going on?" Titus asked.

"We don't know," Dave said, shaking his head, worrying the rim of his top hat in his gloved hands. He used his hat as a toddler did a luv, kneading it for comfort. "Fanny is examining Jasmine now."

The taller man hung his head, releasing a breath. "Tonight's show, we'll need—"

"Titus," Dave said, a quiet warning in his voice. He was admonishing Titus for his one-track mind, always circling around the circus. It had been a contention among the two men. Titus focused on the show and Dave focused on the employees.

"I'm still concerned for Jasmine, but we need to figure out how to replace—"

"Titus, you resigned," Dave said in a hush, hurt stinging his words.

The taller man covered the back of his neck with his large hand, keeping his eyes away from Dave's. "Yeah, bad timing on that, I realize now."

"But how at any time can you resign? And the way you did it, just having a kid drop off a note?" Dave shot his friend a look of serious disappointment.

From fifteen feet away Zuma and Finley couldn't hear the two men's exchange. Finley was reading the body language and knew Dave had the upper hand already, making Titus squirm with regret.

Zuma didn't have to be able to hear to know exactly what was going on between the two. Jack arrived at her side with a look of curious concern. "What's the deal?" he asked Zuma.

"Titus resigned because he's tired of Dave using the 'this is my circus' card and trumping all his decisions," Zuma said, her eyes hinged on the two men in the distance.

"It's just not how I want to work anymore," Titus said, his voice low so as to not attract attention. "You want me to invest my life in this circus and then you don't trust my decisions, you don't even give us the opportunity for discussion. You brought Finley in without talking to me. And then you won't even consider the idea of adding extra shows. I'm just getting tired of having no say in the circus."

"But I was right to bring Finley in midseason," Dave said, throwing his arm in the newbie's direction.

"That's not the point," Titus said. "You could have included me in the decision. We could have had a discussion about the extra shows. But instead you just say, 'It's my circus and no more discussion.'"

Dave sucked in a weighty breath, his face softening as he did. "Well, you know this circus can't lose you so what do you want me to do to make this right?" Dave said and then a beat later he added, "And fair. How can I make our arrangement fair?"

"You know under the best circumstances I will manage this circus with you for the rest of my life," Titus said, his words earnest. "I'm married to Vagabond Circus and the magic and healing it brings to its audiences."

"So," Dave said, stroking his chin, "the question is, what are the best-case circumstances?"

"I want to own part of the circus," Titus said in a rehearsed voice.

"What?" Dave almost choked on the word.

Titus shook his hands in front of him. "Now, now, now. This isn't about money. This is your baby and you gave me this position. I see all that for what it is. But I can't make the best decisions for Vagabond Circus as long as you own it. Dave, you have to give up some of the control. You think with your heart and I think with my head. We make a great team, but not as long as you keep shutting me out. And you feel the weight of it because you know that if it fails then it's on you. Let me own Vagabond Circus with you. Give me ten percent or five percent. Just give me something so that I own a piece of it and you can't make unilateral decisions. Just give me enough so you remember I'm your partner." Titus paused, his eyes studying Dave in that way Titus did when watching an act, looking for the part that was potentially missing.

Again and again Dave ran his fingers over the rim of the teal blue top hat. It was as old as the circus, patched in too many places. The ringmaster hung his head low, his eyes on the dirt under his feet, his mind reflecting on the proposition. After a long moment Dave brought his head up and stuck out a gloved hand. "I'll give you the whole damn circus if you take back your resignation," he said, a smile peeking out under his brown mustache. "Just keep me on as the ringmaster, would you?"

Titus coughed out a relieved chuckle. "Oh, Dave, I don't want the whole circus, you know that."

"I do, my friend, but you're getting forty-nine percent. And maybe one percent of the time you'll allow me to trump your decisions," Dave said with that trademark glint in his eyes. *This was perfect,* Dave thought. Everything was lining up, just as Ian had said. He hadn't expected the resignation but he *had* expected to give Titus part of the circus.

Titus now laughed loudly. "That's a deal," he said, clapping his hand into the ringmaster's.

From the side of Fanny's trailer a contagious smile lit up Zuma's face. Jack was watching the two men. But Finley was watching Zuma, knowing that was all he had to do to know how the decision across the way was going.

"So Titus isn't leaving?" Finley said.

Zuma looked at Finley suddenly. "How did you know?"

He traced his finger in the air, making a circle around her face. She swallowed hard and knew he spied the movement. Finley was always watching her. Never hiding it. But right now his eyes on her felt intimate, more so than usual.

"Yes," she finally said. "Titus is staying and Dave has given him partial ownership of the circus."

"Well, that's going to change everything," Finley said with a weighty sigh, like he was the one who had to draw up the paperwork or something.

"I don't see how it will change anything much," Jack argued.

Finley focused his eyes back on the two men, shaking hands and laughing. It didn't change anything for most at Vagabond Circus, but it meant Finley things had just gotten more complicated.

The creak of the trailer door opening ripped everyone's attention in Fanny's direction. She stood in the entryway, the curls on her head frizzy, no doubt from rushing about and caring for Jasmine for the last hour.

Chapter Fifty-Five

*F*anny hadn't even taken her first step out of the trailer when Zuma's shoulders dropped with relief. "Oh, thank God, Jaz is okay," she said.

Fanny gave her a tired smile. "Shall I give the news or would you rather pull all the information out of my brain and inform the group?" Fanny said, no menace in her voice.

"Sorry," Zuma said at once. "My concern made me anxious to get information. I don't usually get in your head, Fanny."

"I believe you, dear," she said and then turned her attention to Dave and Titus, who hurried over. "The good news is that Jasmine will be all right and after a day or two of rest I think she'll be fine," the woman said, taking turns alternating her clinical, yet warm stare between the two men.

"What's the bad news?" Titus said, the cynical look he wore so well plastered across his face.

Fanny gave him a disappointed look. "Life isn't just good and bad. There's a whole array of in between, Titus," she said in the admonishing tone she reserved for only him. "Anyways, the mysterious thing is I don't know what made her ill. Jasmine is awake now and can't account for anything that would cause her to become lightheaded and pass out. As far as I can tell her blood pressure dropped and her temperature spiked. Those two symptoms alone don't tell me much."

"Maybe she caught a virus," Dave said, his gloved fingertips tapping together nervously, his eyes distant with thought.

"Maybe," Fanny said, looking unconvinced. "I'll keep an eye on her for the next few days but I think she'll be fine. And hopefully whatever it was won't return."

Finley was fairly certain Jasmine wouldn't be sick again. Her passing out was a mistake. She hadn't been the target and that mistake wouldn't be made twice.

"All right, well thank you, Fanny," Dave said, his voice tired from the adrenaline.

"It's my pleasure. I'm going back to our gal now," she said and then the large woman heaved herself up the steps to the trailer.

"And we," Dave said, sweeping his arm at the three people in front of him, "need to put our heads together and figure out how to reconfigure the acrobat acts in Minnie's absence."

Chapter Fifty-Six

*I*t took the better part of an hour for the group to figure out how to replace Jasmine in the show. However, when it was done, Dave knew the show would still receive deafening applause. Vagabond Circus was about change. It moved from place to place, and reconfigured based on available performers. The ringmaster loved that about the circus. "Without change, we are dead," he often said. Titus didn't handle the improvising so well, but he was motivated by the desire to always produce a stellar show. And now the creative director had more of an investment in the Vagabond Circus. It was his and he wasn't going to let it fail, not ever.

The acrobats knew an important part of their act was missing during that night's show. Dave Raydon knew it. Felt it in his bones when he introduced Vagabond Circus. It was as if each performer's energy registered in him during a show and he could feel Jasmine's absence. To Dave a show was an organic being. It was created with real ingredients, by real people. It sometimes evolved and sometimes regressed. It lived and it died. Each show, each day, was alive for a brief period of time, like a human. And then as the audience exited the big top, the beating heart of that show slowed until it was no more.

Zuma for the first time ever completely skipped the after-show festivities. She had already made plans to relieve Fanny and watch over Jasmine for the night. The noise of happy crew members dancing around the bonfire was just noise to Zuma as it spilled through the cracks of Jasmine's trailer. She didn't feel left out of the celebration. There would be other parties. And she'd been to enough. Zuma was like Dave in this way. She was accepting. Fleeting experiences were never really missed by Zuma. And although she wasn't a girl of faith, she somehow always knew if one thing prevented her from doing something it was because something better was in store for her. She trusted life.

Zuma nestled herself deeper into Jasmine's sofa and flipped through the pages of a book. Although she had no intention of reading the book, she liked scanning its pages and stopping randomly to read a sentence. It was like she was stealing lines from the story and creating her own in her head. Jasmine had been sleeping for the last few hours, making Zuma's job of caring for her easy.

From the back bedroom there came a stirring of sheets followed by an "Ugh!"

Zuma set the book to the side and checked on her friend, who was taking an incredibly long time to sit up.

"Z?" Jasmine said as she drew closer to her. Again and again the girl blinked, trying to bring Zuma into focus.

"I'm here, Jaz," Zuma said from the doorway. "Do you need something?"

Jasmine wore a pale face, her eyes unfocused, and her brown hair matted to her head in various places. "A new brain would be nice," Jasmine said, her voice hoarse from sleep. She rubbed at her temples before looking up. "Remember that time that we were rehearsing the trampoline act and I got too close to the platform?"

It was an act they'd perfected recently where the acrobats bounced back and forth from a trampoline to a series of high platforms that resembled a luscious woods. In the act they appeared to be creatures of the forest, hopping and flipping from tree to tree, and running up the sides of massive trunks before flying back to the mossy forest floor.

"Yeah, you smashed your head into the sharp corner of one of the trees. I think you took some paint off it with that hard head of yours," Zuma said, sitting down on the edge of the bed. "The poor crew had to do a bunch of repairs on the set before the next show."

Jasmine almost smiled but stopped herself. "Don't make me laugh, it hurts."

"Jaz, you know I can't make that promise," Zuma said, smiling fondly at her friend. "I can't help that I'm hilarious."

"Well, if you'll stop focusing your concern on some plywood for a second," Jasmine said, the light in her eyes looking to be restored second by second that she spoke with Zuma, "I was going to say, that's how my head feels right now."

"Do you feel nauseous?" Zuma asked.

At that, Jasmine grabbed her midsection, like the question prompted a sudden stomachache. "Yeah."

"Well, I'll go grab Fanny. She might be able to give you one of her homebrewed remedies. I don't think she wanted to give you anything earlier, hoping your body would repair itself," Zuma said, standing. She paused in the doorway and looked back at Jasmine. "Are you all right if I leave you for a few?" Nearly losing Jasmine had almost made Zuma a little sentimental. There were few people she'd really miss if they left or died and Jasmine was one of them. Zuma loved everyone, but to her, most were replaceable.

"I'm fine and go ahead and get that sappy look off your face. It doesn't suit you at all," Jasmine said, her normal spunk back.

Zuma mock scowled at her friend. "Fine, I'll go get Fanny for you so you can feel better. But first, I might stop off at the after-party for a few hours on my way," she said, heading for the door. Then she called over her shoulder, "You'll just have to wait to find out what I do."

Zuma rushed by the after-party, not even throwing it a casual glance. She had thought that she'd find Fanny in her trailer, but she wasn't there. When she was just about to double back to the after-party, thinking the caretaker was there supervising the kids, Zuma heard two low voices in the recreational area. And although usually she'd have ignored them, they were two voices that were incredibly recognizable to her. Finley's and Fanny's. They were speaking in whispers, which Zuma found extremely curious. And even more intriguing was they were sitting at a picnic table both hunched over a book.

To Zuma's disappointment, her presence didn't go unnoticed for long. Fanny turned at once, sensing the girl at her back.

"Well, Ms. Zuma, you found me," Fanny said, a smile visible through the moonlit sky. "I am supposing you were looking for me, am I right?"

Finley turned, startled at first and then brought his eyes low to the table. Zuma watched him for a second before responding. "I was. It's Jaz. She's awoken and has a headache and nausea. Is there something you can do for her?"

"Well, I can sure try," Fanny said, pulling her long thick legs out from between the picnic table and the bench with great effort. She turned back to Finley once she was standing. "I'll be back in just a few, darling."

He nodded, his eyes to the side, a strangeness about him. Finley felt Zuma's scrutinizing glare on him and hadn't had a chance to recover from her sudden appearance. He admonished himself for not being more on guard, but he'd have to make up for it now.

Fanny hurried past Zuma, unconcerned that the girl didn't follow her, but rather stood staring at Finley with curious eyes.

"What are you doing here with Fanny?" she asked, noticing the small flashlight in Finley's hand. He twirled it in his fingers before bringing his focus to meet her.

No longer did Finley look flustered. Across his face was a playful grin. "Would you believe we're having a secret love affair?"

She laughed and he relished the sound almost as much as the fact that he was the one who caused it in her. "No, I wouldn't believe that."

He shrugged indifferently. "Well, then the reason will just have to remain a mystery to you."

"Do you think being a guy of mystery makes you more attractive?"

He smiled. "Is that question implying that you find me attractive?"

Zuma ran her eyes over Finley's spiky dark brown hair, parted on one side and both neat and chaotic. In a better light she'd see the color of his eyes, which couldn't be categorized as either green or brown. But the moonlight did make the angles of his cheekbones and definition of his mouth quite clear. For Zuma there was nothing unattractive about Finley's appearance. But she managed to fake a yawn and through it she said, "I meant in general, to other people."

"So not to you? You're not attracted to me?" he said.

Something in Zuma's stomach rattled, but she ignored it. "I'm your partner," she said simply. Like that answer sufficed.

"Then to answer your question, no, I don't put on an act of mystery so that other people will be intrigued by me."

"Then why do you?"

The truth was, Finley thought, that if people knew who he was they'd be repulsed. He was only preserving the little bit of ego he had left. Instead of telling her the truth, Finley said, "I'm just a private person."

"So I've gathered," she said, stepping forward, eyeing the notebook in front of him. Finley, using his speed, snapped it shut and pulled it close to him.

"It's our love letters, mine to Fanny," he said with a sneaky grin. "I'd prefer you not read them."

"You know there's a no dating rule at Vagabond Circus," Zuma said with smile.

"Rule number two," Finley said, nodding. "But I can't resist Fanny, so we've decided to act on our love."

"You have a thing for older women, then?" she said, unable to suppress the giggle.

"Yes, and I'm a rebel who would break the rules for the person I want," he said, his eyes on her, and because Zuma was so good at hiding emotions, he had no idea that one look torched her insides.

"Lucky Fanny," Zuma said, all the humor in her voice gone.

Finley slid out of the picnic table and approached Zuma, leaving the notebook on the table. "I have a confession," he said, his voice a hush.

"I'm listening," Zuma said, realizing how fast he'd moved and now was only a foot away.

"I'm not really in love with Fanny."

"You're not?" Zuma said with pretend surprise, followed by a smile Finley thought should have been illegal, at least in a place like Vagabond Circus where he couldn't get closer to it. Feel her smile against his lips.

"No, I'm not. And I have another confession," Finley said, fighting past the breathless feeling in his chest.

"What?" Zuma said and held her own breath.

"Mr. Finley, are you ready to get back to work?" Fanny's voice sliced between the two, the woman materializing at their side. Zuma was shocked she hadn't noticed her approach. *How did that happen?* She was always aware. Finley had trouble pulling his eyes off Zuma, who looked to be experiencing the same battle.

He nodded finally.

"Good," Fanny said, her voice warm and rich. "Now Ms. Zuma, Ms. Jasmine is doing better. Maybe check on her in an hour?"

"Yes, of course," Zuma said, not moving, her eyes now on the older woman.

"And if you wouldn't mind leaving us, Mr. Finley and I have an important project we're working on," Fanny said, her tone firm.

Zuma nodded again and turned at once, not bearing to look at Finley anymore. Those eyes. They could trap her. And his words, what he'd said and what he was about to say. It all created a storm inside her chest. She moved fast, feeling his eyes linger on her back.

Zuma was in fact correct, Finley was watching her go, unable to tear his gaze from her until she disappeared completely.

"Lovely girl, that Ms. Zuma," Fanny said, taking a seat at the picnic table.

"Yeah," Finley said absentmindedly.

"Too bad about the curse though."

"Wait, what?" Finley said, turning his full attention to Fanny suddenly. She was wearing a look of knowing. "What do you mean?"

"Oh, well, it's not something most here know." And she wasn't baiting him, but rather determining if he needed to know what she knew.

"I'd like to be one of the few then," Finley said, taking the seat next to Fanny.

She studied him in the way only Fanny could do, where she saw a person and knew exactly what was best for them. Then having made a decision she nodded. "Very well. Ms. Zuma is cursed because she was born here at Vagabond Circus."

"She was?" Finley said in astonishment. "How is that a curse?"

"Well, Vagabond Circus wasn't always a happy place. Twenty years ago there were bad things that happened here, in the beginning," Fanny said, her always cheery face sagging a bit. "Zuma's parents weren't in the circus. Her being born here was a fluke. Bad timing, for sure. Her mother went into early labor when she and her husband were here visiting Dr. Raydon."

"I still don't understand where this is going," Finley said.

Fanny nodded in understanding. "There's all sorts of powers and gifts for Dream Travelers, Finley," she said, leaning forward, her voice a ghostly whisper. It was so different from her normal voice that it made Finley fear she'd been possessed. "One man who performed here long ago had the power of intention, but to most they know that gift as witchcraft."

"Witchcraft?" Finley said, not disbelieving or believing. "Like as in spells and stuff?"

"Yes," Fanny said flatly. "Exactly. And this man with the right intention could produce long-standing spells and curses. It was a subsidiary power, not the one he used in the acts. Most didn't know about it. But there were problems and a falling out." Fanny paused, her eyes troubled as she stared at the tabletop, not really seeing it. "And many things happened, many things that still hold a consequence over the circus to this day. And one of those is that any child born at Vagabond Circus shall forever be cursed."

Finley wanted to laugh, wanted to pretend that curses weren't real and he didn't believe in them. He arranged his face into a skeptical grin, one that said, "why are you playing with me". But Fanny simply brought her large blue eyes up to meet Finley's with a look that chilled him all the way down to his tailbone. The fake laughter caught in his throat at once. "There isn't really a curse on Vagabond Circus, is there?"

"Do you not think it's possible for a single man to command people through something mysterious like magic?" And when she looked at him, Finley knew she saw more of him than anyone else. Fanny, he was certain, knew where he came from. But the fact that she wasn't turning him in was the biggest mystery.

"Yes," he said with a deliberate nod. "I know that can happen."

She gave a nod of approval. So many things were being communicated between them now and so much still left unsaid.

"What was this curse this man put on the circus?" Finley asked, hardly hearing his own voice over the racing pulse in his head.

"He cursed that any child born here could never find true happiness," Fanny said, her words a curse to Finley's ears.

He clenched his eyes shut from the assault to his head and heart. Not only did he believe every word Fanny said, but he knew this man she spoke of and knew his curses were unstoppable.

174

Chapter Fifty-Seven

Jasmine only missed one week of shows, but it was enough that the acrobats never wanted to do the act without her. When the Vagabond Circus threw down stakes in Eugene, Oregon, she was feeling strong enough to start practicing again.

"You're such a faker," Zuma said to her as they sat together. "My head still hurts, and my stomach," she said in a high-pitched squeal, a bad impression of Jasmine.

Finley looked over from his place sitting and chatting beside Jack on the other side of the tent. He was always entertained by Zuma and always having to hide it.

"Right, and why would I be faking being sick?" Jasmine asked, sitting on the mat. "You think I liked being laid up in bed all day? Do you want to even guess how much muscle mass I've lost?"

"I can see it on you, Ms. Flabby," Zuma said, sticking her tongue out. "And I already know you were glued to your laptop, responding to girls from that dating site."

Jasmine shot her a guilty look. "Well...that's kind of true."

"Any luck?"

"Nope," Jasmine said with a defeated sigh. "Being an awesome gay girl is hard. There's just no one good enough."

"Being an awesome straight girl is tough," Zuma said, leaning across her legs, her body so used to stretching, even while dream traveling.

"Yeah, right," Jasmine said, stretching her eyes across the tent at the two other acrobats who were casting their eyes over every now and then. "Real tough for you, Zuma."

"Oh, Jaz," Zuma said in a whisper. "You know it isn't like that."

"Then why does Mr. Fire Eyes always stare at you like that?" she said, indicating Finley.

"I don't know," she said in a pleading tone, trying to stop her friend's questioning.

"Just saying, if I weren't gay..."

"Yeah, I've heard you say this before. You'd rip clothes off," Zuma said. "But you are gay."

"Yep, it runs in the family. No getting away from it," she said flippantly.

"That's totally not true. Sexuality isn't genetic. It's just coincidence that your dads are gay and so are you," Zuma said, wanting to laugh at her friend. "And you've only got one of their blood so there."

"True," Jasmine said with a smile. Her fathers, Papa T and Papa Joe, had worked hard to find the right birth mother for the girl. They found a Dream Traveler who agreed to be their surrogate and the procedure was done in a lab using Papa T's sperm. Jasmine was similar to Zuma in that she came from a good home, but her parents both had demanding jobs in a place more sheltering than the circus, and so she had left them for Vagabond Circus when she was sixteen years old. Now she'd feared she'd outgrown her family and the circus. But if that was true then where would she go?

A scratching noise on the other side of the tent commanded all four of the acrobats' attention. It was incessant and quite loud. And since it was late and they were all dream traveling the noise especially didn't make any sense. Finley stood first, wondering what was happening on the back side of the practice tent that would cause such a commotion. He already had a good working knowledge of the things that did and didn't go on at various times in various places at the circus. And it made no sense to him that someone would have a reason to be over in that area. He soon felt Zuma behind him; her presence was always known to him. With his eyes closed he could sense her nearness to him and then always banished the desires that followed.

"What is that?" he said in a whisper, over his shoulder.

"If you'd get in the telepathic link with me, then we could have already discussed that topic and a whole lot quieter," Zuma said.

Finley turned and looked at her, halting Zuma, along with Jack and Jasmine behind her. "You've already had this conversation with Jack and Jasmine?"

She rolled her eyes and nodded. "Let me in, Finley and you can be in the special club too."

"No thanks," he said and turned around, his attention grabbed by the scratching sound again. *Or is it sawing?* he wondered.

They had already cleared fifteen feet and now they were at the back end of the practice tent where supplies and extra equipment were kept. Only crew members came back that way, and only some of the time, never during practices.

"Are you an ax murderer? Is that why you won't allow me in your head? Are you afraid I'll find out where the bodies are buried?" Zuma asked Finley in a whisper, but still loud enough for Jasmine and Jack to hear. The two then stopped and laughed loud enough that the sound paused.

Finley turned and gave them all a punishing look.

"Go find out what that is," Jack said through a laugh.

"Okay, but I'm coming back with my ax," Finley said. "Come on, Zuma, you're checking this out with me. And if it's something dangerous, I'm using you as a shield." He grabbed her wrist and hardly had to pull to get her compliance.

Jack and Jasmine continued their laughter, strolling back in the direction of the practice tent.

"I bet, when you're not off being an ax murderer, you're a cat burglar," Zuma said, enjoying teasing Finley more than usual. They hardly gave themselves much one-on-one time to talk and they had limited it to "partner talk" as Zuma called it. But having Jasmine back had changed the dynamics a bit.

"That's right, I kill and pillage," Finley said in a hush, scanning the assortment of equipment in front of them and trying to figure out where exactly the noise was coming from.

Zuma took the space right next to him. She was too close for his comfort. Finley didn't enjoy this cozy acrobat relationship she was moving toward. "Oh, so I bet you're the one responsible for all those items that have gone missing lately, aren't you?"

She was only joking, but Finley wasn't in a joking mood suddenly. He twisted around and stared at her with serious eyes. "That isn't me. I'd never steal anything from anyone at Vagabond Circus," he said, his whispered words sharp.

Zuma blinked back at him, taken aback by his sudden turn in demeanor. "Okay…" she said, drawing out the word. "It was a joke. Just a joke." And then she set off in the opposite direction.

More than anything in this world Finley wanted to reach out for Zuma. Explain everything. Hope that it didn't change anything. In his mind, she'd confess her love in reward for his confession, but he knew he was growing more delusional if that was even a thought in his head. Instead of explaining anything he used his speed to cut her off. She sucked in a startled breath as she always did when he raced in front of her. "I just meant that it really bothers me that someone has been taking from people at Vagabond Circus. I don't even want to be associated with it in jest," he said. And what he didn't say was it burned him up that he knew who was doing it and couldn't stop them. They were always a step ahead of him.

Zuma stared up at Finley, startled by how much he'd disclosed when he usually never said anything. But then her attention was stolen away by the warmth on her limbs. She dared to look down and realized he had both his hands on her arms, holding her in place so she couldn't move away from him. And the last thing she wanted to do was move away from him. But she remembered herself, as she was good at doing.

"Yeah, the thief is a huge mystery. Dave can't figure out who is doing it or why," Zuma said, stepping back, away from Finley's grip.

He dropped his hands. They felt like anchors suddenly. "Strange for sure," he said, but Zuma spied the essence of a lie. Finley, she could sense, knew more than he was telling, but maybe that was only because he'd been investigating. She had noticed that he was always watching people, always seeming to be finding covert information. When his attention wasn't nailed on her then it was taking a break to snoop out the people around Vagabond Circus.

Finley's eyes ran over the space between him and Zuma. "I'm sorry," he finally said, bringing his eyes up to her. "I shouldn't always use my speed on you and just now I didn't mean to touch—"

The sound of scratching cut him off. He shut his mouth at once and listened to the sound of what he thought might be metal on dirt. Now that it was close enough, he recognized the sound. It was reminiscent of his childhood.

Finley brought his finger to his mouth and faced Zuma, who nodded. They both approached the back flap, only used for maintenance. Using his speed, and wanting to scout any danger ahead of Zuma, Finley hurried to the exit. Once there, he peered out and took a giant breath of relief. He'd turned to assure Zuma before she was even five feet away.

"It's fine," he said, pointing out the exit.

"Well, what's causing the ruckus?" she asked.

He waved her over. "Just an ambitious ten-year-old boy," Finley said, pointing to the side.

Zuma poked her head out and stared in the direction Finley had pointed. Now she realized that at this location in Eugene, this exit backed up right beside where Dave and Titus's office was set up. Her eyes took a moment to register, but then quite clearly she saw Benjamin clearing dirt out of a hole beside the office tent using a trowel.

"What is he doing?" she questioned Finley at once, who didn't look at all worried.

"He's trying to ensure he gets the best job when he comes of age," he said, proudly.

And just then Benjamin took a submarine-type scope he'd built and put it into the hole. He squinted through it, a clever grin on his face.

"He's spying on Dave and Titus," Zuma said, revolted. Her loud voice couldn't be heard by the boy since he wasn't dream traveling and was in the physical realm. Dave and Titus, who were discussing various acts, also weren't dream traveling. Finley knew that Dave didn't usually dream travel until later in the night, if at all.

"Don't worry," Finley said, placing a hand on Zuma's shoulder and trying to corral her back. "He just wants to know what they want in the best acts. It's his dream to be in the circus. And look," he said, indicating the boy lying on his stomach in the dirt. Benjamin had just set down his scope and was jotting down something on a pad.

Zuma stepped closer, realizing now that he couldn't see or hear her. Over Benjamin's shoulder she read, "What every Vagabond Circus performer needs to know."

Finley was already at her side again. "And have a listen into the conversation in there."

She stopped and listened.

"Oh yes, I agree, Titus," Dave said, speaking too loudly. "I agree that our best performers study a lot and make good grades. They also floss, they floss all the time, because a winning smile always wows the audience."

Zuma's face lit up and then turned to Finley. "Dave knows. They know," she said in astonishment. "They're feeding Benjamin information."

Finley was smiling widely back at her, but it wasn't from the information they'd just discovered, but because of the look on Zuma's face. Her face with a pure smile on it had too many effects on him, but more than anything it made him happy. Then at the thought, his face fell slack. At least Zuma could have fleeting moments of happiness, it seemed, if nothing else.

"How did you know?" she asked Finley. "About Benjamin? How did you know he wasn't up to something nefarious just now?"

Finley turned his gaze to the eager boy, lying on the ground and listening to the conversation on the other side of the tent. "Just look at the kid. He wants to be someone when he grows up," Finley said and then added, "And he wants to be a part of Vagabond Circus when he grows up. It's obvious in everything he does."

"He must have snuck out of Fanny's trailer," Zuma guessed. "But I guess it's safe to allow him to stay here after hours since he's up to something good."

"I agree," Finley said. What he didn't say was that he'd charged Benjamin with the job of keeping an eye on Dave on the nights he had rehearsal with the acrobats. He hadn't realized the boy would dig a hole and build a scope to do it, but now he realized he enlisted the right kid for the job.

Chapter Fifty-Eight

$\mathcal{A}$s Dave had suspected would happen, most of the initial excitement among the circus members had died down after the newness of being the most popular circus in North America had faded. Most relations among the Vagabond Circus employees had gone back to normal. Sunshine wasn't smarting off to everyone. Fanny's kids were mostly calm. And the crew all seemed happy, although there was more work, with a full house every night.

Finley could hardly believe he'd been with the circus for over three months. It felt like no time at all to him and then also, like the longest stretch of his entire life. No doubt the last few months had been demanding for him, but not because of his role in the circus.

What he was most proud about was that he'd figured out how to create a wall between Zuma and him. It came down sometimes, because she had a knack for finding his loose mortar and pushing at it. But for the most part, he'd been able to keep his distance. There were times where he spied a look in her that dared him to cross new boundaries, but he reminded himself of who he was then, and why he was here. And still he cared for her, wanted to help break the curse, one that Fanny said the girl wasn't even aware was on her. Finley didn't have any free time, but he still used any spare second he had to deliberate on Zuma's curse and how to break it.

The autumn winds had started to blow at the big top one afternoon when he caught himself staring at her across the space. They'd just set up in southern Oregon and Finley realized how perfect the schedule was. They'd be out of the Pacific Northwest before winter hit. The Vagabond Circus would spend all of the cold months in California where temperatures are mild. The bad news for Finley was that the further south they got, the more he'd have to watch his back. And there were other problems that were plaguing him. Weighing on him. And yet, he never felt like he had the focus he needed to finally resolve all the problems. To free himself of the mission.

"Why are you staring at me?" Zuma asked from her place on the mat. She had her feet touching in a butterfly stretch.

He blinked rapidly. "I wasn't," he lied and knew his face gave it away immediately.

However, Zuma let it go. She too seemed comfortable with having the wall up between them. Well, not comfortable, but resigned to it. The acrobat had more spare time than Finley and she used most of it to wonder about him. Always she had something else planned, and always her thoughts flocked to the boy of mystery with eyes like a cheetah's. Finley wasn't overtly mean to Zuma anymore, but he also wasn't nice. And still, no matter what, she could turn her gaze to find him staring at her. She stayed away from him, and him her, spending his time with the freaks: Sunshine, the triplets, and Oliver. But every time she looked at him from her place between Jack and Jasmine, Finley was staring at her. His eyes seemed to always be on her. Always watching and trying to piece and unpiece her together in his mind. And Zuma hated that she liked the way his stare felt on her, like silk against her skin.

"Are you ready to get started?" Finley asked, pushing to a standing position. He meant their final act, which Dave wanted them to practice at least once in each new location before the first show.

"I guess," Zuma said. They'd practiced and performed the act so many times that she was sure she could do it under the worst conditions: blind, sick, or heartbroken. Those were what she considered the worst-case scenarios.

She took her place.

"Try not to do that one thing this time," he said, getting into position.

"What thing?" she said.

"The second part of the act, where you rush the sequence."

"Oh, is that what you think I'm doing?" she said, standing tall, not offended in the least by him. "Because I think you're too slow and I'm doing it perfectly."

She was probably right, but Finley found that a slight bit of criticism helped to reinforce the wall between him and Zuma. So he made a point of throwing something critical at her before each practice. "I think you're mistaking the word 'perfectly' for sloppy," he said in his usual offhanded manner.

And for whatever reason, something shifted in Zuma. Her face. The stoic expression she always wore, it cracked. Just a bit. And for a second Finley spied an emotion in her he'd only seen once. That first rehearsal where he'd insulted her callousness toward her family, where he'd actually hurt her. That expression of pain flared in her eyes.

"What?" he said, staring at her, wondering why she wasn't throwing a volley back at him.

Zuma actually didn't know why either. She thought she was hardened enough when it came to Finley, but his criticism just never ceased and she couldn't understand it. She didn't know where it came from. And presently, she wasn't sure why it hurt worse than usual.

"Nothing," she said, shaking her head. "And fine, I'll work on the second half of the act," she said, sounding defeated. "If it will make you happy," she then added.

Finley's eyes shot up to hers. Zuma's expression was troubled and also blank, like she didn't know what was going on inside her.

"Zuma," Finley said, remorse in his tone. He now felt himself shifting too, the wall crumbling. Finley stopped himself, took a deep breath. "Let's just practice, okay?"

"Yeah, fine," Zuma said.

The two took their places and then started in unison, practicing without music. And then as they neared the end of the act Finley hesitated, like he had forgotten what came next.

"Are you all right?" Zuma asked.

His mind had been elsewhere, thinking about her and how she would never be happy. To his horror he realized that he'd just made a mistake because of his distraction. *What if that mistake happens during a show*, he cursed himself. Zuma was indeed his downfall. Not just with the act, but with everything. More and more, he worried about her, knowing the curse over her was real. Sunshine had said it herself, that the girl had everything and still wasn't happy. But what the empath didn't know was that Zuma couldn't be happy. And the more he studied her, the more Finley saw an empty well, unable to be filled. And the worst part was it appeared Zuma was resigned to it. She couldn't be happy, but she could have her highs at Vagabond Circus and that was enough for her.

"I'm fine," Finley said, trying to compose himself. "I just forgot a part, that's all."

Zuma blinked at him in surprise.

"Let's keep going," he said.

The pair started again, but because Finley hadn't fully collected himself on his next move he paused, holding up her hand.

"What is it?" Zuma questioned, stepping nearer to him, staring into his eyes.

He bit his lip and shook off the question. He couldn't tell her the truth, that more and more he was defeated. Defeated by her and the draw to her he couldn't erase. Defeated by his mission, which he felt no closer to than when he arrived. Defeated by himself.

"It's nothing," he said, pushing down the emotions. He took her hand again, then grabbed her by the waist and spun her into the air, the next to last move before the end of their act. He caught her as he always did and then lowered her in one move. And as she was accustomed to he dipped her low as she slid her legs out along the length of his, his figure stretched across her. He then hesitated again, not pulling her up to a standing position beside him as he did before they received their applause from the crowd. However, the tent was empty besides them. There would be no applause. It was only practice. Finley, feeling something in him breaking, leaned down lower, his lips only an inch from Zuma's. She stared back at him, a strange wanting in her eyes.

"Zuma…" he said in a whisper.

"Yes?" she said, leaning back, her weight in his arms.

What he wished he could say was that he wanted to be what made her happy. That for some unexplainable reason he thought he knew how. Instead he said, "I haven't kissed you since that one time." He was certain that the sentence would cause a reaction in her, a snide remark. A rebellion. Instead, she slid her hands out from around his neck and rested them on his biceps. She was fully in his arms, a strange curiosity on her face.

Zuma blinked back at him. "Do you want to?" she asked.

He leaned in close, slid his nose across her cheek. "Yes," he breathed and quickly admonished himself for the statement. But it was already done and Zuma, still in his arms, leaned back and brought one of her legs up and hooked it next to his hip. He grabbed

184

it with one hand and pinned it to him. She was fully suspended in his arms now as he stood in a lunge.

"Then go ahead and do it," she said, her voice tattered.

She hadn't rejected him as he feared. She had just invited him in, given him permission to have the one thing he wanted: her affection. But then Finley reminded himself who he was. How could he allow himself to forget? He wasn't good enough for her. He had deluded himself.

Pulling his face even with hers, Finley stared into her eyes, felt her breath against his. And then in an impromptu decision he yanked his arms away, letting her fall on the rug. Zuma would have caught this, but her desire had clouded her combat sense. Her tailbone took the brunt of the impact. She sat in horror and disbelief, staring at Finley as he marched away to the exit.

"What the hell?!" she fired at him, her words soaked in hurt. "Damn it, Finley! What is your problem?"

He didn't answer. Only left her there on the ground staring at his retreating back.

Chapter Fifty-Nine

The firelight in Dave's office tent danced across Zuma's face.

"Are you sure?" Dr. Raydon said to her.

"I'm sure," she said.

"And you're firm on this?"

"I am," she said with confidence.

He gave her a measured stare. "You know I trust your judgment implicitly."

"I'm honored that you do."

"Very well, then consider it done," the ringmaster said and then reached for his top hat absentmindedly. It wasn't on the table beside him as it normally was. It was gone, he remembered.

"You're not upset, are you?" she asked.

"Zuma, you know I could never, truly be upset at you," Dave said, his hand almost still reaching for the top hat, fingers kneading air.

"Of course you could," she said with a playful grin. "I've just yet to do something that would make you mad. A day will come, you just wait, Dave."

Dr. Raydon sat back in his chair and folded his hands over his rounded stomach as he did toward twilight hours every day, his time to reflect on the day's events. "You've heard the story of your birth before, from me and your parents," he stated, no question in his voice.

The girl nodded, her pink hair looking red in the firelight of the lantern.

"To this day, you're the only child to have been born under the big top. You showed up four weeks early," he said through a tender lump in his throat. He cherished every time he told her this story and tonight it felt fitting to reminisce. "And do you want to know why I think you came early when your other siblings waited dutiful until their due dates?"

Zuma loved this question-and-answer game she often played with Dave. "Yes, please."

"Because you couldn't wait to be a part of the circus. You felt its energy in the womb. You knew your parents were about to leave it and you decided to make a surprise arrival."

"My mother says it's all the extra travel that threw her into early labor," Zuma said, a ghost of a smile still on her face.

"Of course she does," he said, waving his white-gloved hand at her. "Your mother stopped believing in magic long ago. But you, my dear, I knew as soon as I laid eyes on you, right after Fanny had delivered you, that you were born to the circus. I've said it before and I'll say it until the day I die: Zuma Zanders was born to be in Vagabond Circus. You carry its magic in your heart."

She stared at Dave, not knowing what to say. Dave believed in everyone more than they believed in themselves. He saw in people the part in them they longed to see. But this speech he'd been giving her for all these years still confounded Zuma. Yes, she loved the circus and felt owned by it, but she never understood the bit about "carrying its magic in her heart."

"So, don't you see, my darling, Zuma," Dave continued, "I could never be mad at you, for you're the child born to Vagabond Circus. You are, in essence, it's very magic because right after you were born under the big top this circus really started to take on a life of its own and change the people in the audience. "

Dave wasn't lying, Zuma could tell by his micro-expressions. But what she didn't know was he wasn't telling the complete truth. She was in fact the magic given to the circus, but in return her happiness was stolen. All curses operate on the scale of equality, so if something is taken then it must go somewhere. Unbeknown to the spell caster, those born at Vagabond Circus, although cursed, are also its greatest servants. Their happiness is transferred in dividends to the big top, coating it in a different kind of magic. However, Dave would never allow another soul to be sacrificed once he learned this knowledge and so he created rules.

"Okay, well, thanks for understanding on the other matter," Zuma said and stood.

"Whatever it is I can do to make you happy," he said, and silently reproached himself for the statement. But soon Zuma would be happy. He was making the ultimate sacrifice to give her that.

The girl, however, didn't notice this small bit of remorse and emotion building in the ringmaster. She simply leaned over and kissed Dave on the cheek. "Bye, now," she said and turned to leave.

"Bye, my sweet Zuma," he said. "I love you so very much." And he held in the tears until after she left.

Chapter Sixty

The knocking on Zuma's trailer door was loud and incessant. She opened it in a rush, afraid it was an emergency. Her heart had been racing but its speed quickly slowed when she saw Finley standing on her doorstep.

"What do you want?" she said, her tone punishing. He pushed past her at super speed and entered straight into her trailer. His hair was a mess of chaos, like his hands hadn't left it alone all evening.

"You told Dave that you couldn't work with me! That you refused!" he said, his voice loud and overpowering in the compact trailer.

Zuma's eyes scowled but her mouth smiled. "I did," she said triumphantly.

"Well, because Dave will do anything and everything you want he's split us up!" Finley shouted, his words angry, but his face full of fear.

"Oh, is that right?" Zuma said, looking at the clock as if bored by the news.

"Don't play innocent with me, you told him to do it. You demanded that he do it or otherwise you wouldn't perform," he said, his eyes haunted by Dave's words. The ringmaster had thrown his hands up in the air, explaining there was nothing he could do against Zuma's wishes.

"Maybe I did," she said, her voice suddenly sounding vexed.

"And even though losing our act will affect the success of the circus he's doing it, all for his precious Zuma. And you know as well as I do that it's the best act, but you don't care."

"That's the thing, Finley," she said, the hurt in her voice seeping through suddenly. "I do care, but I refuse to work with someone who disrespects me and Dave recognizes that. He won't allow me to be abused. That isn't favoritism, that's good management."

"Abused?" Finley repeated, his eyes lost as he stared out without seeing. "I abused you?" he whispered to himself, his face trapped in self-loathing as the realization dawned.

"You did. I trusted you and you dropped me." Zuma looked away, unable to stomach what appeared to be genuine remorse on Finley's face. She had done what Ian had advised her to do. She'd trusted Finley. Not just trusted, but invited him to kiss her and he dropped her, thereby breaking her heart. She had no idea how something like this could change everything because it felt too personal. All she wanted now was to put as much distance between her and the guy who affected her.

"Zuma, I'm sorry," Finley said, his voice trembling. "You don't understand. I had to. I was so close to…"

"To what?" Zuma demanded.

But Finley just shook his head. The longer Zuma stared at him, the more she felt like she was seeing him for the first time. Everything about him reeked of distress.

Zuma shook off her concern. "And you better be glad Dave's taken pity on you as a confused soul and hasn't kicked your ass out of Vagabond Circus."

"Yeah," he said, his eyes still lost, his voice a hush. "He's reassigned me to work with Jasmine."

Zuma smiled, realizing her friend would be ecstatic about the decision. And Finley wouldn't get away with disrespecting Jasmine. She'd break his arm. "Yes, and I'll work with Jack."

Finley was visibly shaking. It was strange for Zuma to witness this in him. Real fear in Finley. "I don't want to work with anyone else, Zuma," he said, his voice sounding so bizarre to her. His eyes looked earnest, marked by solid stress. "You're my partner. I only want to work with you."

She stepped back from him and shook her head. "You have an awful way of showing it."

"Yeah, I know," Finley said and took another step in her direction. She knew he would reach for her in only a couple of seconds. Sensed it in him before he telegraphed the move. She didn't make to move away but instead allowed him to lock her wrist with his other hand, anchoring her in front of him. "I'm sorry, Zuma. I shouldn't have dropped you." He looked straight at her, his eyes unlike she'd ever seen them. She knew now he wore a mask and presently it was off. "I keep trying to make you hate me. I keep pretending that I don't care about you. Since the moment we met, I've been trying to resist the gravitation I have toward you. And it might ruin everything but I'm tired of pushing you away from me. That's why I dropped you. That's why I insult you. The way I feel about you scares me." She watched his face for the normal hint of mischief. For anything to tell her he was playing a trick. There was nothing.

"That's why you're mean to me?" And it made perfect sense to her. Zuma often welcomed the insults, needing reasons to not be swept away by her own desire for Finley. Too often she'd felt that his lingering gaze was ripping her resolve apart. It would take little from Finley to unravel her heart.

"Yes, that's why I've been cruel to you since the beginning," he said, pushing one hand through his wild hair. "I don't know another way. I'm afraid of how I feel about you. It's unlike anything and it threatens my very survival. Whatever it is about you, it owns me. And I didn't want to be owned, Zuma, not anymore."

And in that moment he could no longer look at her. Finley dropped her wrists and his eyes. He shouldn't have come here, to Vagabond Circus, months ago. To Zuma's trailer tonight. Shouldn't have allowed this emotion, but he couldn't fight it anymore. He was a slave to the way he felt for the girl in front of him. And it was time he stopped avoiding it. If his life was going to be a series of enslavements then he needed to give himself over to Zuma. At least with her he'd be happy and safe. He had been afraid she would distract him and she did. Everything about her distracted him, and he didn't care anymore. He was failing at his mission and now he'd lost Zuma. Whereas before he was afraid she'd be his downfall, now he didn't care if he was defeated, not if he lost her. Not having Zuma was his worst-case scenario. Now that he had had her attention, he couldn't fathom another reality.

Zuma studied him, taking in the details only she could see. Finley hadn't lied. In every word he spoke there had been more sincerity than she'd ever witnessed from him. But she didn't have to look at him to know what he said was true. In her own heart, Zuma knew Finley was right. She'd never been drawn to anyone the way she was to him. He stole her focus. He owned her attention just by existing. He did to Zuma what she did to the world.

They were quiet for less than a minute when Zuma stepped in closer. Her slender hands found Finley's chest and she stared up at him, begging for his eyes to look at her. She didn't have to wait long.

"Finley," she said up close to his face. "You're not alone in the way you feel."

He blinked back at her in astonishment. "I'm not?" And then he brandished a pirate's smile. "Tell me more."

"Tell me first who you are," she said. "I know nothing about you. Tell me something. Anything."

He sucked in a breath and eyed her hands on his chest. To have her willingly touching him was beyond all hope. Finley brought one hand up and pushed a strand of blonde and pink hair away from her heart-shaped face. "Zuma, I'm the guy who's incredibly in love with you. That's all you ever need to know about me." His hand found her chin and tilted it slightly. She stood up on her tiptoes as his other arm came around her waist and encouraged her forward. Their lips sank down on each other's and the kiss that followed flowed like a large wave in the ocean, powerful and overwhelming.

Zuma allowed Finley to wrench her into him tighter, and still she recognized they weren't close enough. Tying her arms around his neck she then parted her lips, allowing a deeper, more passionate kiss. She couldn't believe she was kissing Finley and yet there had never been anything that felt so exquisitely perfect as being in this moment with him. And he seemed to feel the same way as his mouth sped up with hunger against hers. She was breathless and yet didn't mind the lightheadedness that followed. Zuma thought that her heart would beat out, that it would lose its rhythm in her chest and fail altogether and yet, the idea didn't pull her away from Finley. It was her logic that did. Her logical side came rushing in and she realized at once how wrong everything about this was. Dave would never approve and she couldn't afford to lose his support. Three times she tried to break away from Finley and three times he encouraged her back. Finally she placed her hands on his chest and pushed him back as she stepped away. He stood staring at her with new eyes. An expression she'd never seen on his face.

"Finley," she said, between breaths. "We can't. This isn't right."

He nodded but there was something in his unsatisfied eyes that said he didn't really agree.

"We have to talk about this. Figure out what to do," Zuma said, and dared to step forward and grab his hand. She led him to the couch built into the wall. "Sit," she said, pointing to the cushions.

He shook his head, looking at her defiantly. And he did sit but then promptly lay out, stretching his long legs across the length of the sofa. Then he waved her forward. "Lay with me. I promise to be good. We can talk."

She looked at him lying on her couch. He was more than handsome. Finley was raw beauty. There were scars in his eyes and they were beautiful too. Now that she was allowing herself to admit it, everything about him was alluring. Zuma didn't nod but instead crawled into his arms, laying her head on his chest. She had never lain with anyone in this way and yet it felt natural to curl herself against this guy.

Finley released a full breath when she was snuggly against him. To feel Zuma like this was more than he ever thought possible. More than dreams.

She angled her head up and looked at him, a sly smile on her face. "Seriously?" she said. "You're being serious with all this? You promise?"

"Yes, Zuma," he said, running his finger over the curve of her jaw. "This is who I really am."

Her fingers slid over the fabric of his shirt. It felt real. He felt real. And yet, the moment was too surreal. How had the wall between them, built to the clouds, come crashing down so quickly? "So before…you were just acting?"

"Yes, to keep you at a distance," he said, picking up her hand and bringing it to his lips, kissing her fingertips with a tenderness she didn't know he possessed. "And I'm so sorry. So sorry I hurt you. You have to realize I didn't know what I was doing. I was acting out of fear and self-preservation."

"Then tell me why. Tell me where you came from."

"Zuma …" he said, sounding defeated. "It's not important."

"It is to me." And then seeing the look in his eyes she added, "It won't change anything, but I want to know about you."

"But you care about me, right? Without knowing much about me? I'm not misreading that, am I?"

"Of course," she said, scooting up in his arms and laying three kisses, each on a different place on his cheek, until she found his lips and kissed them once tenderly. "I've been drawn to you since the beginning, and for different reasons than yours I've been afraid of how I felt. I can't risk losing my job here, it would kill me."

Finley nodded. "That's why you and Jack never—"

"Stop. Jack doesn't even compare…" Zuma trailed off, a hesitant look in her eyes. "And I don't want to confuse the issue by talking about him."

The truth was Jack had never been as bold as Finley. Never given her that look of desperate wanting. She would have kissed Jack a hundred times, but he never pushed the boundary like Finley. And what she almost said was nothing compared to the way she felt about Finley.

"Dave isn't stupid, Finley," Zuma said after a long pause, her chin on his chest, her eyes always watching him.

"No, he's the smartest man I know," Finley admitted. "But Zuma, I love you. I want this, and we have the most incredibly poetic act in Vagabond Circus, which now that I'm speaking openly, that is no mistake. You and I are strangely connected. Dave must know that. He will understand. He will accept it."

"Finley, you don't understand, if he allows us to be together, then he'll have to allow everyone and that's something Dave can't do."

"Well, then we will promise secrecy," he said, his voice full of a new hope. It tightened Zuma's heart, made her want this more. "Our act is based on two lovers," Finley continued. "No one will suspect anything and Dave will see that once I talk to him."

"Finley!" Zuma said, her eyes bulging.

"Shhh," he said gently, stroking his hand through her hair. "Zuma, I don't think telling you everything about me is necessary. But I will tell you that I have gone without my entire life. I grew up in a bad place, and hardly ever had anything I needed. Usually I didn't have food. I was rarely warm. And I definitely never had love. Please give this a chance."

And she couldn't help but stare at the guy before her with a quiet reverence. There was no one like Finley. And no one she'd risk her place in the circus for but him. And how could she not. He had made her a star in the circus and a star in his heart. She leaned down again, relishing his mouth against hers. *Love. This is what love feels like,* she thought as her lips pulled away from his and her head snuggled into his chest. Zuma didn't feel happy as she rested on Finley's chest, but she felt like she'd looked through a window and knew what happiness looked like. It was pure and unadulterated and just on the other side of a distant ridge through a murky window. And still she was closer to happiness than she'd ever been. She fell asleep listening to his breathing, which was steady and calm.

Chapter Sixty-One

*F*or Finley, everything felt too perfect about holding Zuma. People like him didn't get a chance at true love. His type of people worked until they exhausted themselves. Until they were demoralized. They settled for squalor and cheap thrills. They died alone or forgotten. He was one of those people, and yet, he was holding Zuma to his chest.

He awoke an hour later, feeling excited for the possibilities again. Finley knew more clearly than ever what he'd say to Dave. It was like a voice was telling him exactly what to say to get what he wanted. It felt like divine intervention. It felt like destiny.

The last thing he desired to do was to leave Zuma's arms, which were still wrapped around him, holding him with a silent need. She wanted him. He felt that now, allowed himself to relish in the idea. Finley had felt their connection like one does a diamond and knows it's real and unbreakable. However, he'd convinced himself again and again that she could never *really* want him. Not like he wanted her. Needed her.

Finley was careful to slip out from underneath Zuma without waking her. The smell of lavender in her hair caressed his nose as he gently arranged her on the sofa. He stared down at her, for the first time allowing himself to suck in her beauty with his eyes. She was enchanting when she slept and he couldn't help but notice that for the first time she had a look of peace about her. Maybe it was because she was sleeping, but Zuma almost appeared happy. And because Finley wanted to return to her arms as soon as possible he pulled his greedy eyes away from her and headed out the trailer door.

It was still early and Finley expected that the ringmaster would just have returned from his office. Finley knew Dave's schedule better than anyone since he had been watching him all these months. Protecting him. It had been difficult to keep up with his acts in the circus, his sessions with Fanny, and also his watching over Dave. However, his job involving Dave was his first priority. It was the reason that had brought him to the circus. Everything else was extra. But finding and falling in love with Zuma wasn't extra. It was a rare gift and now he realized he had never breathed properly. Before being granted Zuma's affection, he had never been whole. Not until that moment.

The moon rose out of a pillow of clouds as Finley half skipped to Dave's trailer. The man should be settling into his recliner right about now. Then he'd pull the pills that Fanny made for him from the side drawer. Finley had watched him do it a hundred times. To say Dave Raydon was a creature of habit was a grand understatement. Three things are forever consistent: the passing of time, the rotation of the Earth, and Dr. Raydon.

Chapter Sixty-Two

Zuma awoke like someone had rattled her shoulders. She was alone. Squinting through the darkening trailer, she tried to remember what was out of place.

Finley. He was gone.

She had thought that he would stay the night. It was an unspoken agreement, she felt. But she now guessed that he had gone back to his own trailer. However, she'd felt the tingling excitement in his hands on her. That was not the type of reaction someone gives and then retreats to their own space.

Zuma stood suddenly, now completely lucid, the grogginess of sleep instantly pushed away. She knew where Finley had gone. With the certainty that she knew he was connected to her in a mysterious way, she knew where he was.

She didn't even bother to put on her shoes, but rather bounded out the door. Zuma was both exploding with excitement and panic. This was all happening too fast. But no matter what happened she wanted to be there. The girl wanted to be by Finley's side when he made his case. And she wanted to have a chance to convince Dave that she never meant to break his rules. She wanted to be there for both Dave and Finley. This did involve her.

Chapter Sixty-Three

$\mathcal{F}$inley froze when he rounded the corner. It was ten at night and Dave's trailer was dark. The light on the side table should be on in the ringmaster's trailer as it was every night at this time. He scanned the area, his senses switching into hyperdrive. His greatest fear was that the person he had been protecting Dave from was somewhere close by. Finley's eyes roamed down his bare arms and he instantly wished he'd grabbed his jacket before heading out. He should have, but he'd been too distracted by Zuma.

Behind him he heard the sound of a twig cracking into two. Finley spun around. He knew better than to race toward the sound. Away from it was the smartest option. For the last few months his presence outside of Dave's trailer had been effective at deterring the imposter from getting close to the ringmaster and killing him. But Finley hadn't been here tonight. He'd been with Zuma. He'd let down his guard and now what was the result? He feared the answer.

"Come out," Finley said to the quiet night. "Come out already and face me, you coward."

A boy's laughter filled the air. "Cowards don't face people," someone said from a distant shadow. "They run and hide, which is what I'll be doing now that my job is finally done."

Finley whipped around and stared at the darkened trailer. "No!" he said, his voice cracking. And he could have used his speed to track down the murderer, but it wouldn't be wise. This wasn't a person one went after, but rather stayed away from. And he'd been effective at keeping Dave from this person until now. The sound of running footsteps told Finley that the boy was on the run. Escaping.

He turned his full attention on the trailer and now he noticed that the door was partially open. With deliberate paces Finley cleared the distance to the trailer. He found a stick along the way and used it to urge the door back the rest of the way. Dave had in fact made it home and probably at his usual time. He had not made it to the lamp to switch it on. There, lying just inside his trailer, was the ringmaster. Dead.

Chapter Sixty-Four

Zuma froze at the sight in front of her. It confused the girl and she wasn't sure why. Finley was standing just in the doorway of Dave's trailer. Just standing. Not moving. She wanted to call out to him, but the way he stood was wrong. His shoulders were pinned up high. His back tense. Her combat sense told her one important thing. Finley was extremely stressed. He felt in danger. *But why?*

Chapter Sixty-Five

There was two feet of space between the threshold of the trailer and where Dave lay. Finley stood in the doorway searching, trying to figure out what had killed him. There were so many possibilities and it was almost impossible to know for certain. In the end, it would be a guess. Finley moved farther into the trailer, skirting around Dave. He wasn't even sure what he was still doing in the trailer. There was nothing he could do. And then a grief so raw struck him in the chest and he realized that he was in shock. It was sorrow that kept him there, standing over the dead man's body. He had failed the ringmaster and now Dave was dead.

He heard the footsteps first. As if stuck in a daze he turned too slowly. Finley moved the opposite way he normally did, like he was locked in quicksand. His eyes blinked a few times, working to bring the person outside Dave's trailer into view. Her face took several seconds to register for him. And then Finley's mind and eyes caught up with each other in real time and he realized how utterly doomed he was.

Chapter Sixty-Six

Zuma froze two feet from Dave's trailer door. Her racing heart crashed like a train in a collision at the scene in front of her. She sucked in a breath and choked on it. Finley stood before her, Dave at his feet unmoving.

"What have you done?" she asked, her eyes shifting between Dave's body and Finley, standing just as frozen.

Finley's eyes widened as he focused on her. "Zuma, don't touch anything," he said, his voice panicked.

"Finley!" she said, gasping for air in a throat that was quickly tightening. Her eyes searched him. "Who are you? How could you?" She backed up a step, almost tripping on her feet.

"No, Zuma," Finley said in a rush. "I didn't do this."

She shook her head erratically, her long hair whipping her in the face. Tears not ready, but building in her, like poison in a syringe.

"It's not what it looks like. I can explain," Finley said, taking a step toward her.

"Stay away from me," she said and turned to run and knocked straight into Finley, who had teleported to catch her.

He gripped her arms. Held them in front of his chest. "Zuma, you have to listen to me. I tried to stop this from happening."

"Did he tell you no? Is this what you do when you don't get what you want?"

"God no," he said and yanked her closer to him, but she used everything in her body to pull away from him.

"Titus!" Zuma screamed. His trailer sat beside Dave's. It was always set up adjacent to the ringmaster's. The creative director's trailer was a blaze with light from within. And Zuma didn't have to wait long before Titus tore through his door, scrambling out at the sound of Zuma's frantic voice. Finley released Zuma at once, afraid of what the scene looked like to a worried Titus. And then behind him Jack poured out of the creative director's trailer. The two had been discussing changes to next year's show when or if Jasmine left

Vagabond Circus. They'd bolted out of their seats at the sound of Zuma's screams.

Finley clasped his hands to the sides of his head. Things could not worsen in this moment. He wanted to run, but he had nowhere to go and a responsibility to these people.

Titus raced to Zuma and clutched both his hands on her shoulders since the girl was shaking wildly, every part of her trembling.

"What is it, Zuma?" Titus asked. Jack was at his shoulder immediately, eyes protectively on her and also watching Finley.

"Da-da-Dave," she said, pointing at the still open trailer door. "H-h-he's dead."

Titus's eyebrows shot up to meet his receding hairline. "What?! That's impossible." His head whipped in the direction of the trailer. The door was still open, but the scene inside was too dark to make out. "No-no-no," he said in disbelief, but Titus couldn't understand why Dave's trailer would be dark at this hour. Why the door would be ajar. He knew the ringmaster better than anyone else and he knew that Dave's light should have still been on.

Jack stepped for the open door.

"Stop," Finley yelled. His voice drenched with panic. "Don't go in there! Don't touch anything!"

Jack halted and looked at Finley, gauging him.

And before he could respond Zuma said, "It was Finley. I found him standing over Dave. He killed him." And now she was crying, tears gushing down her cheeks as she collapsed into Titus's arms. The first horror she'd ever witnessed played over and over on the inside of her eyelids. She saw Dave's dead body again and again, and she saw Finley standing over it.

Finley shook his head erratically. Titus and Jack exchanged a look of apprehension and then the creative director indicated to Dave's trailer with a nod of his head. "Check it out, Jack, but be careful."

Jack approached the trailer, his shoulders pinned back. And it was Zuma who spied the first bit of shock sprint through his body as he tensed at the sight made visible by the waning moonlight. "Oh my god," Jack said, backing away at once, a crazed look in his eyes when he turned around. "You did this to him?!" he roared at Finley.

Titus, who was still holding onto Zuma, shot a look of disbelief at Jack. "It's true? Dave is…" And his voice fell away, like it was sucked up by the night, his eyes emptied like the stars had robbed him of his soul.

Jack nodded, his eyes still on Finley. Menace covering his face.

"Check his pulse," Titus demanded.

"Don't touch him," Finley said. "It might kill you too."

The three turned and stared at Finley, horror in their eyes.

"You did this," Jack said, spit flying out of his mouth.

"No," Finley said, holding up both his hands in the air in surrender. He knew Jack was considering tackling him and trying to tear him apart with his hands. Finley knew that look in Jack's face. Had seen it on too many faces throughout his life. But Jack couldn't catch him and they both knew it. That's why Finley held up his hands, to show he wouldn't fight or run. The innocent have no reason to fight or run. "It wasn't me. I found him and I know who murdered him."

Zuma pulled out of Titus's arms. "What? Did you see it happen?"

Finley ran his hand through his hair. "No, I didn't see it happen. But I know without a doubt who did this. It's why I came to Vagabond Circus and took the acrobat job. I came here to protect Dave from this happening." And Finley lowered his hands as the grief set in, pulling him deep inside himself. "But I failed," he said in a whisper.

"What?!" Zuma said, stepping closer to Finley. She needed to be closer to him, to see his face. Zuma needed to see if he was lying. Titus and Jack arrived on either side of her. The three faced Finley with threatening demeanors.

Chapter Sixty-Seven

*I*t was clear they all were in shock and needed to grieve, but such rights aren't granted as long as an ominous threat continues to hang in the air. And unfortunately for Finley, he was that threat until he proved otherwise.

"Son, I think you have a lot of explaining to do right now," Titus said, his face tight.

Finley nodded. One of the last things he wanted in this life was to divulge the truth. It involved so many secrets he thought he could keep buried. But the very last thing he wanted was for Dave to be murdered and his failure to prevent it brought with it many curses. "Sebastian did this," he finally said, pointing to the trailer where Dave's dead body lay.

"What?" Jack said, an almost laugh in his voice.

But Zuma knew Finley was telling the truth. "Go on," she said, no emotion in her voice.

He slid his eyes over to her, a look of pleading in them. "I didn't come from the street, like I told Dave. I belong, I mean I belonged, to a group run by a man named Charles Knight."

"Ohmygod!" Titus said in one word, his mouth hanging open.

"Who is that?" Zuma asked, turning to him.

"He was Dave's first performer," Titus said, his voice heavy, almost sounding hoarse suddenly. "And in one year Knight ripped Vagabond Circus to pieces along with Dave's life."

"And you work for this guy?" Zuma said to Finley, everything about her intimidating.

"Yes, but not anymore, so no," Finley said.

"But you used to work for him?" Titus said with disgust.

"You don't understand. No one has the choice to work or not work for Knight. I was born to work for him," Finley said.

Zuma blinked at him in surprise. He wasn't lying and yet what he said didn't make sense.

He closed his eyes, understanding how confusing this must sound, but the truth was a series of complex stories and he wasn't sure which parts were necessary to tell. He wanted to keep them all to himself, but that privilege was gone now.

"How can you be born to work for someone like Knight?" Titus asked.

"I was manufactured, in a way," he said and paused. Real people with real families, like Zuma, wouldn't understand. She would think he was a freak, and he was, he admitted to himself.

"Go on," Zuma said. "How do you manufacture people?"

"Not just any type of people," Finley corrected. "Specifically Knight manufactures Dream Travelers."

"Wait, you're telling me there's a man who produces Dream Travelers?" Zuma said. "How?" And that was only the first of many questions in her overloaded head.

"He has surrogates he uses to create his kids. They're all Dream Travelers and carry that gene. Then he has male Dream Traveler sperm donors. I was, as are all of Knight's kids, created to serve him," Finley said, keeping his eyes on Titus, unable to look at Zuma.

"So you're saying that you and Sebastian worked for Knight?" Titus asked, his hand pinned to the back of his neck.

"Yes," Finley said.

"So you lied to us and have been spying for Knight all this time," Titus stated, heat building in his tone.

"No, I came here to protect Dave," Finley said, throwing his hands in his air. "And I realize what this looks like because I've lied and failed. But you have to believe me when I say I don't work for Knight anymore. I work…" he hesitated, "I worked for Dave."

"I want to know why this Knight guy manufactures kids." This time it was Jack who spoke, a hint of hostility in his voice. "Is he creating an army or something?"

Finley's head was exploding with the truth. He didn't know where to start and how much to tell. What he told was up to him, and he needed to be careful only to divulge the story in the most relevant way. And still that would involve divulging too much about himself. He slid his eyes over to Zuma, whose gaze was boring into him. Finley cleared his throat and brought his focus on Jack. "Not an army, not like you think. Once we are old enough then we are released to Knight. He breaks us down like they do in the army, but he doesn't build us back up as a team. He does things to ensure we're weak, to keep us weak. And keep us separated. He's the worst kind of person you can imagine. All of his kids, we're all Dream Travelers, except that we don't even know we have that skill. I learned it by accident. And when we come to Dream Traveler age and get our special skill he trains us. It the only thing he ever gives back." Finley stopped, thinking he'd suffocate on his words.

"Why? Why does he do all this?" Zuma asked.

Finley took three hyperventilated breaths. "We're thieves," he said, making himself look at her. "We are, I was, one of Knight's Kids."

Titus let out a gigantic sigh. "Oh man, I'd heard of them, but I thought it was rumor. And I had no idea it was actually run by Charles Knight," he said, shaking his head. "I didn't think they were..." He looked at Finley. "I didn't think *your* group was real. But you all are associated with some hefty crimes."

"It's not my group." Finley bit on the words. "I'm not with them and none of the other kids have a choice."

"Okay, fair enough," Titus said, nodding. "So you say you came here to protect Dave? Explain that."

"Yes," Finley said. "I learned on accident that I could dream travel, but kept it a secret since I didn't know how to escape physically. Knight keeps us imprisoned when we aren't working. And when we are working he has eyes on us. I started dream traveling to spy on him and learned he had a grudge against Dr. Raydon and planned to use Sebastian to murder him. He had been planning this for a while, waiting until the perfect kid was produced with the right skill. Curious, I dream traveled to spy on Vagabond Circus. I started watching Dave and realized he was a good man."

Finley paused, but couldn't bring his eyes to meet Zuma's although he knew this talk about Dave was hurting her. And what he was about to say would make it worse, but it was important to the story. "I learned what you all have known for a long time, that Dave Raydon is...was one of the best men to ever live. He was a true inspiration and I saw that when I observed. I knew I needed to save him. It took some time to plan, but I was able to manage my escape from Knight's compound, and I'm certain I'm the only one who has ever gotten out, thanks to my gifts. It isn't a place people break out of. And Knight isn't a man people can easily rebel against," Finley said, and the look in his eyes impaled a piece of Zuma's heart. She found that her hands had clasped her chest, almost as if trying to keep the organ inside of her from falling out.

Aside from the obvious pain, Zuma didn't know how she felt in that moment. Finely wasn't who she thought he was, but she had to remind herself that she never knew who he was. This was just not who she expected. And still she looked at him and saw the affection she had for him that she couldn't push away, not even in that moment full of pain and confusion.

"So you have been here all this time knowing Dave was endangered and you didn't tell him or any of us?" Jack said, his words scorched with heat.

"I decided the best way to protect Dave was to watch over him and keep Sebastian away from him. I knew what Sebastian was doing and I kept intervening to save Dave. He should have been dead months ago but I shielded him," Finley said, his confidence growing as he spoke. It was because of him that Dave had lived as long as he did. Then Finley shrunk in on himself. And it was because of his mistake tonight that Dave was dead.

"But why couldn't you have just informed us an assassination was being attempted?" Jack asked.

"I don't know," Finley said, momentarily baffled by the question. That idea hadn't occurred to him. Becoming a part of the circus and protecting Dave had always been the plan. "I knew I could protect Dave and when I could get close enough to Sebastian I'd take him out, but I had to be careful."

"You were going to kill a boy?" Jack asked, his voice dripping with revulsion.

Finley shot him a frustrated look. "He's not as young as you think. He looks young for his age. Sebastian is fifteen."

"What? Does he have his gift?" Titus asked.

"Oh, yeah. He was faking not having it," Finley said. "And he's not an innocent little boy, he's a murderer who does all Knight's dirty work."

"Well, why didn't you just take him out?" Jack said, his eyes narrowed at Finley. "You've been here for months."

"It's not as easy as you'd think," Finley said, a frustrated edge in his voice. He'd exhausted himself trying to trap Sebastian, but the boy was smart and knew how to avoid Finley. "Sebastian is dangerous and also Fanny keeps her kids guarded. I couldn't just stroll into the trailer and take him out, not without creating a lot more problems."

"Is that why you kept going to see Fanny?" Zuma asked, her voice sounding strange to her.

"It was one of the reasons," Finley said, knowing lies wouldn't help him. "I was trying to earn her trust, hoping she'd grant me alone time with Sebastian. I knew if I tried to go after him with the other kids around he'd use them as a hostage or shield."

"What was the other reason?" Zuma said, studying Finley, watching him for any hint of a lie. "You said that was only one of the reasons you visited Fanny."

"It doesn't really matter," Finley said, not looking at her. "It had nothing to do with this at all."

"Dave's dead," Titus said. "You're the only one who supposedly has information about his murder. I think at this point, if you don't want the blame on you then you're obligated to fill us in on everything. We will need to decide what's pertinent or not."

A growl ripped out of Finley's mouth. *I should just run*, he thought. Instead he said, "I told you all that Knight keeps his kids weak. He breaks us down and doesn't give us any way to empower ourselves. Fanny was helping me."

"Helping you how?" Zuma asked, all her emotions centered on these words.

Finley grunted with frustration. He couldn't lie or run or make this go away so he sucked in a breath and looked Zuma straight in the eyes. "I can't read."

And her heart sank suddenly. It was one of the cruelest punishments she could imagine. How alienated this man made his slaves. And suddenly her eidetic memory pieced it all together. The multiple times Finley avoided reading, faked it when around her. And although she wanted to feel sorry for Finley, the weight of Dave's murder deadened her to any sympathies.

"How do we know what you say is true?" Jack asked.

"It's true," Finley said adamantly. "Everything I've told you is true and Zuma knows it." He locked her in his gaze, as only he could do. But too clearly she remembered his hands on her, his whispered words of devotion. And the memory made her feel foolish.

"But everything about you *has* been an act, hasn't it?" Zuma said, looking at him with contempt. "You acted to get your position and to keep it." Anger flared so sharp and hot in her head she thought she'd charge Finley, knock him to the ground and assault him until he begged for mercy. If anyone could take him down, it would be Zuma. She knew how to fight him.

"No, Zuma, no," Finley said, his hands up in front of him, shielding him from her penetrating stare. "What I told you tonight is true. I was not acting in any way tonight. When I told—"

"Shut up," she said, backing away from him. "If you would have told us any of this, then Dave wouldn't be in there dead." Zuma pointed a shaking hand at the dark trailer, which already felt like it possessed a ghost. "You came here, made Dave think you were homeless, and never told him a boy in his circus was trying to kill him! How can you live with yourself? You allowed this to happen," she said.

"Zuma, I didn't think—"

"Don't you say my name." She said like it created an intimacy between them she couldn't bear.

"This isn't my fault," Finley said.

Titus held up a hand to stop Finley, who looked more flustered than the three had ever seen him. "I'm sorry, son, but you are absolutely responsible for this. Dave took you in and gave you a job, and you owed him this information." He shook his head in disapproval. "And now we have to figure out what to do," he said, turning for the trailer, a new weight on his shoulders. Then he took a few steps in the direction of the RV.

"Wait!" Finley said. "If you go in there then you can't touch anything. Especially don't touch Dave."

"Why?" Titus said, almost sounding offended.

"Because he was poisoned but it could be anywhere. He probably didn't ingest it, but it's most likely on a surface that he touched."

"Wait. What?" Jack said.

"Sebastian," Finley said. "He secretes an oil from his skin and it's lethal. A drop of the poison is enough to cause cardiac arrest to another person."

"That's his gift?" Titus asked, completely perplexed.

"Yes, and the poison stays on objects," Finley said. "That's how he kills his victims but I've been wiping down things where I saw he'd left poison. Also Dave wore gloves, so that prolonged him. But Sebastian obviously found a way to get the poison on Dave."

"Jaz," Zuma said in a hush, the realization entering her mind. "Was her illness Sebastian's doing?"

Finley nodded. "Yes, he delivered the letter from Titus. I'm sure he hoped it would make contact with Dave's skin at some point, but Jasmine touched it first."

"But it didn't kill her," Zuma said.

"It obviously wasn't enough poison," Finley said. "Paper is a poor carrier of the oil. Fabric is much better, as Sebastian can soak more of the oil into it, ensuring it's a deadly dose."

"And when you ran off, after Jaz passed out?" Zuma said, remembering every detail of that memory.

Finley nodded. "I was trying to stop Sebastian, but he had already disappeared."

"And that's why you wouldn't help me carry Jaz?" Jack asked. "Because you knew she had poison on her?"

"Yeah," Finley said, dropping his eyes with shame.

"I could have been poisoned too though," Jack said, repulsed. "And you were just going to allow it?"

"What was I supposed to do? It all happened too fast."

"You could have told us there was a murderer in our midst," Jack said, his voice cold. "Told us to be careful."

"It wouldn't have done any good at that point. You had to transport Jasmine and I figured she'd be fine since she was still breathing," Finley said, his eyes earnest on Jack. "And I then knew that Dave realized Jasmine had been poisoned, although he was wrong about the means, so I thought there wasn't any reason to blow my cover."

"Dave knew?" Titus said, unconvinced.

"I think he had an inclination," Finley said.

"And all those thefts?" Zuma said, her question directed at Finley, but her eyes unwilling to look at him.

"Yes, also Sebastian," Finley said. "He's Knight's perfect kid, a born thief and murderer."

Titus turned to Jack. "Go to Fanny's trailer and I want—"

"Sebastian is gone," Finley said. "I heard him go."

Titus scrutinized Finley. "You realize this doesn't look good for you, right?"

"Yes," Finley said, sliding both hands over his head. But Zuma knew he was telling the truth. She could see it in him so plainly and wondered how she hadn't seen he was hiding something so unforgiving.

Titus turned back to Jack. "I want you to go still. Confirm this and alert Fanny, but keep this quiet. No announcements until I investigate."

Jack nodded before turning away and running off.

Titus carefully entered the trailer. Zuma, behind him, willed herself forward. She felt like she was floating and might drift into something laced with poison at any point. Finley watched her carefully, ready to bolt forward and protect her if she got too close to a wall or piece of furniture. They stood in the trailer, too close to each other and too close to Dave's stocky dead body.

"We can't see anything," Zuma said.

"No turning on the lights," Finley said, wadding up his shirt and wrapping it around his fingers. He was just about to use his swaddled hand to find a light when Titus put his hand on him.

"No need for that," he said and he laid his palm out flat and a bright orb of fire lit up in his hand.

"Whoa, what's that?" Finley said.

Titus's face didn't shift, but he still looked eerie under the glow in his hand. "It's my gift. I illuminate."

Chapter Sixty-Eight

$\mathcal{T}$he scene that came to life in front of Finley, Titus, and Zuma emptied each of them of all words. Dave lay on the ground, face down in his usual jacket and slacks. Finley watched Zuma, who was cradling her arms.

Titus scratched his head. Finally he said, "What happened here?"

"He was poisoned," Finley said, feeling irritated. "I told you."

"But how? How was he poisoned?"

Finley scanned the figure and the surroundings illuminated by the strange orb in Titus's hand that glowed like a fluorescent bulb. "Why is he wearing his top hat?" Finley asked. The ringmaster usually had it with him, working his gloved hands across the brim dispelling his nervous tension, but he rarely wore it unless it was during a show.

"Oh, he just got it back," Titus said, his voice removed, like he was speaking from a script. "He had a rip in it for the longest time, but he was superstitious about getting it repaired. Fanny finally convinced him and did the repair and she had..." Titus's words stopped abruptly as his face fell slack.

"Fanny had Sebastian deliver it, didn't she?" Finley said.

"Yes, he dropped it off at the office this evening," Titus said with a small shiver. "And Sebastian didn't say a word, just laid the hat on the table top and smiled."

"And Dave wore it home, probably happy to have it back," Zuma said, her eyes lost.

"Yes," Finley said. "Sebastian could have drenched the inside rim of the hat with poison. There's no way that part of the hat wouldn't come in contact with Dave's skin. It would have been the perfect vehicle, since I know Sebastian was running out of ways to get the oils on Dave."

Titus shook his head with frustration. "All things if we knew about we could have prevented," he said, not staring at Finley, although the remark was directed at him entirely.

Finley now looked back at the last several months and realized he'd made fatal errors. He always thought he could manage the situation. That he could protect Dave. That at some point he could stop Sebastian entirely. But once he set eyes on the big top and Zuma he wanted to have it all. He didn't want to compromise, although he saw now that coming clean from the beginning would have saved Dave's life. How had a noble gesture turned so wrong and made him a villain? His eyes swiveled to Zuma and he realized she was never going to trust him. Not like she did before.

A quick presence entered the trailer, startling everyone but Zuma.

Jack stood in the doorway, breathless. His eyes fell to Dave's body and then flew away at once. "Sebastian's gone," he said between inhalations. "We have to go after him."

"It's no use," Finley said, defeated. "He would have had someone waiting for him. He'll be down the interstate by now."

"Then we have to call the police to investigate this," Jack said irately.

"They won't find anything," Finley said without inflection. "Sebastian's poison isn't traceable. It's an oil that hardly registers on tests. And it produces something that looks like a heart attack. When they find a man in his fifties like this they'll call it cardiac arrest and close the books. Believe me, that's why Knight uses him."

"Then we go after him ourselves," Jack said.

Finley realized that everyone was looking at him this time, waiting for his response. "I can tell you where he's going. Where the compound is, but it's guarded, it's going to take more than we have to get in there."

"You're not a part of 'we,'" Jack said, tearing across the space and almost stepping on Dave to lean over Finley. "*We* will simply tell the police that—"

"You're going to tell them this was foul play when there's nothing to suggest that it was?" Finley said, a cold laugh in his voice. "Are you then going to say a kid with super powers is responsible and he's in a warehouse in LA? Yeah, I'm sure they'll run to help. While you're at it, tell them you belong to an elite race known as Dream Travelers. I'll visit you in the mental hospital."

"The hat though," Titus said. "What if we have it taken in for evidence?"

"Well, if the person who investigates the evidence doesn't die from exposure then they probably won't find anything of use either," Finley said, now speaking with such confidence that he had everyone's attention. "Sebastian is untraceable. His poison is so similar to natural body chemicals that it doesn't trigger any alarms."

"Then we tell them we have a lead on Knight's Kids," Jack said. "If Titus is right about them being associated with hefty crimes then they'll want our tip-off."

"You think Knight doesn't know how to dodge suspicion?" Finley said, shaking his head. "He has his act down. The police knock at his door and all they find is a warehouse full of sailboats in various states of disrepair. They meet a cordial man who offers to take them out sailing once he gets one of the boats going again. There isn't a trace of evidence. Nothing that would cause a judge to issue a search warrant. He doesn't have his kids out where they can be seen and I don't even know what he does with the things we steal. We never see them again after our job is done."

"So then what do we do?" Zuma asked, cradling her arms in tighter.

"I don't know," Titus said, the orb still lighting up the trailer and their faces. "I need time to search this place and figure this out, but I definitely don't want the authorities or the circus alerted until I have time to think. I can do some time travel while sleeping tonight and try and learn what was going on, but I'll have to be careful."

Dream Travelers can go back in time to witness certain events, but it's exhausting, difficult, and can lead to a schism in a person's consciousness. All Titus would have to do is accidentally pick a time when his consciousness was present in that reality and he'd scar himself forever. Past self-interaction was never advisable and illegal in most societies of Dream Travelers.

"Titus, I can help you," Zuma said, but her voice sounded defeated as she stared blankly at the dead body before her.

"Thank you, but I think the fewer people involved the better," he said to the girl. "For now don't breathe a word about this. We're just going to close up this trailer and pretend we haven't found this until I have more time to investigate, all right?"

Everyone nodded.

"All right, Finley," Titus said, sending his eyes in his direction. "I'll need you to write down where this compound is. I've got to figure out how we are going to go after Knight and the location is key to the strategy."

Finley ground his teeth together, his eyes cast on a dark corner. "I'd love to, but as you might remember I can't write. Thanks for reminding the group though," he said.

"Right. Sorry," Titus said at once. "Follow me back to the office and give me the information, would you then?"

"Sure," Finley said, stepping out of the trailer. He waited until Titus and Jack stalked past him, leading the way to the office. When Zuma moved by him, he stuck out an arm to block her. "You have to know that I thought I was doing right. I'm sorry. Please don't—"

She pushed his arm down with a brutal force and stepped in closer, putting her nose even with his. "I didn't love anyone more than I loved the man inside that trailer. He represented everything that was right in my life. And you, whether you meant to or were just too much a coward, ripped that away from me. I won't ever be able to tell him how much he meant to me and that's *your* fault. Since you entered this circus, you've cursed it, Finley," she said, her words spilling out of her in an angry mess.

"Zuma," he said, reaching for her, knowing she couldn't mean all this.

She marched past him immediately. Jack reached out and shoved Finley back. "Lay off her, man. You have to realize you've put this on yourself. Don't make it worse with false apologies."

And suddenly all of Finley's past behaviors at the circus seemed wrong. He thought he'd been strategic, playing things just right. But now he realized that everything he did wasn't considered normal or serious by these people. He'd been trying to protect himself, and them, by not opening up. And now they didn't trust him. Couldn't trust who he was showing them now, which was his true self. How had Knight won again? How had Knight swept in and taken everything dear to him yet again?

Chapter Sixty-Nine

The group marched to Titus's office tent. Zuma really thought she'd go in there, but as she neared, she realized that she couldn't. She needed to get away from all things that reminded her of Dave. As her eyes skirted around the trailers, she realized that was going to be difficult. This grief felt impossible and yet, she hadn't even begun to deal with it. What she wanted was a break. A reason to get away from this group. She needed to be alone. Jack was in front of her, marching with his shoulders high, and he was beside an also tense Finley. Titus led the group.

"So what did you steal?" Jack asked Finley, not sounding curious, but rather intimidating.

Zuma noticed Finley's head drop. She didn't know how she could love and hate someone so much, but that's how she felt for Finley right then. She wanted to wrap her arms around him and tell him he was good enough and also shove him down and kick him in the ribs and tell him he was no one to her. The competing desires ripped at her, tearing her into pieces that could never be sewn back together.

"Everything," Finley stated without inflection.

"Elaborate," Jack said as they walked.

"Stuff," Finley said, easily keeping pace. Zuma thought it must have been difficult for him to move with normal-speed humans since he always had the option of super speed, which she felt was more natural for him. "Cars, money, jewels, artwork…you know the stuff people steal. The stuff of value."

"So you stole whatever that guy told you to?" she heard Jack ask. She wished he'd stop. Leave Finley alone. No, the guy wasn't perfect and had done something unforgivable, but it was doing irreparable damage to her insides to hear the extent of his past. *Maybe that's why he kept it from me?* she thought.

"I did whatever he told me to," Finley said matter-of-factly, "until I realized I could think in my own head, but that took some time. I'm certain none of the other kids ever got there. I have an advantage on them though."

"That's ridiculous," Jack said, scoffing at Finley. They were nearly to Dave and Titus's office. "Of course you can always think in your own head."

"Ever heard of Maslow's Hierarchy of Needs?" Finley asked.

"Of course. How have you, without reading?" he asked and didn't sound like he was trying to insult as much as having a burning curiosity.

"I've spent a lot of time dream traveling, once I realized I had the skill. I've learned by listening to others, by attending lectures at Ivy League universities."

"Uhhh...why didn't you use that time to learn how to read?" Jack asked.

"Because it was more important to me when I entered Vagabond Circus that I sounded educated, rather than actually being educated," Finley said.

"That's pretty smart," Jack admitted. "But what's your point, about Maslow?"

"Well, when your basic needs aren't met then you don't ask questions. You do whatever you're told to get to that next meal. You do whatever you're told as long as you aren't beaten. You may be able to find your own food or fight back, but until you get to that higher level then you don't know that," Finley said.

"So the prisoner remains in chains until they realize there aren't any chains there in the first place...which doesn't happen if they're never given sight?" Jack asked in a hush of poetic disbelief.

"Yeah, I guess," Finley said, turning his head and startling at the sight of Zuma behind them. He had thought she was farther back or had stopped off. His eyes rested on her for a moment before she sent hers to the ground.

"You said you had an advantage on the other kids. What was it?" Jack asked.

"Knight can't get in my head," Finley said.

"Like the way you keep Zuma out?"

Finley tensed at the mention of her name, knowing she was just behind them and listening. "Yes, but he doesn't read thoughts."

"What does he do?"

"He gets into kids' heads and causes them the worst pain, apparently a headache like no other. With the right motivation he can cause an aneurism."

"What?" Jack said, completely grossed out by the idea. "That's how he controls the kids?"

"That's part of it," Finley said, his voice calloused. "He isn't normal, not like most Dream Travelers. He's different. Stronger."

"But why doesn't his power work on you?" Jack asked as they walked, their pace slow in the dark.

"I don't know," Finley said. "I've always had a permanent shield built into my head it seems, but Knight doesn't know it. I pretend his skill works on me. I pretend to be in pain when I know that's what he's doing."

"You're good at acting, aren't you?" Jack said, cold contempt in his voice.

"Look, man, I did what I had to, to survive. I don't expect you to understand."

Jack ran his eyes over Finley's face, still so unsure what to make of him and all he'd shared. "So the other stuff Knight does to get compliance…did he starve and beat you?" Jack asked, and he wasn't trying to pry unthoughtfully. He was trying to make sense of the person who strode beside him and had made so many fatal errors in the last few months.

Zuma's eyelids pressed together with a sudden memory. The three long scars down Finley's back. He'd remembered how he'd gotten them after all, but he didn't want to tell her who he was and where he came from.

Finley threw another look of longing over his shoulder at Zuma, who refused to look back at him. "It doesn't matter, does it? The point is that I'm here." *And screwed up everything*, he thought to himself.

Chapter Seventy

Zuma stopped, her legs unwilling to bring her any closer to the miniature big top. Inside that tent, Vagabond Circus was created. Every single employee had sat in that office across the table from Dave and listened to his speech.

"I refuse to allow the world to turn into a series of gray emotions," Dr. Raydon said to Zuma on her first day. She remembered the smell of dirt and hay in the air. The cool breeze wafting through the open tent. And the excited eyes of the ringmaster as he sat before her. He focused his gaze fondly at the top hat on the table before returning it to her. "In my psychiatric practice grown men told me there was nothing to live for. Women with perfect health told me they were lost. Children complained about having too much responsibility. It was then that I realized how defective the population was. And, you know, the cure was so simple to me."

Dave had then smiled broadly, a knowing look in his eyes. "There's no reason anyone should ever feel lonely when there's love everywhere. There's no excuse for talented people to trudge through life. And if we weigh down our children, the very source that makes the stars blaze in the sky, then we may wake to realize we've lost something irretrievable." He then sucked in a breath and released a fond sigh as he stared out at nothing. "Vagabond Circus has one main goal and that's to inspire. We want to reach those who have lost the spark in their eyes, and the repercussions to that will be tenfold. If we show these people, these lost souls, that magic exists in us, then they will find it in themselves. If you, my friend, want to remind the world that true magic is in each and every person then I invite your talent in my circus. But this isn't just an agreement you enter into with me." His tone suddenly had grown cautious, while still inviting. "You are making this agreement with your fellow humans. You are agreeing to save them from monotony and starched suits and deadlines. You're agreeing to make them feel something. And part of that agreement is to give them the gift to smile for no reason. To laugh unabashedly. To revert to who they used to be before they forgot how incredible life is." Then Dave would stick out a gloved hand, offering it to the would-be Vagabond Circus member. "If this sounds like the right place and job for you then no words are necessary, let's just shake on it."

And the ringmaster was strategic in his approach, because most had been so inspired and reenergized by Dave's speech that a handshake was all they could manage. But now that speech was dead, just as the man who had given it hundreds of times was too. Would his circus die now? The idea made Zuma want to throw herself to the ground. Beat the earth under her feet. Kick until the bruises and gashes she caused on her body from the tantrum stole her attention from her bleeding heart.

"Zuma," Jack said, turning and realizing she hadn't moved. Her eyes were frozen on a single spot, not seeing it. She had made herself momentarily catatonic to keep everything locked inside her.

Jack retreated back to her, his face kind. "Are you coming?"

Zuma tried to shake her head but it was useless. "No," she finally whispered.

"Okay, do you want me to take you to your trailer?" Jack had a worry in his tone, like he was afraid his voice could break her.

She was acting fragile. That was unacceptable. Zuma pulled her eyes up and found Finley staring at her like he didn't recognize her suddenly. *Stone. I'm stone,* she thought.

"No," she said with a deliberate force. She pulled her gaze to Jack standing in front of her. "Help Titus. I'll see you later."

He nodded and then she turned and took calculated steps away. Each stride she took peeled back her determination and the beast inside of her threatened to break loose, bringing tears of unending grief to the surface. Once it was loose then it would never be tamed. She would be its prisoner.

The trailer door shut behind her and Zuma jerked the last remaining strap off the beast. She always knew she was meant to be broken. The girl crumbled to her knees, her arms gripping her abdomen as the tears tore out of her. Her cries spasmed through her core, bringing a pain unlike any she'd experienced. Last year she broke three ribs and this felt worse. *How can emotions bring such physical agony to the body?* she wondered. Those ribs were healed by Fanny, but there was nothing the older woman could do for Zuma now. She was forever broken.

Chapter Seventy-One

*J*ack didn't knock on the trailer door. He knew Zuma wouldn't hear him over her tears, her muffled cries. And he'd been able to operate out of adrenaline, but staring at Zuma, curled up in a ball and sobbing, ended his stoic sabbatical. He kneeled to the ground and covered her with his arms, and joined her in her grief. Large sobs raked through his chest as he came to terms with what Zuma had faced ten minutes prior. Dr. Dave Raydon was dead. The founder of Vagabond Circus was never coming back. Their ringmaster had been murdered. People fear the worst and this for Jack was it. Just the realization that Dave was gone made the old anxiety race through the acrobat's head. He didn't know who he was without Dave to remind him.

"You're a star, my boy," the ringmaster told him before his first show. "I'll remind you of that as often as you need, but one day you'll need to believe it on your own."

But Dave couldn't slap Jack on the shoulder and boom those three words. And Jack hadn't gotten to the place where he believed it on his own. He always thought he had time. Time for Dave's words to sink in. But they hadn't and now without Dave he was "just Jack," the boy who hadn't met his family's standards. He was a loser.

Zuma shifted to a sitting position, cradling Jack as he cried on her shoulder. They had switched positions, and that was fine by Zuma since for the moment she couldn't squeeze out another tear. This state was fleeting, though, and soon she'd crumble from the tears that had only momentarily retreated.

The two acrobats held onto each for a good part of an hour. Finally Jack stood, pulling Zuma up with him. Then he sat her on the sofa, taking great care to ensure she was okay before he fetched them both water from the refrigerator.

"How can he be gone?" Zuma said, staring blankly at the wall.

"I don't know," Jack said, his voice raw.

He handed her a bottle of water but she simply shook her head at it.

"And who would ever want Dave dead?" Jack said, setting the bottle beside her on the table.

"Dead! He's dead," she said and brought her hands up to catch the tears that had returned. "I...can't...take...this..." she said through hyperventilated breaths.

"Shhh," Jack soothed, sitting beside her and wrapping her trembling body with his own. "You are my girl of stone. You can deal with this, but you don't have to all at once. We will deal with it together."

She nodded into his shoulder, her sobs having dissipated briefly. "God, Jack, what would I do without you? I'd be an even bigger mess."

Jack pulled back, his eyes weighted. "I know. Me too." Then he reached up and pushed away a strand of hair that was matted to her cheek by tears of glue. "I'm here for you, Zuma. Lean on me and I'll lean on you. We will need that so we can be strong for the rest of the circus. They will find out soon."

Zuma released a strained breath. "Yeah," she said in a croak. And then realized Jack's hand was still resting on her chin. She looked at him. Really looked at him and recognized the expression in his eyes. She made to pull away from him just as he leaned into her, like he was going to hug her but then his lips pressed against hers. A raw ache in the kiss. Their pain echoed in the act of affection. He pressed his mouth to hers for only a second and then pulled back. It had been a chaste kiss, but it communicated so much. It made so many things clear for the both of them.

"Sorry, I didn't mean to..." Jack said. "I'm not thinking."

"We are both trying to find comfort right now. It's okay, Jack," she said, pushing back on the sofa, away from him.

"I always pictured that..." Jack said and then couldn't finish his sentence.

Zuma knew he wanted her to make it easier by her just reading his thoughts, and she needed to. Needed to know they shared the same thought.

Just lips. Jack's mouth on hers just felt like lips. No spark. No power. The kiss didn't stop her heart or speed it up. And the only relief that day came when she read the thoughts sitting on top of Jack's head.

"Well, at least we know now," she said.

223

"Was it the same for you?" he asked, sitting back on his heels, away from her.

She nodded. "Good thing we never screwed up our careers trying to find out before now." And then the implications of that statement brought their current reality back to the forefront of her mind. None of it mattered anymore. Her career. The rules. Her passing desires.

Dave was dead.

"Jack, we cannot allow the circus to fail. If we owe Dave anything then we have to keep it going. No matter what," she said, standing, realizing she wasn't crying. The dull ache smothered the tears for now.

Jack nodded. "I promise, we will keep it going."

Zuma didn't know what he was going to do, but she knew that if there was one person she could stake certainty in, it was Jack Fuller. He would never let Dave down.

"I have to go now. I feel like I'm about to pass out," she said, retreating to her bedroom, stumbling on her feet. Jack watched her go, knowing what he had to do. Even if it killed him. He couldn't let Zuma down. He couldn't let Vagabond Circus down. He had to do it for Dave.

Chapter Seventy-Two

*F*inley described where the location of Knight's compound could be found to Titus. He didn't really know street names, except the ones he'd learned from George Anders when he escaped and was looking for a hiding spot. Still, he knew how to describe the things around the compound. He'd been in and out of there so many times, on so many different jobs. LA was large, but the compound had a few things surrounding it that were distinct. Titus jotted all this down, asking follow-up questions as Finley spoke. It burned him up the way the creative director could form questions and write at the same time. Titus probably didn't even realize what a gift he had, and that he was just flaunting it in front of Finley's face.

He left the miniature big top without being dismissed, needing fresh air. Jack had left it twenty minutes before, saying that he thought someone should check on Zuma. Finley wanted to be that person. Needed to be, but there was no way for him to create that reality for himself, not after how everything happened.

The people of Vagabond Circus would find out the news of Dave's death tomorrow. The authorities would be brought in. Titus was only going to allow himself that night to investigate, but Finley already knew what he'd find. Little evidence and no way to identify the murderer, except by the deadly poison he left behind. And that was inefficient to catch Sebastian. He was already back under Knight's protection. Finley knew this.

The grounds were almost silent as Finley walked through the trailers, his mind tearing at itself. He stopped, struck by a stream of light. It stood out in the dark trailer area, everyone else's curtains drawn for the night. And the person in the trailer was like her light, she shone in the dark. She was what always captured his attention. Zuma was the light in Finley's life and he had ruined everything. He had done the one thing she'd never forgive, failed to stop a man she loved from dying. Finley had almost allowed it, he saw now. He had allowed himself to be distracted by Zuma, and the circus, and by spoiling his needs and desires for the first time ever. Could Zuma ever understand that she had been the reason he didn't catch Sebastian? Was it incredibly unfair to tell her that once she entered his life he lost sight of everything as he feared he'd do? He wasn't thinking clearly, that was certain. Anxiety and loss were creating chaos in his head.

Like he had months ago, he stood watching through the open window as Zuma crossed the space in her trailer. To Finley's relief she sat on the sofa in full view. Looking at her made him feel almost human again.

A breeze drifted through the campgrounds smelling of pine and leaves. Medford was just a few miles away. Their first show for its people was tomorrow, but he and Zuma wouldn't be performing together again. He knew that for certain. She'd never work with him in the big top again.

Zuma wasn't laughing as she was the first time he'd spied her through her window. It tortured him in new ways to watch her cry. Painful moans escaped her, seeming to vibrate her chest. He wanted to comfort her, needed to wrap his arms around her. He knew they had a bond unlike any other. He could make her feel better. Finley remembered her lips on his, the way they filled him with a love so pure they erased so many scars inside of him. He knew he could do that for her. There was something they did for each other. To each other.

Finley bolstered his confidence and took three steps in the direction of Zuma's trailer and then he froze. Through the window he spied Jack crouch in front of her. He didn't hesitate before wrapping her in his arms. She reciprocated pulling him closer, burying her head in his shoulder as she cried. Finley couldn't move. He was frozen, forcing himself to watch the last thing he wanted to see. He'd *had* Zuma. She was his to hold and he lost her. Made her hate him.

Fire burned in his chest as the pair held onto each other. Jack finally pulled back, but not enough. He stayed close to Zuma, whose face was red from crying. Jack slipped his hand across her cheek, probably pushing away tears. And then Finley watched his fingers pause on the side of her face. He knew what was coming. Knew watching this was creating new scars, but still he remained focused, spying. And then Jack leaned in and kissed Zuma. It wasn't a passionate kiss, like the one they'd shared, but it was still a kiss, a slow one, reeking with their pain. And then Zuma pulled away, her hands at her side pushing her back on the couch. *Was she pushing away from Jack?* Finley couldn't tell. Maybe he was believing what he needed to. But then she shook her head. Stood suddenly. Disappeared into the back of the trailer. Finley's focus blurred, his head suddenly spinning with confusion and pain. It didn't matter what he'd just seen. He knew before witnessing Zuma kiss Jack that he'd lost her forever.

Chapter Seventy-Three

Zuma fell asleep less than a minute after Jack left. She hadn't meant to abandon him, but she couldn't grant him company when she desperately needed to be alone. Having not slept since she was in Finley's arms she fell asleep immediately, her mind falling straight into REM sleep, dreams and nightmares crashing down on her.

It felt like awakening in a nightmare when Zuma stirred the next morning, her head heavy from crying. In her dreams she'd forgotten her reality, but now it pressed in all around her. Dave was dead.

She showered and pulled on a pair of jeans and a knit top she never wore. She really only wore workout clothes but she wasn't working out today. She didn't care if Titus decided not to cancel the shows, they'd go on without her. She couldn't look in the direction of the big top. Who would replace Dave as ringmaster? It was wrong to replace him, and then to lose Vagabond Circus was also wrong. It was Dave's legacy and couldn't just crumble in his absence. Tears again streamed down her recently powdered cheeks. Zuma didn't want to leave her trailer sobbing but soon she had to get out of there.

She dug through her drawers, searching for keys she hadn't used in a long time. Finally she found them at the back of a drawer of art supplies. She hardly used her car, but it was on the lot somewhere. Dave always had it moved with the circus and ready for her if she cared to drive it. She ran her fingers over the Audi emblem on the car fob, her head swimming with the multiple things Dave had done for her. It was overwhelming. He took care of her. He cared for everyone at Vagabond Circus. Who would do that now?

She exited the trailer with her head down. People were starting to stir. Soon they would get the news. Titus would call a meeting or something. Zuma wouldn't be there. She'd be as far away from the circus as she could get. And since she'd pushed him away last night she decided that she'd invite Jack to join her. She didn't think he'd want to stay here either. He always wanted to get away from the circus when things got too difficult, and what was more difficult than Dave being murdered? Nothing.

Zuma hoped that Jack kept his distance though. They were friends and that's what she needed now. Her life couldn't grow anymore complicated with choices and frustrations. She knocked on his trailer door and was surprised when it swung open from the small force of her rap.

"Jack?" she called.

No answer. The trailer was dark. Empty. She didn't care for dark, empty trailers anymore. It felt like a curse.

But on the bulletin board over his sofa there was something out of place. Her eyes swiveled to it immediately. Over the pictures of the acrobats performing nationwide was a white piece of paper. On it in large black letters was her name: "ZUMA."

She crossed the space and ripped the note down. Her eyes moved too quickly across it, taking in the important words: *protect, circus, left, revenge.*

A hive of fear started to swarm inside her chest. She took a deep breath and forced her eyes to the top.

Zuma,

I know that Vagabond Circus will never be the same without Dave. But it is doomed to be half of what it was with his murderer roaming free. I trust Titus with most things, but I don't think he'll take the risk to really go after Knight. He'll take the safe option: keep an eye on him, up security, recruit with more scrutiny. I'm going to protect what Dave created. I'm going to save the circus. I've left to exact Dave's revenge. Please take care of the circus. I'll be back soon.
Love,
Jack

"No," she said out loud. She didn't know what he was thinking. He was obviously motivated by his grief. Why had he left her? Why had he left her behind?

Zuma turned and raced for Titus's office. Maybe it wasn't too late. Maybe she could still catch Jack.

She raced to the mini big top Titus and Dave shared as their office. She choked on tears at the thought of Dave. Could she really enter his sacred office space knowing he'd left it for good? Her thoughts turned to Jack as she pushed the flap back and stepped into the tent.

Chapter Seventy-Four

$\mathcal{T}$itus's head flipped up, startled when Zuma entered. His eyes were rimmed with red and he was hunched over a mess of papers.

"Oh, Zuma. It's you," he said, seeming distracted. He shuffled through a stack of pages filled with numbers. "I don't know what to do first. Do I tell the circus what's happened or call the authorities? I've been dream traveling all night and Finley's right, there's no discernable clues." He looked up at Zuma, an expression of real fear in his eyes. "What do I do?" he said and she realized how alone he was. Dave always made the plans. Titus carried them out. He was lost to run Vagabond Circus and worse than that, he had lost his best friend and had no time to grieve with the decisions weighing on him.

"Titus, have you seen Jack?"

"Well, yes, he came by last night when I wasn't dream traveling. It was late though."

"What did he say?" Zuma said in a panic, rushing forward and planting her hands on his table top.

Titus squinted at her. "Nothing really. He kept me company for a few minutes and then asked to borrow my car. He said he wanted to go somewhere to clear his head."

"Titus, you didn't give him your car, did you?"

"Yes, Zuma, of course I did."

She planted both of her hands on her head. "He went after Knight!"

"What? Why would he do that?" Titus said, suddenly standing, causing papers to spill from his lap.

"He wants revenge."

Titus nodded solemnly. "Right. And he didn't think…"

"You'd do it fast enough," she said, completing his thought.

Titus winced from the statement. But then recovered with a look of relief. "But he won't know where to go. Finley gave me directions to Knight's warehouse directly. Jack wasn't here for that part. He won't know the location."

"Where are the directions?" Zuma said, sweeping her eyes across the various pieces of paper lining the office, using her eidetic memory to assist her. Worry coated her face at once. "Titus, I don't think it's here."

"Don't fret," Titus said, sensing her stress. "I put it right here under the lamp," he said, and went to lift up the Tiffany lamp on the side of the table. It was where he kept his working notebook; important pieces of paper were tucked into the folder on the inside flap.

He slipped the notebook out from under the base of the lamp.

"It's not going to be in there," Zuma said, her head beating with adrenaline.

Titus's head shook. "What? Of course it is," he said and then sucked in a sudden breath as he found the folder empty of the last paper he stuck in it. His startled eyes slid up to Zuma's.

"He kept you company, you say? Did Jack flip through your play book?"

"Yes," he said in a hoarse whisper. "But he often does."

"Damn it," Zuma said. "He's really gone then. And he's going to get himself killed."

"What are we going to do?" Titus said, gripping his hair in his hands.

"I'm going after him," Zuma said, forming a plan in her head.

"How?" Titus said in sudden worry and disbelief.

"Someone here still knows the address," she said, and dreaded the words at the same time.

Titus nodded with understanding.

"Call a meeting and then the authorities. Maybe the forensic team will find something that you didn't," she said. She knew she probably sounded like Dave, bossing him around, but she didn't care.

"I doubt it, Zuma. It looks like he had a heart attack."

"Well, then also report Sebastian's disappearance."

Titus nodded.

Zuma was about to race out of the tent and paused. She reversed her direction and ran up to Titus and he folded her in his arms. His chest rose and fell several times as he battled to keep his tears inside.

Zuma pulled away. "You can do this, Titus. You have to. The show has to go on. I'll bring Jack back, but you take care of Vagabond Circus, okay?"

He nodded as she turned and left.

Chapter Seventy-Five

*T*he one person Zuma needed right then was the last person she wanted to ask for help. She wasn't her usual stoic self in the wake of Dave's death and Jack's disappearance. Emotion was knocking on her chest, begging to come out. But she had to lock it away.

Zuma rapped on the trailer door. A few seconds later Finley pulled it back, his eyes regretful and confused. She tried not to allow her gaze to land on his, but immediately she was swept into a hazel green sky of him. She hiccupped on a rogue emotion that burst past her walls.

"Zuma?" Finley said in disbelief. He stood frozen, everything about him tortured as he studied her.

"Can I come in?" she said, her voice careful.

Finley nodded, stepping back. Everything about him had changed in the past twenty-four hours. He was trying, where before he didn't. He was paying silent penance, whereas before he banished his guilt.

She turned to him when he closed the door. Zuma opened her mouth to ask her question but the way he looked at her, it ripped her fragile heart to pieces. He'd betrayed her and he knew it, and it strangely hurt her to see him with his remorse.

"Stop looking at me," she said finally.

"Where would you like me to look?" he said, his voice raw with emotion.

"I don't care. Away."

Finley took in a strained breath and moved his gaze to the open window. "Why have you come here?" he said, his voice dead of his normal life.

"I need you to take me to Knight's compound," she said, trying to sound natural, entitled.

And he disobeyed her wishes at once, jerking his eyes to her. "What? No!"

It was Zuma's turn to shift her eyes away. To the blank wall. Finley's trailer was bare of personal effects and she realized that was because he had nothing. "Fine, then don't take me, but you have to tell me where it is," she said.

"I already told Titus," Finley argued.

"And that information has disappeared," she said at once.

"Then I'll give him the information again."

"No, give it to me," Zuma urged.

Without looking at her it was so hard for Finley to see her true conviction, and yet he still felt it and it hurt him in ways he didn't understand. "Why?"

"Because I'm going to Knight's compound," she said.

And Zuma knew he was moving for her before he did. She didn't budge, didn't pull her eyes from the window, although he moved until he was only inches away. From her peripheral she could see the urgent panic in his eyes. "No, Zuma. You can't do that," he said, his voice pulsating with fear.

"Jack took the address and left. He's going to try and take Knight out himself," she said, pulling the note from her pocket, and then, remembering Finley couldn't read it, she tucked it back in her jeans.

Finley blew out a tight breath. "What is he thinking?! He's doesn't stand a chance in Knight's compound."

"He isn't thinking," Zuma said. "He's stricken by grief. Grief that *you're* responsible for."

Finley reached over with his super speed and grabbed her jaw, but gently pulled it so she was facing him. "Look at me," he commanded.

For a long few seconds he waited, but she didn't bring her stubborn eyes to his, instead kept them angled away.

He dropped his hand, exasperated. "To hell with this all, Zuma, but I'm not responsible for Dave's death. I came here to prevent it and I'm sorry I failed, but I'm not to blame."

"If you would have told us though…" Zuma said.

"Don't you see that I tried to stop this? I watched Dave every night. I stood guard outside his trailer so Sebastian couldn't touch him in his sleep and kill him, or go into his trailer and put poison out for him. And so many times I broke into Dave's trailer and wiped it down, endangering my life to keep him safe," Finley said, almost breathless, but still he pushed out another sentence. "I failed, but don't you see I tried?"

"But you don't see that Sebastian found a way around all that?" Zuma said. "There was no way you could have saved Dave last night. The only way would have been to tell him the truth so he could have gotten rid of Sebastian. If only you'd told him...or me."

"If I told you then you'd know where I was from. You'd look at me like you're doing now, like I'm an uneducated thief."

"I'm not looking at you," she said, her eyes pinned on the carpet.

He shook his head at this. "I really thought I could stop Sebastian. I made mistakes. I couldn't stop him," Finley said and sucked in a breath, trying to loosen the tension in his chest. "But, Zuma, you have to see that I didn't do this."

"But you could have told Dave!" Zuma screamed so loud, everything seeming to pour out of her at once.

"It wouldn't mean he wouldn't be dead," he said at the fraction of the volume she'd just used.

And then they were silent, but not long.

"Finley, please help. Tell me where to find Knight."

"No," he said, his voice haunted.

"Then take me there."

"Zuma, you don't know what you're asking me to do. I can't go back there," he said, pinning his head in his hands. Just then she allowed herself to look at him. She saw him for who he was, a survivor. If she represented the mystery of the circus then he was the power. He was strength, even in his weakest moment.

"Finley, if I don't go then Jack won't return, will he? They'll kill him, won't they? He'll be caught. Am I right?"

He brought his head up, but kept his eyes off her; the pair were taking turns looking and not looking at each other. "Yes," he said. "There is no way an outsider can get in and out of there alive. There's so much security. So many traps."

"Then you see why I need you," Zuma pleaded.

A cold laugh fell out of his mouth. "Oh, is that why you need me?"

"Finley," she said, half begging, half frustrated.

"I saw you kiss Jack last night," he said, his voice dead.

"You what?" she said and turned, putting her back to him. "How dare you? You were spying on me."

236

"I wasn't spying," he said in an almost whisper. "I was just passing by. I wish I hadn't seen it, believe me."

"I didn't kiss Jack, for the record," she said, her face hot all over suddenly, her ears on fire.

"That's not what it looked like," Finley said, and wasn't even sure why. Zuma wasn't his, never would be. It didn't matter.

"He kissed me. And…"

"And what?" Finley said, desperate to know what came next in that sentence.

"The kiss, after all this time of waiting and wondering…it…"

"It what?" Finley thought he was going to explode. Zuma couldn't speak fast enough for him. He needed to know it all. Good or bad or heartbreaking. He couldn't not know.

"It…I…I didn't feel anything," she admitted out loud for the first time.

"Are you telling me that so I'll help you rescue Jack?"

"God no," she said so fast he wanted to believe her. "I just want him back safe. That's all."

"Then *I'll* go. *I'll* get Jack and bring him back," Finley said, surrendering in that moment.

"No, I'm not letting you go alone. We would be better as a team."

"Zuma, you have no idea about these people," Finley said. "The things they'd do to you…I can't allow it."

"I get you see me as sheltered but—"

"No!" he barked, making her jump. "I see you as perfect and I don't want anything to happen to you. Even if you'll never be mine."

"Finley," she said and turned and looked at him. It did exactly what she feared. It made her feel that she was truly broken. How could she want someone and not allow him into her heart although he was willing? How as humans had they screwed up so much? She stared into his wanting eyes and felt cursed by them.

"I'll help you," he said, sounding defeated. "I'll take you to Knight's compound, but you have to listen to me."

Zuma stayed silent, sensing there was more.

And just as the five senses operate naturally she felt the power of her telepathy opening up like Finley was pulling her into his thoughts.

One day you have to give me another chance, Zuma. You have to forgive me, she heard so plainly in his thoughts.

She dropped her eyes, unsure what to say. And she'd expected that Finley was just trying to relay one message to her and then he would close the door to his mind again. Bolt it shut. But he didn't. He invited her in and allowed Zuma to sense his mind, to realize she was everywhere in his thoughts. And after only a few seconds of perusal she knew his mind was like him, so very enchanting to her.

With a great effort she pulled her focus out of Finley's mind and shook his thoughts away from her. "Please don't ask that of me, Finley. I won't lie to you, I can't ever forgive you for what you've done," Zuma said.

He nodded, seeming to have expected this answer. "Fine, I'll still take you," he said.

And then his mouth closed but she heard his voice in her head again. *I was foolish to ever think you'd love me anyway.*

Zuma wanted to reach across the space and tie her arms around Finley. Not because he had scorned her with that exact thought. She did things because she wanted to and not out of persuasion. But Zuma always knew what true love's kiss would feel like, and she was broken by the fact that she would never be with her true love, because she could never forgive him.

To continue your journey with Vagabond Circus, purchase your copy of Paralyzed, Book II in the series. It's available starting February 15, 2016. Enjoy a sample chapter at the end of this book.

Acknowledgements:

Thank you so much to my readers. It goes without saying, but I can't do this without you. What you probably don't know is that I read every email, every message, every single thing you send. Sometimes it's hard to respond, since I can't seem to stop writing, but I do love hearing from you. And in truth, now I write because of you. In the beginning, I did because I was driven to, and now I do it more and more because people read my books, send me encouraging letters, and leave lovely reviews. I'm not going to lie. If I published my first series and it tanked, I probably would have quit. But it didn't and you all kept me going. It's not that I'm a quitter, as much as a realist.

Thank you to my fan group on Goodreads. Dominque and Maja are such great supporters. And your family too. Thank you to all the members. I love my Goodreads family. I've found the best people there. Thank you to Oak and the support of the people in the Book Trailers group. Another wonderful bunch of people. I've loved connecting with the readers and authors there.

Thank you to my editor Christine LePorte. I love working with you. You're work makes mine salable. And your feedback keeps me sane. I plan to do this for a long time, and I hope you're there to edit all the books. It's such a blessing to have a long time editor who has worked on all my books. I think it makes my books better.

Thank you to Andrei Bat. Seriously, do you just wake up every morning and say, "I'm a freaking genius"? Because you probably should. This cover was having some dimension issues because, as I tend to do, I overcomplicated the idea. However, you swooped in with the perfect design. I was blown away.

Thank you to my beta readers, Colleen, Heidi, Melinda, Kimberly, Elizabeth. My editor does an incredible job, but you all serve such an important role in making my books great! Thank you!

Thank you to the awesome blogger whose support is crucial to my success. I really can't express how much it blows me away that you all lead lives, have jobs, and also run fantastic blogs that support readers and authors. You're incredible. Thank you!

Thank you to Carole. I hope you know how helpful all your advice is to me. I take it all, stuff it in my pockets and use it every step of the way. A lot of my recent success is because of you!

Thank you to my fans and readers. Seriously, you all amaze me with your support. Thank you to Kathy, Kelly, Heidi, Alicia, Sarah, Katy, Maria, Marie, Kit, Lesley, Nicole, Becca, Stephanie, Susi, Chelsea, Anna, Kariny, Katie, Kimberly, Karen, Michelle, Christina, and Jamie.

Thank you to BOD. I was reviewing marketing strategy and where most of my sales have come from. No big surprise. If it wasn't for BOD readers then I wouldn't be writing. My most faithful supporters come from that group. You know who you are and I know you rock!

Thank you to Linda. You have always supported me. Encouraged me. Believed in me when I thought I was just a loon. You're such an incredible person and half the state of Oregon wouldn't be as awesome as it is if it wasn't for you.

Thank you to Dave. You were my first boss and you may not realize this, but you taught me so much in those first formative years. I constantly spout Davism. Can't help it. Anyway, you're the inspiration behind Dave Raydon. There you go. Now you know. Or you don't. This is why people should read the Acknowledgment page. Anyway, you're an incredible manager and I watched time and time again as you took people and pulled the raw talent out of them. Oh, and you're just an inspiration for the character, so don't worry about the whole killing off Dave thing. That's not what I want for you. Or the plump part either. We all know you're rugged and handsome.

Thank you to my family. Seriously, I know you all have to love me because it's required, but I think you also do because you just plain love me. Thank you for everything. XOOXOXO

Thank you to my husband, Luke Noffke. Not only are you an amazing beta reader, a wonderful supporter and lend me a boatload of encouragement, but you're also super smart, a great father and a loving husband. Thanks! If you weren't who you were, I wouldn't be who I am. And we're kind of cool.

Thank you to my daughter. How do you get better every year? You stun me with your love and the sparkle in your eyes. And if it wasn't for you this novel wouldn't have happened. It was that trip to the circus with you that sparked the idea for this series. The best ideas really start with you.

Thank you all!

Love,

Sarah

About the Author:

Sarah is the author of the Lucidites, Reverians, Vagabond Circus and Ren series. She's been everything from a corporate manager to a hippie. Her taste for adventure has taken her all over the world. If you can't find her at the gym, then she's probably at the frozen yogurt shop. If you can't find her there then she probably doesn't want to be found. She is a self-proclaimed hermit, with spontaneous urges to socialize during full moons and when Mercury is in retrograde. Sarah lives in Central California with her family. To learn more about Sarah please visit: http://www.sarahnoffke.com

Check out other work by this author:

The Lucidites Series:
Awoken, #1:
Around the world humans are hallucinating after sleepless nights.

In a sterile, underground institute the forecasters keep reporting the same events.

And in the backwoods of Texas, a sixteen-year-old girl is about to be caught up in a fierce, ethereal battle.

Meet Roya Stark. She drowns every night in her dreams, spends her hours reading classic literature to avoid her family's ridicule, and is prone to premonitions—which are becoming more frequent. And now her dreams are filled with strangers offering to reveal what she has always wanted to know: Who is she? That's the question that haunts her, and she's about to find out. But will Roya live to regret learning the truth?

Stunned, #2
Revived, #3

The Reverians Series:
Defects, #1:

In the happy, clean community of Austin Valley, everything appears to be perfect. Seventeen-year-old Em Fuller, however, fears something is askew. Em is one of the new generation of Dream Travelers. For some reason, the gods have not seen fit to gift all of them with their expected special abilities. Em is a Defect—one of the unfortunate Dream Travelers not gifted with a psychic power. Desperate to do whatever it takes to earn her gift, she endures painful daily injections along with commands from her overbearing, loveless father. One of the few bright spots in her life is the return of a friend she had thought dead—but with his return comes the knowledge of a shocking, unforgivable truth. The society Em thought was protecting her has actually been betraying her, but she has no idea how to break away from its authority without hurting everyone she loves.

Rebels, #2
Warriors, #3

Ren: The Man Behind the Monster:

Born with the power to control minds, hypnotize others, and read thoughts, Ren Lewis, is certain of one thing: God made a mistake. No one should be born with so much power. A monster awoke in him the same year he received his gifts. At ten years old. A prepubescent boy with the ability to control others might merely abuse his powers, but Ren allowed it to corrupt him. And since he can have and do anything he wants, Ren should be happy. However, his journey teaches him that harboring so much power doesn't bring happiness, it steals it. Once this realization sets in, Ren makes up his mind to do the one thing that can bring his tortured soul some peace. He must kill the monster. *Note* This book is NA and has strong language, violence and sexual references.

Spanish version of The Lucidites Series:
Awoken: Despertada
Stunned: Atonita

Sneak Peek of Paralyzed

(Vagabond Circus Series, #2):

Chapter One

Summer had died along with Dr. Dave Raydon. Winds laced with hints of pine and an icy chill swept through Vagabond Circus. Soon the cool nights would turn the leaves on the trees in Medford, Oregon to dazzling yellows, vibrant reds and bright oranges. The people of Vagabond Circus would be gone before the change. That was Titus' plan. He didn't have many plans now that his circus partner was cold and rigor mortis was setting in, but he knew they'd stick to the schedule. In one week they'd pack up the big top and caravan down to Redding, California. That had been the schedule before Dave died and Titus was holding to it. The show must go on.

The ringmaster had been dead for twelve long hours and still his body lay on the floor of his trailer, everything was how it had been when he died. Everyone knew that Dave didn't exit his trailer until nine each morning. It was only after he'd meditated, ate a breakfast he prepared for himself, and fashioned his gloves did he step out of the trailer with a wide smile, greeting the open air and the members of Vagabond Circus. When his round face didn't pop out of the trailer at its normal hour, Titus knew his time was limited. People would start to wonder. They would come looking for the ringmaster, Titus knew this. Dave's presence was the sun to Vagabond Circus. His round happy face started each day for most. And his presence marked hope and growth and light. And now he was dead. It was like the sun had burned out for Vagabond Circus. How would its crops grow without their ringmaster to shine on them?

At ten past the hour people began looking around, wondering if Dave had snuck past them. But Dave wasn't the sneaking type. He bounded out into open spaces welcoming a new experience and all the magic that a new day brought. When Dave Raydon entered a space, people knew it. Felt it. Things shifted. Usually people's demeanors shifted too. Even Sunshine, the girl with an affliction to smiling, softened in Dave's presence. He was a person who brought goodness to everything and everyone. "How may I serve to bring more love?" was the mantra he practiced during his daily meditations. And it's how he lived his life, and his life was one that did make the world better.

But Dr. Raydon was dead now. He wouldn't be springing out of his trailer or greeting the children who were playing in Fanny's area with open arms. The caregiver hurried over now to Titus who stood between his own trailer and Dave's. The Creative Director's tentative eyes shifted between the various onlookers, Dave's door, and the phone in his hand. Titus was paralyzed, unsure which thing to do first: tell the circus or call the authorities. He was the sole person remaining at Vagabond Circus who knew the fate of the ringmaster. And what happened next was *his* decision. This was *his* circus now.

Fanny regarded him for a long moment, her fist on her meaty hips. "Titus why don't you relieve some of your obvious stress and tell me what in God's name is going on? Where is Dave?" she said, motioning to the trailer door, her voice a hush. "And why do you look so troubled?"

He tucked the phone in his jean's pocket. "Fanny we need to call an all-circus-meeting. Have everyone meet me in the big top in five minutes."

Paralyzed, Book II in the Vagabond Circus Series coming February 15, 2016.

Sneak Peek of Defects (The Reverians Series, #1):

Prologue

My fingers tremble as I assemble the pieces.

He'll be back in a few minutes.

I blink away the sweat dripping into my eyes. I can't afford to swipe it away.

The two ceramic pieces chip at the edges as I try to match them up to how they should align. I know he keeps glue in his front desk drawer. Everyone does. *We fix things that are broken.* I slip the tube from the drawer and dab a glob of adhesive on the center of one of the broken pieces and then press it against its counterpart. I'm so used to fixing things, but now I'm not doing it because it's the law. I'm doing it because if he finds out I was here he'll punish me with night terrors again.

The pieces slip just as the glue is setting. Ragged breath hitches in my parched throat. *If he finds out I was here, that there was a trespassing...* I press the pieces together so firmly the glue seeps out and threatens to cement my fingers to the statue. Footsteps in the hallway. Soft-soled shoes. His. I know *his* gait.

I release my fingers from the statue. It teeters but stands, looking unmarked by the fall it recently experienced. But will it stay up?

The envelope still sits neatly on the mahogany desk. It was my own nervous reaction to it that shook the statue down from its high place on the shelf. I knew I should come here and look first. Knew I'd find information. My father always told me, "Instinct is the gods tapping you on the head." Still, I wish I knew what lay inside the folds of that envelope that bears my name.

The key slides into the lock, a sound like a reluctant bell. I close my eyes and dream travel back to my body, pulling my consciousness out of its current location.

Chapter One

My house is haunted. I've never seen a ghost in it, but Tutu, whose gift is seeing the dead, says there are many who reside in our home. I haven't received my gift yet. At age seventeen that's rare. My sister, Dee, teases me that this is a sure sign our mother had an affair with Ed, the mailman, who's a Middling—a person who can't dream travel, has no gifts. I pretend this is a joke but with each passing year I believe it could be a possibility. My family is pureblooded Dream Travelers and they're all gifted with strong talents since puberty. And although I dream travel I have no other talents, which is a first in the Fuller family. My grandmother, who I call Tutu, has three abilities. My mother, two. Even my older sister, Dee, has her gift—which she spends every single opportunity rubbing in my face. Since I have no super power I've reverted to spreading false rumors about her all over Austin Valley.

"You're going to be late again," Dee says, sounding pleased by the prospect.

"Thanks for the reminder," I say, not meaning it.

I slip my favorite organic bamboo blouse over my head and hurry out of the room I share with my sister. With one hand I smooth my hair and the other guides me down the banister as I take the stairs two at a time.

"I'm sure his mother would love the opportunity to be interviewed," my mother says to a visitor in her usual subdued tone. I don't even chance a glance at her as I scurry to the entryway, head low. Maybe this visitor will actually save me from being scolded. The brass doorknob is cold under my palm. I wrench the door open and pull it back, a rush of warm June air greeting me at once.

"Not so fast there, Em," my mother says.

I freeze. Push the door closed. Turn and face her.

My mother stands in the threshold of the sitting room, her hands firmly pinned to her hips. "You're late for your meeting with your father."

"Which is why I'm rushing to get out of here," I say, sweeping my eyes to the person my mother was talking to. Zack. He's giving me a curious expression, arms crossed in front of his suit jacket.

"Have I not instilled in you the proper manners to know you should greet and say farewell to everyone you come in contact with?" she says, shaking her head at me.

"Hi, Mother. Hi, Zack. I'm leaving before Father kills me for being late. Goodbye," I say, turning on my toes. I slip my hand onto the door handle again, but don't even dare to open it.

"Em?"

I turn and stare at my mother. Her red hair is pulled back into a tight low bun. Her sleeveless black turtleneck must be stifling in this heat. "Yes, Mother?" I say, working hard to keep the irritation out of my voice.

"You weren't planning on leaving the house like that, were you?" she asks with a disappointed glare as she sizes up my appearance.

"I was—"

"Looking for your blazer, right?" Zack plucks my black blazer from underneath a cushion on the settee behind him and holds it out for me.

Reluctantly I eye it and then him. He's wearing his most encouraging look. It partners well with his slick blond hair and winning smile. He's right, politics is the right career for him.

I take my blazer from him and slip it on. "Thanks," I say, pulling my tangled blonde curls out from underneath the jacket.

"Oh, you're still here?!" Dee says, tromping down the stairs behind me. "You really take advantage of our father's unending patience, don't you?" Her black heels make note of each of her steps. When she meets me at the landing she pushes my hair behind my ears. "And really, if you're not going to at least dress like an upper-class Reverian you could brush your hair once in a while."

I bat her hand away and clench my teeth together. Insulting my sister will not release me from my mother's wrath, which seeks to make me even later for my appointment. Still, someone should say something about how my sister looks more and more like an obsessed Goth whose only mission in life is to give the Catholic clergymen a heart attack. She wouldn't understand that reference though. Most people in Austin Valley wouldn't. My sister is wearing her usual get-up: short pleated skirt, starched black button-up shirt open to reveal too much, heels, and an assortment of gold jewelry.

Instead of commenting on how she looks like a confused Catholic schoolgirl I lick my finger and press it to a flyaway by her hair line. "You have a hair out of place. Here you go, dear."

She steps back, grotesque horror written on her face. "Eww, don't touch me." My sister turns to our mother. They don't just share the same disapproving scowl, but also the same straight red hair, which they wear similarly. "Oh, Zack, you're here," my sister says, strolling in his direction. "I had no idea."

"Are you blind?" I say dully.

She throws me a contemptuous glare over her shoulder before turning back in Zack's direction. "You could obviously teach my sister something about dress, couldn't you?"

He coughs nervously, flicking his eyes over her shoulder to me. I know Dee makes him nervous. Hell, she makes the devil nervous, probably because she's soulless. I shrug and sling my bag over my shoulder.

"Well...I..." Zack begins.

"There are not many students who choose to wear a suit before they're chosen for positions," Dee says, having cleared the space between them. Her long pointy fingernail has found his shoulder and is now tracing its way down his pinstriped sleeve until she finds his hands. She pulls his fingertips up close to her face and inspects. "And such clean nails. This says so very much about you. Obviously you take a great deal of pride in your appearance."

"I'm merely tryin—"

"Zack is actually here because he'd like to interview your tutu in order to better understand cultural changes which have transpired within our society over the generations," my mother informs Dee, pride evident in her tone.

"Impeccable dresser and ambitious," Dee says, her hand still gripping Zack's.

"Yes, I dare say that if you stay on this track then you'll make great contributions for the Reverians once released from your studies," my mother says, her stare not on Zack, but rather on my sister.

Although I realize I'll be punished later for interrupting this crafty attempt at mating I dare say something. I have other punishments way worse I'd rather avoid. "Well, I really must take my leave," I say, injecting pleasantry into my voice. "I don't want to keep Father waiting any longer than I already have. Goodbye." Again the brass knob greets the palm of my hand.

"Yes, you are *so* late," my sister says, eyeing the ancient grandfather clock in the entryway. "He's going to be livid."

"I'm going that way too," Zack says, taking hurried steps in my direction. "I'll walk with you."

Just over his shoulder I catch a fiery glare flash in my sister's eyes.

"Sure," I say with a shrug and turn at once and hurry out the door.

The humid breeze is a welcome relief from the frigid air in my house. Sunlight greets my eyes with a quiet satisfaction and I smile at the blue sky like it's an old friend.

"You always do that, don't you?" Zack says, hurrying to keep up with me.

"Make my mother and sister furious? Yes."

"Well, yes, that, but I was referring to your reaction to the outdoors. You always break into a relieved smile when you walk outside."

I snuggle my shoulders up high, enjoying the warm sun on my cheeks. "I do love it," I say, pausing to allow a group of elderly Reverians to pass in front of us. Zack pauses with me but gives an irritated expression while we wait. "I'm already late," I finally say to him when they've moved on and we continue down Central Boulevard.

"I don't get you, Em," he says, shaking his head. "Why do you make your life harder when you know what they want you to do?"

"I just find it difficult to conform to their standards. I mean, why in the hell should I have to wear a blazer in the middle of the summer?" I say, scratching at my forearms which are already sweating under the tight-fitting jacket.

"It's just customs. If you followed them then they'd leave you alone and let you do what you want."

"Somehow I doubt that," I say, raising an eyebrow at Zack.

"It seems you're looking to get in trouble: being late when it's easy to be early, dressing inappropriately when they supply you the right clothes, and not following etiquette."

"And may I point out that you seem to only notice my shortcomings," I say, taking an early turn. It's a shortcut down a less than desirable neighborhood, but still completely safe and will save us an extra minute on the commute.

Zack's hand clamps down on my shoulder. I stop and look at him, ready to defend the route I've chosen. His denim blue eyes lock on mine. "That's not all I notice," he says, a firmness in his voice.

"Mmm…" I say, gauging his expression which is so familiar and also year by year growing indistinct, like my father's. "Yeah, what else do you notice?" I say, turning and continuing our trek. The alleyway here is a little more crowded, but only because this is a Middling street where they build the houses too close together and the insides are too small for the families who are forced to reside within them.

"It doesn't matter," Zack says, eyeing a man leaning in his doorway up ahead. "We can finish this conversation later. Let's just get you to Chief Fuller's office quickly."

"Right," I say, kicking the contents of a puddle, which is no doubt a result of poor drainage from the sprinkler system. It splatters droplets on my shoes and bare legs, but doesn't irritate me in the least.

At my father's office Zack stops, eyeing the door and then me with an uncertain expression. "You know I'm just trying to help, right?"

"Then you shouldn't have offered to escort me here," I say, pushing him playfully in the chest. "Dee will probably set fire to my bed while I'm sleeping tonight as retribution." Literally she's done that a time or two. I have no idea why the most hostile Dream Traveler born to the gods was given the gift of pyrokinesis.

Zack doesn't respond, but instead gives me his usual commiserative expression. He doesn't know what to say. I get that. "Yeah, I know you're trying to help," I finally say. "You may want to consider there's no help for me. I'm a Dream Traveler whose only talent is I disappoint my family."

"Oh, Em, I've told you that your gift is delayed. It will come on soon and when it does you'll blow all of them away."

"Thanks, Zack," I say, reaching out and straightening his tie. It isn't even that crooked, but I know he likes when I do it because it

254

sharpens his appearance. "Are you off to go take over Austin Valley?"

"Not quite yet," he says with a wink. "I've got a thing or two to learn still."

"Don't we all," I say, returning the wink and then dismissing him by facing my father's ornately carved door. I've stalled long enough. Now I must face that which is certain to be extremely unpleasant.

To continue reading, please purchase Defects (The Reverians, #1)

Sneak Peek of Awoken (The Lucidites Series, #1):

Prologue

The howling wind always marks his arrival. Tonight I'm not sleeping when it shakes the trees and sends debris flying around outside. The recurring nightmare woke me an hour ago. I wipe away the sweat beading my hairline and steal a glance out my window. The figure lurks in the shadows. He's never any closer than the old oak tree, but that's near enough. A chill shakes my core. I can't do this one single night more. Shaking fingers scroll through my phone contacts until I find the right one.

"Hello," a groggy voice says on the other end.

I speak in a whisper. "I'm not sure I believe what's happening, but I'm ready to let them protect me."

"Good," the voice says with relief. "You'll be glad you did."

"What do I do now?"

"They want you to meet someone. He'll explain what happens next."

Chapter One

Forty-eight hours later

I wouldn't believe any of this was real if it wasn't for the two-inch gash in my arm. Still, denial has rented a room in my head and frequently stomps around slamming doors. I have never considered myself normal, but only now do I fully realize how extremely abnormal I am. That's not the part I'm denying anymore. It's my potential fate.

Now I have to do the one thing that feels impossible: focus. It's difficult when my life has quickly turned into a mass of confusion. I force myself to shake off the distractions. The answers I seek reside in a place I can only get to if I let go.

With immense effort, I relax enough to concentrate. In my head, I see the dam. The concrete stretches out like a barrier, pushing the water away. I pay attention to the water, how it voyages down the spillway. Slow breaths intensify the meditation, giving it color and sound. I continue to visualize until I sense the change. It's polarizing, in a good way. My body remains planted in the comfy bed while my consciousness dream travels. Now I'm racing through the silver tunnel—my transport to the other dimension. Adrenaline tastes like salt water in my mouth. And too quickly the journey is over, leaving me panting as I'm tossed into a vast space.

The tunnel deposits me at the edge of the spillway on a concrete embankment. A cursory glance behind reveals a calm lake reservoir; ahead the spillway plummets for a hundred feet or more before cascading into the lake. The moon overhead is full. Beside me is a woman.

"I was beginning to think you were lost again," she says.

"It's nice to meet you too," I say.

"I assumed you already knew my name."

Apparently the Lucidites don't believe in greetings. "Well, some ID wouldn't hurt."

Shuman's black hair resembles strands of silk. She wears a leather vest and blue jeans. I straighten, feeling smaller than usual next to her.

"Did you decipher the riddle on your own?" Shuman says, ignoring my comment. The moon reflects off her high cheekbones, making her appear angular.

"No," I admit, "Bob and Steve helped."

I'm confused why Shuman gave me a riddle instead of just telling me where to dream travel to meet her. I guess as the Head Mentalist for the Lucidites she has to make everything as perplexing as possible. She must be great at her job.

"Yes, it was forecast that they would assist you," she says.

"Right, of course," I say, not masking the irritation in my voice. It isn't Bob's and Steve's help I resent, it's that the Lucidites are privy to my life through psychic means.

"And we are here because of a different prediction."

"Yes, I've heard about it."

"Have you also heard that it involves you?"

"Well, I know there's a *potential* I'll be involved."

"We have new information. Your name is the only one in the forecast now."

"What?" I breathe with quiet disbelief. "No, that's impossible."

"It is possible and I assure you it is true. The speculation of predictions solidifies as the approaching event draws closer. Now forecasters see you as the true challenger."

"No," I say too fast, denial evident in my tone. "And I'm not here because of the forecast; I'm here because they said you'd help me."

"They are correct. The first way I can help is by getting you to accept what has been predicted."

"Predictions are just guesses though. What if they're wrong?" I say.

Shuman raises her eyebrow in disapproval, shakes her head. "Roya, do you doubt it because it involves you?"

"Mostly I doubt it because it's absurd. None of it makes sense."

"Maybe not yet, but it will," Shuman says. "Unfortunately we are running out of time. The forecasters have determined the static moment to be twenty-one hundred hours on June thirteenth."

That's in a month. My throat closes and my chest shrinks in on itself. "What? I can't…There's no way…" I trail off, lost in morbid thoughts of my impending death. "Why not you or someone else more qualified?"

"If I was chosen I would be honored, but I was not. You were." Shuman gazes at the full moon, her silver earrings highlighted by its white light. "I have tracked Zhuang for decades without success. Many of us have." She turns and looks at me for the first time. Her dark eyes resemble amethysts. "This fixed point in time is the only chance anyone will have the opportunity to challenge him. And the forecast states you are the person with the best opportunity to end his brutal reign."

"That's ridiculous. I'm not a threat to anyone."

"A few days ago you saw yourself very differently than you do now, is that right?"

"Well, yes, but—"

"Then consider it possible that in a month you will be a deadly force."

After what I've learned, I'm almost willing to believe this might be true. I sigh. "So what do you really want from me?" I ask.

"Make a choice," Shuman says at once. "You must decide whether you accept this role. If you do, then I can give you the help you asked for."

"If everything you've said is true then I *don't* have a choice."

"It is all true," she says through clenched teeth. "And in waking life and dreams, you *always* have a choice. This is what makes Dream Travelers different from Middlings. We do not sleep and fall into dreams that happen to us. We create our dreams. We choose where we travel."

I rub my eyes, frustrated and strangely tired. "It's just facing Zhuang sounds like a death sentence. I don't want to go through all this just to die in June."

"If you make the choice to be the challenger then you will face many dangers. You may not even make it to June. You may die tonight." Shuman's face lacks any compassion.

"If you're trying to convince me to do this then you're not doing a very good job," I say.

Shuman stares at the moon for a minute as if she's calculating something. "I will need your answer."

"What? Now!?" My voice echoes over the spillway. "Just like that? I don't get a minute to think it over or go home and weigh out my options?"

"You do not have a home," she reminds.

My foot connects with the concrete curb in front of me. I want to throw an all-out tantrum. Running and hiding also sounds like a good idea. Shuman's oppressive demeanor, indifferent to my predicament, makes it tough to think. I wait for her to say something, but she just stands motionless watching the moon. She's starting to creep me out.

"What's going to happen to my family?" I ask, the last word sounding strange as it tumbles out of my mouth.

"I suspect Zhuang will maintain his hold on them, but who he really wants is you," Shuman says indifferently. "Your family is officially classified as hallucinators. He has the ability to keep them like this for a long time. Or he could finish them rather quickly."

Finish them? Does that mean what I think it does? This man, this parasite, is stealing my family's ability to dream, causing them to fall into hallucinatory states. And I'm powerless to stop Zhuang if he decides to drain them of their consciousness. Then they'd be shells, sleepwalkers. Dead in no time. A shiver runs down my spine.

Shuman continues, "Zhuang's plan was to make you panic and surrender to him. It is fortunate we found you first. My guess is your family will hang in limbo. Zhuang's attention will be on finding you. If you want to help your family then stay away, otherwise he will use them against you. And if you want to release them then you need to fight Zhuang."

"And win," I say, doubt oozing all over the words.

"Well, of course."

"This whole thing makes no sense." I rub my head with a shaky hand. "Why me? I'm barely old enough to drive. I've only known about this mess for a few days. How was I chosen? How am I the best person to face him?"

"I do not know the answers to these questions," she says, still fixated on the moon.

"Then why should I do this!? Why should I jeopardize my life without knowing why I've been chosen?"

Shuman takes one long blink as though contemplating or meditating. Her words are airy and quiet when she finally speaks. "The great Buddha once said, 'Three things cannot be long hidden: the sun, the moon, and the truth.'"

I bite down hard on my lip. So this is the way it is? Either I live my life alone on the streets and watch as Zhuang ransacks humanity's dreams. Or, option two, I volunteer to kill him and most likely die trying, but my consolation prize will be I'll know why I'd been chosen. I'll know who I was and where I could have belonged...if I hadn't died in Zhuang's hands. This seems like a scam, although an ingenious one.

A sincere part of me wants to return to my family and shake them until they're released from their hallucinations. Then we can go on living our lives where the most interesting things that happen are football, church, and barbeques. It's not a great life for an agnostic vegetarian, but is it better than death? I may be a product of the East Texas soil, but the winds here have never agreed with me. I've been looking for a way out of this town, but not like this.

"I cannot grant you any more time," Shuman says. "I need your answer."

I scan the surface of the water, looking for nothing in particular. She *can* wait for my answer. She will.

I push my fingers into my eyes and inhale deeply. This duel is inevitable. Zhuang and his challenger's futures are intertwined. Any attempt to evade the other person will only bring the two together. And somehow I was elected by people I don't know, for a danger I only recently knew existed. Still none of this makes sense, which is why I know I have to rely on instinct. It's all I have left. "Fine," I say a bit pathetically. "I'll do it."

A smile would be nice, or maybe a "good for you." Instead Shuman, who appears to be all business, all the time, begins spouting instructions. "Your next step is to find the Lucidite Institute. Since you are relatively new to dream traveling there are many risks you face."

No big surprises there.

Shuman continues, "You must dream travel to the Institute while fully submerged in water."

Um, what? "Are you serious? I'll drown."

"There is that risk, yes, but the only way to enter the Institute is through water. To travel there you must return to your body and then immerse yourself in water. I advise you to *know* you are one with it. It is through this knowledge that you overcome the fear of drowning and focus on the higher task of dream traveling. If you remain calm and focus properly then you will travel and arrive at the Institute. If you are unsuccessful, then yes, you will drown."

"Oh, is that all? Sounds like a piece of cake." I'm wondering now if I made the right decision.

Shuman narrows her eyes, but doesn't respond otherwise.

I rub my temples as an overwhelming pressure erupts behind my eyes. "This is all so strange, it sounds like a recurring dream I've been…" My words fall away as the inevitable truth dawns on me. "You put those dreams in my head, didn't you?" I accuse, staring at her rigid persona.

"The Lucidites are responsible, yes," she says, her tone matter-of-fact.

"What! That's insane! That's awful. Night after night I dreamed I was drowning myself. Do you know how horrifying that is?"

"You should be grateful. We have prepared you for the journey you are about to take. Your subconscious mind has already practiced much of what you are going to do."

"Grateful!?" I shake my head in disbelief. "I thought I was losing my mind. I didn't sleep well for weeks. No. I'm not the least bit grateful. You invaded my subconscious," I spew, more frustrated now than frightened.

Shuman takes a long inhale and says, "Everything that has been done was to protect you and the future."

How do I argue with that statement? How do I argue with any of this? I want to run, to abandon this farce which has become my life. However, my instinct is concrete around my legs, pinning me in place, assuring me this is where I belong.

"Roya, we are running out of time," Shuman says, breaking the silence. "Do you have any questions?"

"Why does it have to be so complicated to dream travel to the Institute? Isn't there an alternative?" *Like a spaceship or a drug?*

"No, there is not," Shuman says. "The Institute is heavily protected by water. The difficulty it takes to travel there is what makes it the safest place on earth."

The idea settles over me like a down comforter. Safety. What would that feel like? Every moment has been cloaked with a hidden threat for so long. When the recurring dreams weren't plaguing me, the paranoia lurked in the shadows and was all but incapacitating. It was almost enough to make me take the pills the therapist kept pushing. Almost.

"If I do all this"—the words drip out of my mouth— "if I don't drown, then I'll be at the Institute? I'll be safe? At least for a little while, right?"

Her eyes jerk away from their focal point. There's a twitch at her mouth. "Yes."

I sigh. It's the first one of relief in a while. "All right then, I'll do it," I say halfheartedly.

262

She turns and faces me, resting her arms across her chest. Around one of her forearms is a tattoo of a rattlesnake. The serpent's tail lies on her elbow and its head on the back of her hand.

"There is one last thing," she says, a warning in her voice. "Only Lucidites can enter the Institute. You must want to be one of us, or you will be forbidden from entering."

I blink in surprise. My mouth opens to voice hesitation, but she disappears, leaving me alone and feeling as though I'm standing on the edge of the earth.

To continue reading, please purchase:
Awoken (The Lucidites, #1)

Sneak Peek of Ren: The Man

Behind the Monster:

Prologue

When I was born the doctor said I wouldn't live the night through. I had a problem with a valve in my heart. My pops called a secret healer who lived a few towns away. And now I write this to you as a grown man. I'm not spoiling anything for you from the tale you're about to read. It isn't a spoiler that all these years I've survived. The true secret is that I lived at all. Actually I lived on an edge, one so dangerous most don't even know it's there. I didn't sell my soul to the devil or dance with her on a clear night. I ran up to the devil and I stole the mask she wore and I wore it comfortably for quite some time. But then I met an angel and she made me want to die. I didn't though. My secret isn't even that I lived. It's that I lived pretending to be the devil, wishing God would save my soul. I knew this was a wasted wish. I have no soul left to save. It's why I could steal the devil's persona. It's why I lived when I should have died too many times.

I don't hold babies or pause for the elderly. It's not because I'm unkind. I'm kind. I'm kind enough to never put myself close to anyone vulnerable. I'm afraid I might break them. I'm afraid of myself. I live alone or with the strong and arrogant. But I don't live close to those who are vulnerable. I don't live close to those who might dare to love me. I don't trust myself otherwise.

When I was born God made an awful error. He allowed a healer to save me. He allowed me to live. I'm a mistake. Not because my parents didn't intend to have me and God failed to kill me. I'm a mistake because of what I can do. I'm a mistake because people like me aren't destined for happiness. We are the miserable. The lonely.

The people you warn your children not to become. The ones you warn your children to stay away from.

I'm Ren Lewis and I was born with too much power.

Chapter One

April 1985

*T*he antique clock on the wall had the most irritating tick. It seemed extraordinarily loud. Probably because the old grandfather was a knockoff. It most likely was manufactured the year before in some backyard by a wanker who failed clock-making school and decided to go into forgery. I instantly liked the clock a lot more.

Snap. Snap.

The middle-aged Middling therapist dared to snap his dried fingertips in front of my face. Sure, I wasn't paying attention to him. Sure, he'd asked his question to me repeatedly, and without answering I continued to stare at the clock which had too much lacquer and the detail work was a bit rough in places. How much did this shrink shell out for such a phony piece of furniture?

Unhurried, I pulled my gaze around to face the irritated therapist. I had to give him credit. He almost appeared in control of this situation. Bravo. This is the only thing I think he had control of, since I was guessing his overweight wife probably bossed his skinny ass around all day and his three kids owned the parts of him that she didn't. But this guy had a mock sense of authority over me; at least he had been trying to make a show of it.

I blinked at him blankly. "What was the question?" I said.

"Ren, are you paying the least bit of attention during this session?" Dr. Simon said, pushing his wiry glasses up the thin bridge of his nose.

I took a deliberate moment to actually think about the question. Should I answer honestly or should I save his ego and make him as the poor therapist feel better about himself? Yeah, saving egos is someone else's job, for sure.

"Not really," I said, stretching out my arms with a long yawn. "But if it will make this whole mess go along a tad faster then I'll give it a bit more of my attention. How's that, doc?"

He bristled, pulling his yellow pad of notes closer to him as he crossed a skinny ankle over his bony knee. "What do you have to say for your actions? Are you the least bit remorseful about what you did to poor Widow Johnson?"

I felt my eyebrows rise with surprise. Yeah, I was remorseful, but not about what I did to the old bag. I was remorseful that I'd been so foolish. Still new to my gifts, I had a lot to learn about limitations. Using my mind control, I convinced the old lady to give me her husband's old Bentley. Give it to me. No questions asked.

"Here you are," she said, her Scottish accent much fainter than I remembered in years past. "It's all yours." Old Mrs. Johnson handed me the keys to the Bentley Continental, which had only been driven on Sundays. Then she gave me one little bit of advice. "Be careful around the corners. Henry didn't like the tires to get dirty."

I'm sure he didn't. But this car had only one destiny in my hands. It was going to get dirty. Inside and out. I was going to drive it to London. Park it in front of the finest clubs and tempt the finest of women to join me inside it. And my plan would have worked and I would have been laid by a model at the early age of fifteen years old. *However*, it didn't work because I didn't have a license to drive or the know-how to do so.

Instead of driving that sleek ride to London, I crashed it into old man Miller's stack of hay bundles on the other side of Mrs. Johnson's farm. I knew then I'd never see a pretty lady undressing herself in that backseat. I had the know-how without all the actual "know-how." I could control minds, but didn't know how to do things…simple little things like driving. I needed to learn how to do these small tasks. But being fifteen provided all sorts of disadvantages. And namely, the first disadvantage was sitting squarely in front of me, fidgeting with his note pad.

"The last time you were in here was because you let all of Mr. Gretchen's sheep loose," Dr. Simon said, reading from his file on the side table. He needed to have his orderly notes. Needed to be able to refer back to them. He didn't have the advantage of a flawless, photographic memory, like me. Poor soul with his weaknesses and many shortcomings. How he made it through graduate school is ever a wonder to me.

My green eyes narrowed at the accusation. It was all wrong. As usual. Just like with the Bentley. They thought I stole it, when it was actually given to me. And I didn't let the sheep loose. I made Mr. Gretchen do it using a bit of hypnosis, partnered with mind control. However, I made silly errors in the process. Firstly, I'd hung around to watch the mayhem of sheep patrolling through our muddy streets. I'd also done a sloppy job of mind control on the dumb farmer. He remembered me. Didn't know what I did to him, but there was enough suspicion that the whole thing was pinned on me. They thought I just let the sheep out, which is a lot more innocent a crime than what I really did.

"Tell me, Ren, why is it that you keep acting out?" Dr. Simon said, almost looking a little afraid of me, but bent on acting his part as the parish therapist. The church wasn't just paying him to sign off on the health and well-being of most of its members. They also expected him to fix the lot of us who were intent on the devil's rule.

I sized the guy up. We'd had at least half a dozen sessions. None of my usual lies had worked, so I decided he was ready for the truth. The truth I always saved until I was in the most amount of trouble. The truth invariably set me free, but not because people believed me. Rather because they thought I was crazy, which I probably am.

"I keep acting out because," I began in a rehearsed voice, "well, it's complicated, and it's actually a secret. I'm not sure if I should tell you. You may get mad at my parents since it was their insistence that I keep this private."

"Ren, I won't get mad at your parents," Dr. Simon said in his soothing therapist tone. "You can tell me anything and we will work through it together. Your parents will suffer no harm by your truths."

I nodded. Inside I smiled with glee. "The truth is that I was born half Dream Traveler, and not only can I travel through space and time using my dreams, but as this special race of humans I'm also gifted with a skill. Some Dream Travelers have one or maybe even two gifts. I can control people using my mind, hypnotize people with movements, *and* if I touch someone I can hear their thoughts." I scuffed some imaginary dirt off my shoe. "That's the truth. The big secret. Don't be mad at me or my parents for it."

The therapist took in a long annoyed breath. "Until you, Ren, are ready to actually talk about your crimes in a real manner then these sessions are futile."

A slow smile formed on my face. The truth was always the better option in these situations. No one believed it and therefore just assumed I was a no-good teen. A troublemaker. A pathological liar. The truth was I kept telling the truth over and over again and no one believed me. My father, who had spent his life hiding the fact that he carried Dream Traveler blood in him, hadn't especially liked that I did this. But he was smart enough to realize no one was ever going to believe me. I was Ren. The boy who had been there when my teacher pulled her knickers down during my solo detention last year. The boy who had been the one to call authorities when my entire church group, including our teacher, fell into inexplicable comas. I was the strange boy. The one who things happened around. But people thought it was because I was a troublemaker branded with the word "cursed" across my head. They had no idea it was because since I was ten years old I'd come into my gifts and could control most using my mind and hypnotize anyone I dared. I told them to hold my hand so I could read their thoughts, but they'd totally shrugged me off most of the time. Even though I kept telling the truth, I was dismissed. And that's what made the whole thing even more fun. What fools they all were. Utter, stupid fools.

But my mum saw through it and knew I was manipulating the lot of them. And her look of heartbreak did cause me a bit of stress. She kept professing her faith in me though. She thought that a heavy hand would never make me see my awful ways, but rather the hand of our Lord and Savior. That's why she kept convincing the church to take me in after each of my crimes. Counsel me. Absolve my sins. Steer me in the right direction.

However, my mother was as short-sighted as the rest. As a Middling, those who are without gifts or the power to dream travel, she'd never see how much fun it was to manipulate. My mother didn't see a lot. Mostly because her life was so limited. And I wasted too many years of her life with my antics when I could have been with her, learning the lessons only she could teach me. The ones I only now realize Middlings can teach. Those of the heart. Dream Travelers are too distracted by our minds, by our gifts, to fully understand how love works. However, Middlings aren't complicated in that way.

"Ren, we've been doing this regularly," Dr. Simon said to me that evening. He was thoroughly done with my shenanigans, and soon the poor chap would sod off to his meager dwelling on the outskirts of Peavey, where his family would abuse him with neglect and pesky remarks about his feeble appearance. He sighed deeply. "Ren, when you get caught, your mother makes her case to the vicar and somehow you end up seeing me instead of the constable. These opportunities for you to have rehabilitation instead of punishment are running out. I suggest you be real with me. I want you to tell me why you act out. Many of your teachers describe you as having a chip on your shoulder. Of being hostile. Do you want to tell me why? This is your last chance."

More than once throughout my life I've been asked what it is that made me so hard, so hostile. Why would something have to make me the way I am? I've known dozens of happy people who have nothing to be happy about and still they plaster stupid grins on their faces every bloody day. There are those who are all scared and tortured and they've got no good reason for the self-pity. Nothing more than a few trivial things have ever happened to them. Forgetting their lunch. Missing an exam. Not getting the girl. And yet these lowlifes go through life like they were given a curse at birth.

It's mostly just a choice. Life doesn't make most of us any certain way. We wake up, and usually without knowing it, act in a way that fits our personality. Nothing made me the way I am. Not really. Things colored me. Persuaded me. But no experience is responsible for making me hostile. It's just the way I prefer to be. Also, who I am is a result of something inside my bones. Probably a monster who feeds off my unhealthy behavior. I'm not a victim of circumstance. I'm a man who believes that the best strategy involves being extremely cynical and even more conniving. And if there's one thing I'm more excellent at than all the other things, it's strategy. I'm a bloody master at it. Hell, I'm fairly certain God takes notes out of *my* book. He should. If he knows what's good for him.

I brought my eyes up to meet the therapist's gaze. I'd made a great show of putting real emotions on my face. My bottom lip quivered a bit. My eyes were filled to the brim with fake tears. And when I opened my mouth an actual croak happened out. "It's my sister, Lyza," I wailed. "She abuses me. She abuses me badly," I sang.

"Your older sister, Lyza?" Dr. Simon said, sitting forward, almost knocking the pad off his thin lap.

"That's right," I said, furiously nodding my head. "The one due to graduate early this year and with an acceptance to Oxford. That one. But what you don't know is she does things to me," I said, putting a look of shameful hurt on my face.

"Don't you worry, Ren," Dr. Simon said, leaning forward, placing a hand on my shaking arm. "We won't let her hurt you any longer."

Truth be told, Lyza only hurt me with dirty remarks and cold stares. But Lyza had told our mother since she was thirteen that our mum was no better than a servant in our house. She had despised our mum for being a Middling and I in turn despised Lyza. And now I was going to make her pay for every hurtful thing she did to our mum. See, the thing is, when Ren gets in trouble, so do other people.

I allowed the doctor's hand to linger on my forearm. Now was probably not the time to tell this homosexual that I didn't quite enjoy his touch, but definitely go and cart my sister away for abusing her little brother. I grabbed one more thought out of the doctor's head before he slipped his hand away. That one thought was enough for me to know that the punishment Dr. Simon saw for Lyza would fit the bill until I could up the ante.

To continue reading, please purchase:
Ren: The Man Behind the Monster
(Ren Series, #1)

For more books by this author or to learn more about
Sarah Noffke, please visit:
http://www.sarahnoffke.com

Made in the USA
Charleston, SC
17 January 2016